W9-CGX-966

Refinements *of* Love

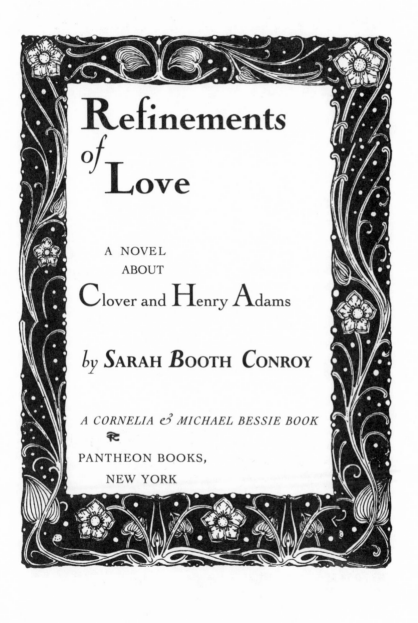

Refinements *of* Love

A NOVEL
ABOUT
Clover and Henry Adams

by SARAH BOOTH CONROY

A CORNELIA & MICHAEL BESSIE BOOK

PANTHEON BOOKS,
NEW YORK

Copyright © 1993 by Sarah Booth Conroy

All rights reserved under International and Pan-American Copyright
Conventions. Published in the United States by Pantheon Books, a
division of Random House, Inc., New York, and simultaneously in
Canada by Random House of Canada Limited, Toronto.

Library of Congress Cataloging-in-Publication Data

Conroy, Sarah Booth.
    Refinements of love : a novel about Clover and Henry Adams / Sarah
Booth Conroy.
        p.   cm.
    "A Cornelia & Michael Bessie book."
    ISBN 0-679-42050-9
    1. Adams, Marian, 1843–1885—Fiction.   2. Adams, Henry, 1838–1918
—Fiction.   3. Washington (D.C.)—History—Fiction.   I. Title.
PS3553.051987R44   1993
813'.54—dc20   92-50468

Book design by Cheryl L. Cipriani
Text is set in Perpetua

Manufactured in the United States of America

9 8 7 6 5 4 3 2

To Richard Timothy Conroy

TABLE OF CONTENTS

Table of Contents

A century ago, in Washington's Rock Creek Cemetery, a bronze figure by Augustus Saint-Gaudens was mounted on a granite slab to cover the grave of Clover Adams—and, a third of a century later, of Henry Adams. The sculpture has an eerie power. A brooding, shrouded figure sits frozen in time. Its hand pulls aside a winding sheet, revealing a glimpse of a stoic face; the rest of the grave clothes fall in deep folds over the figure.

The statue has no sex, no name, no inscription, no message.

The "un-Christian abomination" repelled the 1892 rector of St. Paul's Church, proprietor of the graveyard. But he could not keep the monument out of the century-old cemetery. So he had the memorial walled off, hiding it inside a grove of holly. The incensed architect of the site, Stanford White, suggested Saint-Gaudens treat each tree by "making a little hole in the ground near the root, a little vitriol would do the rest." Evidently they didn't get around to pouring it, or the rector must have laid a powerful blessing on the holly.

For, in spring 1992, a century after Adams first faced the artwork, the trees had grown belligerently. The thirty-foot-high trunks pushed against the statue, and the roots stretched out to disturb the dust to which all return. Branches of spiky green leaves reached over to weep blood-red berries and cast dark shadows on its dispassionate visage. The family talked of removing or thinning the trees.

The enigmatic effigy remains as a memento mori, a reminder of the unsolved mystery of the death of Clover Adams—and the paradox of Henry Adams who made every effort to obliterate his wife's name from memory. After she died on December 6, 1885, he burned her diaries and cherished letters from her father and friends. He burned even his own journals. He destroyed all photographs of his wife except for two in the possession of others in which she is barely visible. In his autobiography, *The Education of Henry Adams*, the years between 1872 and 1892 are discarded, as though they were out-of-date calendars fit for the trash.

From the day of her death until shortly before his own, he would not speak nor listen to the sound of her name, as though its two syllables might cause the earth to shake and crack. Yet Henry, whose only contribution was the $20,000 commission fee to the sculptor, became obsessed with the ambiguous creation of Saint-Gaudens.

"Every now and then, in a certain light," he wrote the sculptor in 1892, "I see or think I see, an expression almost amounting to defiance in the mouth and nostrils. You did not put it there, nor did I, nor am I sure of it, nor is it intended in the conception, nor am I consciously seeking it, nor can you perhaps see it even when I say it. Is it there?"

Thousands still come to the mysterious monument in Rock Creek Cemetery, shake their heads, and wonder, "What does it mean?" Eleanor Roosevelt in times of travail came to sit on its granite bench and meditate. She said it represented one who had "transcended pain and hurt to achieve serenity." Earlier, onetime Secretary of State John Hay, who knew Clover well, said the silent one is the image of "infinite wisdom, a past without beginning, and a future without end, a repose after limitless experience, a peace to which nothing matters."

Adams angrily rejected labeling the sculpture: "Grief, Despair, Pears Soap or Macy's Suits . . ." But he revealed more than he intended when he wrote Homer Saint-Gaudens, Augustus's son. Adams said the figure is meant to "ask a question, not to give an answer." And he added a curse, to one who would try: "The man who answers will be damned to eternity like the men who answered the Sphinx."

Adams himself, like the sculpture, gave no answers to questions about the life and death of Clover. His threat tempted me to try to solve through imagination what can never be proven by evidence. How fortunate I am that Adams did not bother to lay his malediction on women.

Refinements *of* Love

CHAPTER 1

October 31, 1885

The Night of the Dead on La Fayette Square

∞

Tonight, I, Clover Adams, pulled the mauve velvet curtains aside, jingling their brass rings and shaking their ball trim. I stood close to the window and watched as the miasma rose from the swamps of the Potomac. The noxious effluvium drifted slowly up to the White House. I wondered if Grover Cleveland studied his papers in his office in the Oval Room on the family floor, lured into an unaccustomed feeling of privacy. I pictured his sister Rose collapsing in the west sitting hall after the last tea party guest departed the Red Parlor, grateful for the fog curtain close against the great arched window. Neither had been in Washington long enough to know the dangers of that exhalation, the ectoplasm of riverbank dead matter.

3

Octo-
ber 31,
1885
The fog—to give it a good name—spread over La Fayette
Square as surely and insidiously as a scandalous story. The effusion
moved wetly over the ornamental bronze urns, chilled the scantily
clad nymphs who danced around them, and filled the interstices
of the fence that defined the square. I could just see the tip of
General Andrew Jackson's hat, as he eternally salutes his troops,
but nothing of the man and the eighteen tons of bronze horse
underneath it.

When the emanation reached Decatur House, it slid over
General Edward Fitzgerald Beale's new sandstone-furrowed eye-
brow window trim and made shades for the recently elongated
windows. On the east side of the square, Dolley Madison's old
house was dark, not a glint of its New Orleans–style porch trim
recalling the trim on her famous turbans. I wondered if the Widow
Wilkes will be able to sell the house to the Cosmos Club. She's
wanted to sell since the Admiral has, as they say here, been gathered
to Abraham's bosom. Next to our own door on H Street, I could
see only the yellow light from the gas lamps in front of William
W. Corcoran's house, once Daniel Webster's podium, now the
most elaborately decorated house in town, including the White
House.

The fog slipped under the cracks of our front door, 1607 H
Street, as though it were an invitation no one wanted to answer.
It slithered into the upstairs tri-part window bay, between frame
and glass.

Henry used to say, "If I ever take too much laudanum, the
coroner's jury may bring in a verdict of willful murder against the
month of November."

We learned to live with fog when Henry researched his
histories in England. We grew accustomed to the yellow cloud
that shielded murderers, thieves, dirt, and starvation for months

on end. But in Washington the fall is full of Indian summer days, October 31,
1885 so warm that roses bloom and residents rejoice. The brilliance of this sun makes the foggy chill that much more depressing when it comes.

As I felt the damp reaching me, poking my dress, looking for a way to chill my spine, I glimpsed a white and gold hearse, like a large bonbon on wheels. From it issued a short line of black-coated men. Vapor disguised as smoke rose from their stovepipe hats. They marched across the square, respectfully following the black bier resting on six shoulders.

Without thinking about it, I knew they were headed for St. John's, the church of the presidents. The sanctuary, also on the north side of the park, but across Sixteenth Street, was out of my sight line, but I imagined its gilded spire shining faintly through the mist, like a good deed in the murky morality of the capital.

I, who eschew religion, have never been inside St. John's and often have said I would never go except "feet first," as indeed the present parishioner seemed to be doing. I wondered if he were ready to go. Had he had time, as my father did seven months or so ago, to pronounce benedictions, to bestow his worldly goods, to renounce life, to plan his funeral?

Did the corpse before me order up the vapor to make it harder for the devil to find his soul in the murk before his body reached the safe haven under the golden spire?

A hundred years ago, the body would have gone in the Pearce family burial ground in their Jamaica Plantation not far from where I stood. I used to think the Pearce family graveyard, surrounded by an apple grove, stood where our house now stands. Henry said that was another of my morbid fancies and, to prove me wrong, found "Early Recollections," a small pamphlet published in 1866 by Christian Hines. He'd lived in Washington since 1796 when he "went to see the President's House, which was then just rising above the basement story."

The old man said the graveyard of the Pearces—whose plantation covered the whole area before the establishment of the federal district—was on the north side of what is now Pennsylvania Avenue, just opposite the President's house. When Hines heard the land was to be plowed and leveled to make the present-day La Fayette Square, he ran to Georgetown to tell a latter-day member of the Pearce family. Mrs. Pearce pleaded with him to take charge of saving the remains, an appropriate appellation. Hines found "little else to take up but a few bones and a little black dust, besides, I believe, a piece of hair-comb, some plaited hair, et cetera. After gathering the remains together and putting them into the case, we had them placed in a cart and proceeded to Holmead burying ground, where we deposited them."

Hines's story came back to me as I enjoyed the foggy funeral this evening more than anyone but the dead man's heirs. I suspected, with no evidence, they came only to be polite before the reading of the will.

Henry says I have a graveyard gaiety for every season. Perhaps I do, but November in Washington is a month appropriately preceded by Halloween. And the scene before me, though in dead earnest, seemed like a parade of All Saints' Eve revelers.

In the park, the shadows grew deeper and longer, giving the illusion of strange hollows in the ground. Before I could steady myself, I felt a shudder shake me from head to toe.

My observations were interrupted by a noise from the street. A ruffled and flounced parasol wielded by a ruffled and flounced Mrs. John McLean banged at Henry's study window on the ground floor. I was appalled to see—as if Mrs. McLean is not unbearable enough—she was accompanied by General William Tecumseh Sherman's niece. Elizabeth Sherman, Mrs. Senator Cameron, was saying saucily to Henry's head, stuck out the window to hear her: "Let us in. Let us in. We must have some of your good tea to take away the taste of that bilge we've been drinking." October 31, 1885

Mrs. McLean struggled to hold onto the parasol and keep her giant staghound from carrying her further down H Street. When she finally mastered him, she handed the dog over to our Johnson. I was relieved to see he tied the leash to the hitching post at the curb. Boojum, our brave—foolhardy is a better word—Skye terrier, despite the difference in size, is ever ready to challenge the hated staghound. I stiffened as I heard the tip tap of their heels on the stair to the piano nobile and the giggles of Mrs. McLean, Emily Beale that was.

"We caught Mr. Adams. It's better to slip up on him than ringing because he can't say 'engaged.' "

"Why, Mistress Adams, what a sad scene you watch. Come, give me a cup of tea, laugh, and forget that pitiable procession," said the fashionable Mrs. Cameron.

I stood still. I gave her no answer. What tormentors, that pair! I despise guests before 5:00 P.M. Discouraging them is, I once wrote my father, "a process of picking off burrs, which is not pleasant." Everyone should have the right to their days. I share my teatime, but my days belong to me, and to Henry—if he wants them. Time is not shared but wasted with Mistresses Cameron and McLean.

"Clover," said Henry, not as easily ignored as La Dona Cameron, as he called her.

I turned, deciding to put a good face on it. "Hello, you two. Have you been here long? I was fog gathering, letting it seep

through my brain to cushion the sharp places. Is it already teatime?"
This a slam because both should know I always ordered tea for
5:00 P.M.

"Where has your mind been, Marian?" When Henry is annoyed by me, he always calls me not by my flowery family name,
but my proper given name. It rather had the effect of making me
feel like two people. "It's already 5:30, and I am perishing for tea.
Did you order the cucumber sandwiches made?" said Henry,
accusingly.

"Anytime is time for your excellent tea!" said that corn-
mush mouthed Cameron. "You must tell me where you get it."

Henry beamed. "You shall have a tin of ours. Straightaway.
I settled on A. H. mixture when I taught at Harvard. The right
tea might not turn a bore into a wit, but it wets the whistle," he
said.

I made no motion to pull the bell rope. When Elizabeth
Cameron's back was turned, Henry made a face at me and motioned
his head toward the bellpull. I pretended not to notice. Finally,
Henry pulled the bell himself, saying as he did, "Marian, you must
be fog-bound, Mesdames Cameron and McLean are come to cheer
you up."

Elizabeth Cameron is tall, taller than the short Henry, and
sweetly rounded. Her slow smile is in itself an aphrodisiac to her
many followers. Under the fluffy curls, her face is almost heart
shaped. She is a flirt, certainly, but hardly a femme fatale, though
she is sometimes called "the most beautiful woman in Washington." Her beauty, her soft skin and luxuriant curls, her enormous
eyes give her a curious air of innocence, or naïveté. Henry, perhaps
making a pun with his own name, once called her Eve, but then
he settled on La Dona—he said the appellation was in tribute to

Don, her husband's name, but was Henry suggesting virgin purity?
If so, I think him mistaken.

Mrs. Cameron spread her skirts on the right of the sofa with
the air of one who is at home. She stuck her hand between the
cushion and the frame of the arm and said, "Why, I believe I've
found my earring. I wondered what had become of it. Let me see
. . . Oh yes, you remember, dear Mr. Adams, I told you I'd lost
it on the day you first fed me those delicious blueberry scones.

"I must have misplaced it, the earring, not the scone, thank
heaven, while we were sitting here. Mrs. Adams, that was while
you were nursing your father. Do you remember the earrings?
Large garnet stones dangling from strings of smaller ones." She
opened her hand to show a single earring. "I am so fond of
them—and the delicious friend who gave the pair to me. Of course
I won't tell you who," she said firmly, though no one had asked.
"That's a secret."

With considerable effort, I decided to ignore the tantalizing
tidbit offered up by the Cameron cat. If rumor were right, more
than one candidate might be suspected of bejeweling Mrs. Cameron. To keep from seeming interested, I turned my gaze away
from the feline Cameron and to Henry.

His face was flushed as if he'd turned a glass of whisky bottoms
up. What was this? Why should Henry's face redden at Elizabeth
Cameron's tease?

I felt my face go as white as Henry's was red.

The maid arrived with the heavy silver tray, the teakettle on
its stand with the candle below it; the big silver pot that Robert
Cunliffe, an English baronet and a dear friend, had given us; the
cream pitcher and the basket for sugar lumps, the tea caddy and
the waste bowl, all in heavy sterling, wedding gifts of a Sturgis

relative. The maid had put out the old Berlin china cups, another wedding present, from Brooks Adams.

I went about my job with careful attention, giving the impression that this difficult and complicated task was far too important to allow me to join in their inconsequential chitchat. I supposed that short of fainting I couldn't get out of measuring the tea. I concentrated on the seashell thoughtfully provided by "Messrs. Twining & Co., By appointment to the Queen"—I read it all off in my mind to dampen down the awful thoughts that threatened to float up to the surface like a wayward tea leaf.

I poured the hot water over the dark leaves, giving it a stir, thinking that the Danish blue and white porcelain would have been quite good enough for the Mistresses Cameron and McLean. What had the maid been thinking to bring out all the wedding gift silver? Though, come to think about it, what I really needed was a silver bullet, for the vampirish Cameron—I didn't think Emily Beale McLean was worth shooting.

I hoped my face was set in its usual slightly sardonic look, as if the conversation were rather ridiculous and beneath my notice. Actually, I began to pay their words close attention. They sounded as if they were speaking in code. The sensation was eerie, as though all of a sudden I no longer understood English. Were Henry and Elizabeth Cameron speaking a secret language to each other?

I shook my head and realized that after Henry's blush, the two of them had paid me no mind. Mrs. McLean, for once, was silent, though watching the two closely, turning at first to one and then another, as though they were playing tennis. I couldn't stand my thoughts anymore. I'd talk, that was the thing to do, I'd talk, so I couldn't hear myself think.

"You're very dressed up, Mrs. Cameron," I made myself say. "And Mrs. McLean, you must have started out with that brand-new parasol when there was sun to excuse it. Surely you and Mrs. McLean are not wasting all those French furbelows on Henry and me. Faith! We're certainly not worth it. Don't tell me, let me think. You've been to your mother's house for tea. How is she?"

Mrs. C. laughed. "You are wrong. We went to Miss Cleveland's tea. This is her day, don't you know. As usual it was quite grand. Her flowers are quite wonderful."

Ah ha, thought I. So that's why they've come, to boast that they've been to the White House tea.

She rattled on, "Miss Cleveland, however, seems very bored with society."

"I suspect she has more serious matters to think on." I admire Rose Cleveland's career as a teacher, lecturer, and writer. I had no intention of telling Mrs. Cameron that I have spent pleasant hours tête-à-tête with Miss Cleveland. That worthy had confided to me the most delicious secret of the new administration—that she amuses herself by conjugating Greek verbs while smiling and shaking hands in receiving lines.

Emily McLean piped up, "She's very old maidish. The men are annoyed because her temperance beliefs prevent her from serving wine at her own luncheons or receptions. Her principles, thank heaven, didn't keep Mr. Cleveland from serving six different kinds of wine at his first dinner. Anyway, the President is certainly fortunate to have a sister like Miss Rose. What would the poor bachelor do if he didn't?"

"Serve wine at lunch and at receptions, I suspect. Anyway, after Chester Arthur and his sister, I am perfectly inured to bachelor presidents. I suppose them all to be provided with sisters who are superb hostesses. But I am surprised that you deign to join us in our humble tea after having been so regally entertained, Mrs. Cameron."

"I thought you'd like to hear all about it. I know you seldom go. I don't want you to miss anything. Have you been at all since Cleveland was inaugurated? I know dear Mr. Adams has. He's always in the thick of things." She rattled on without waiting for an answer. "Have you heard? Cleveland may marry the Folsom girl, Frances, though some say it's her mother he's interested in. They're both in Europe at the moment."

"It could be," said Mrs. McLean. "Maybe that's why he's waiting to redecorate the White House. So far, President Cleveland hasn't changed any of his predecessor's decor. Though I think he might've had the ivory embossing on the wallpaper in the Blue Room cleaned. People *will* rub their hands over it."

"I hope the President doesn't take down the Tiffany screen." During the fashionable Arthur's administration, I walked through the house with Artful Arthur and his decorator, Louis Comfort Tiffany, marveling at the flags and eagles entwined in the great glass screen that cut the drafts off the cross hall.

"No such luck, we're stuck with it," said La Dona.

"I rather like it," I said, and went back to watching the fog, hoping to see the funeral procession leave. "When we were in England, I became quite interested in the New Art."

Mrs. Cameron, wrapping a curl around her finger, leaned over to Henry and said in a whisper just loud enough for the first balcony to hear, "She is a bluestocking, isn't she? All advanced aesthetics and such. I, for one, like decoration for my man's comfort. Not lily-back chairs and limpid teapots."

Henry looked over at me to see if I'd heard. He couldn't decide. So he said, "My wife takes tea and taste seriously." And he turned, thinking only my tormentor could see him, and winked.

I saw the wink reflected in the window from the mirror on

the opposing wall and looked at both of them. She had her hand to her lips. Laughing at me.

October 31, 1885

Suddenly, her companion leaned over to ask, "Are you all right, Lizzie?"

Mrs. Cameron nodded, but her eyes carried no such conviction. Mrs. Beale fumbled into her reticule and brought out her cloisonné bottle of smelling salts, removing the stopper and handing it to her friend.

Finally, I realized Mrs. Cameron was not laughing at me, but her pale skin was rapidly turning a celadon green. I went to her. "May I help? Would you like to lie down a moment? Henry, go fetch Dr. Hagner."

"No, no," she said. "I'll be fine. Emily, your salts are very restorative. Mrs. Adams, I'll just totter into your morning room and stretch out for a moment."

We women disdained Henry as useless in such circumstances. We left him behind, protesting his desire to go get the doctor, to pour a glass of brandy, to do anything to help. The three of us moved slowly into the next room. Mrs. Cameron draped herself over the chaise longue, arranging her skirts with some art. But there was no denying her vapors were not assumed. At least she looked very much the color of the jade pieces in the cloisonné bottle.

I found an extra pillow to prop behind her and said, "Would you like a damp cloth? Or a basin? Do you feel ill?"

My remarks were perhaps too suggestive.

The maid had to be summoned to clean up the ensuing deluge on the India carpet the color of the Nubian desert, to replace her dress with one of my negligees (distinctly short, since Lizzie towers over me), to feed the fire and pull a quilt over the delicate stomach.

"Dear me. All that couldn't have been caused just by Miss Cleveland's bad tea, or, oh dear, my cucumber sandwiches."

"You can't imagine how bad the tea was, Mrs. Adams. But Lizzie didn't eat any of your sandwiches so you're excused. Come on Elizabeth, tell our hostess your news."

Suddenly, it was as if the haze had made itself into a feather boa, encircling my neck and flinging itself down my backbone with a cold whoosh. I managed to say, "Yes, do tell us, Mrs. Cameron."

Her lips were beginning to lose their tremor and her face began to regain its sunrise color. She smiled, with a smugness that was plain to read.

"Do I have to tell you? Can't you guess? Don't you know? Isn't it obvious? I'm going to have a baby. In the spring. Isn't it wonderful! After being married seven years! Isn't that splendid news? Don is ecstatic. He's so thrilled he hasn't drunk over a pint of whiskey a day since he heard! And I may have anything my heart desires! I think I'll be like that woman I saw at the White House the other night and ask for eighty-five diamonds to wear all at once on a chain."

I mumbled something I hoped would be heard as the correct congratulations. And then I turned, saying, "I'll just get you . . ." exactly what was lost in my flight from the room.

Henry was in the next room, standing stupidly, wondering what he should do. As I fled up the stairs, I said, "Tell her she's made me sick at my stomach. You and Emily get her out of my sight. Send her home. I can't take this."

My last look at Henry, his face a fencing court of emotions before he pulled down its visor, made me wonder how much he thought I knew.

Upstairs, I eventually calmed myself by going again to my window. From my bedroom, a floor above where I began my vigil, the atmosphere seemed even denser. I could barely see the funeral procession, illuminated in the gas light, now leaving the church.

The efflux turned La Fayette Park into an impressionist landscape, W. Holman Hunt's *The Ponte Vecchio, Florence*, perhaps. Or more a dirge than a nocturne by James McNeill Whistler. I prefer his etchings. No film or camera would record that eerie light. I etched it onto my mind, as Whistler might on a copper plate.

The last mourner disappeared into the murk that was Pennsylvania Avenue, unless, of course, they had all dropped off into the Potomac. The fog might well be hiding the earth's jumping-off place.

I pulled slowly away from the window and went to the dressing table, put my elbows on its top, and stared in the mirror. It was immediately obvious that I do not look like Mrs. Cameron.

Having just had my forty-second birthday on September the thirteenth, I am reconciled to the fact that I'll never be taller than 5 feet, 2 inches, that my nose at best is aquiline, my cheeks too puffy for beauty—no interesting hollows for Clover—and my chin—well.

My husband, as he has made no pains to hide, does not think me handsome. "Her features are too prominent," he once said. Though when I was twenty-eight, and we were first affianced, he wrote to his friend, Charles Milnes Gaskell, that I would not be "quite called plain, I think."

"A charming blue," an acquaintance familiar to us both called me. Then I laughed at the thought of being a blue. I think I was said to be a bluestocking primarily because I was not beautiful enough for people to forget I could read German and Latin and a very little Greek—and had opinions. No one would call Elizabeth Sherman Cameron a blue, no matter how much Greek she knew.

I stared again at my face in the mirror. I know not only my own mind, its hills and hollows, but the bones and bumps of my face, the way gardeners know their flower beds or cartographers the terrain.

I tried that curious way Mrs. C. has of tilting her head and looking up at a man—even Henry who is shorter than she. I bent my head, flirted with the mirror, and shook my head at the unlikely result.

I tried my version of my enemy's soft voice: "I am, as always, guided by your opinion, Mr. Adams," she said, ad nauseam. My efforts were neither ethereal nor seductive, only ridiculous.

I gave up looking at my face; at best it would not scare the horses. I relieved my eyes by admiring the photograph on the dressing table of Boojum, Marquis, and Possum, the Skye terriers, having a tea party. I could feel—and see—a red flush starting at the base of my neck and going up to the edge of my hair as I thought of the party where everyone was showing their babies' pictures, and like a fool, I pulled out my photographs of the dogs. Now, at the thought, I took aim at the photograph, and threw a powder puff, a large, soft ball of net trimmed with ribbon, that Lizzie Cameron gave me.

Oh well, as Mr. Corcoran says, if you need a friend in Washington, get a dog. And that I have, I have.

I closed the window, locked the door. I tumbled my clothes over my head and left them in a heap on the floor. For the first time in my proper Victorian life, I went to bed naked and lay there, feeling the strange sensations of unconfined body against the texture of the Dresden linen sheets, aching with desire, grief, and perhaps most of all, anger.

♣

CHAPTER 2

November 1, 1885

All Saints' Day — The 85th Anniversary of the Day
Abigail and John Adams First Occupied the White House

∞

Dear Posterity,

This morning the fog is gone, along with the funeral march.
I have only my thoughts—of this day, of Elizabeth Cameron, of
Henry Adams, of his grandparents, of our marriages. I will, as
usual, purge my thoughts by writing them down. I went to my
sixteenth-century Spanish writing cabinet, opened the carved
screens and gilded metalwork which serve as doors, caressing them
as I did, and worked the catch that revealed the secret drawer
and its contents, my pen and my last present from my father, a
burgundy leather-bound journal. Not even Henry—I believe—
knows of this secret drawer. I hope he never does.

He would find written here thoughts that might disturb even
that Boston hard clamshell protecting his amour propre. And what

17

then would he do to my protective shell? Though I like to think of mine as more of a soft-shell crab.

Henry is forever talking about writing an autobiography to chart his "Education"—by which he means the people he has known, the accomplishments he has made, and the influences on his life. Though I doubt anyone cares about my own life, I too am dedicated to setting down its salient experiences. For years, I wrote my father every Sunday. After his death, I put the letters in order, a memoir, of sorts, rather like a sundial, marking only the sunny hours. Now I write in secret to a correspondent yet unborn, and thus am free to tell a darker tale. For these epistles are written, to be pompous about them, for a time when Clover Adams and La Fayette Square have passed into oblivion. I don't intend Letters to Posterity to be read while either Henry or I are alive. This is the record book of my life. I write all I know—give lengthy explanations; record my dreams; divulge intimate secrets of the marriage bed; describe at great breadth the architecture and other attractions of the city; detail the curious societal customs practiced in this late nineteenth-century capital; tell the histories and stories of the principal characters (including of course, Henry and me) who live within La Fayette Square. These are the boundaries of my subject. Here are my own, if warped, views of Washington 1885—and of Clover Adams.

What matter if I sound crazy, unhappy, paranoid, or worse yet—verbose? I shall send this volume, sealed, to Mr. Corcoran's bank, where I will hire a safety deposit box, not to be opened for a hundred years. My mother wrote for her children. I, who have none, nor am likely to, think I shall require my journal to be salvaged and read by a woman who can prove she is not even a collateral descendant to the Adams family. Dear Miss Posterity—

what will your life be like? I wonder what a hundred-year lease Novem-ber 1, 1885
on a box will cost me? And how I will explain the expenditure to
Henry?

∞

I once wrote my sister that I felt as though I lived and
dreamed behind a wall of ice. Ice is a metaphor that occurs to me
over and over again. I have always felt cold. Maybe not always,
but certainly since my mother died when I was five years old.
There is a story that Betsy tells. Kind Betsy took care of us from
the time we were born because Mother was ill. When Mother
died, Betsy said she told me my mother had gone to heaven. And
I asked, "When will she be back?" That's the way Betsy tells it.
I remember it differently. I don't really recall being told at all.
I learned of her death by touch, not by hearing. When I was
brought to her room, she was gasping for breath, her eyes wide
open, wider than open, as if she were stretching every orifice
searching for air, for some way to get the giant ton of pain off
her chest.

When Mother saw me, she tried very hard to smile—I think
she loved me very much, but then I was the smallest and had the
shortest list of transgressions. I think now that my birth must have
shortened her life, but I believe Mother never held it against me.
I touched her hand, and I almost flinched because it was very hot,
the consumption was burning her up. And then someone moved
me away, over to a big chair on the opposite side of the room.

The room was dim, shadowy—perhaps that's the reason I've
always loved light, chandeliers filled with candles, rooms flooded
with south light, bridle paths illuminated with sunshine, the coming

of spring, the comfort of summer. I die each year at the December solstice, I am born again with the summer solstice.

In Mother's soft chair, its big arms hugging me, soft cushions snuggling me, I felt consoled. I could still feel Mother's fever on my hand, now warming, not burning. I must have gone to sleep. It is perhaps not surprising that no one picked me up and took me to my room. Maybe they thought my presence would be a solace for my mother. Most likely it was simply that no one was paying much attention to me, since I was quiet and no trouble. When I woke again, only a single candle cast a flickering light that was almost worse than total darkness, since it distorted what it revealed. The room was very dark, so dark I had no idea the dawn would ever come again. When you're five, you aren't so sure about these things; in winter you have no confidence in summer, in night, no certainty of day.

I could see only the bare outline of my father, asleep I'm sure from the exhaustion. In his lap, my sister Ellen slept as well. I don't remember Ned, but he must have been there, because in later years he recalls it all. Betsy, dear Betsy. She was awake, standing by my mother and the candle on the bedside table. I went to her quickly, almost in a single motion. Betsy reached out for my hand and held it tightly, a warm hand, lending her life's heat to me. I looked at my mother in the candlelight and thought how beautiful she was. Her eyes were closed. Her mouth was barely open, not a smile or a frown. I suppose she gave up trying to breathe and died. I was overcome with my love for her. I wanted so strongly to be part of her again, but I didn't know how. I hadn't kissed Mother in a long time. I know now she worried for fear Ned or Nella or I would catch her tuberculosis. Though the idea of germs was not as clear then as it is now, my father was advanced in the knowledge, and he saw that she protected us as best she could. Kisses, then, were rare and great pleasures between us. At November 1, 1885 that moment, in the late of night, since her eyes were closed and she was very still, I thought she must be asleep, or at least not aware of me, or what I planned. Before Betsy could stop me, in a trice, I leaned over and kissed her white, smooth cheek. My lips felt as though they froze to her, as though she were a chunk of ice. I will never forget that coldness. Never. Cold, cold, cold, cold, cold. The river's winter ice. The slabs of ice in the milk house. The icicles hanging from the roof. The snow as it falls, covering over the windows, heavy against the door, piling atop the roof, a great huge pillow, a satin pillow suffocating us below it. I felt all those things in the cold flesh of my dead mother. I knew very well that Mother was no longer there. She had gone away. If I called, Mother would not hear me. If I laughed, she would not smile. If I cried, she would not comfort me. Mother had left me and I was forever alone, and eternally frozen.

On good days, rationally, I know this harsh feeling is untrue. Betsy loved me then and loves me now. My sister Nella and brother Ned loved me and love me still. Most of all, my father loved me from my birth to his death. Though I had lost Mother, they had lost her too. Betsy lost a kind friend more than mistress. My father lost a lover as well as a wife. Nella and Ned knew her longer and loved her as much as I. They did their best to keep me warm. It was not their fault that I refused to thaw.

Oh, what a silly fool I am! Oh, how tragic a poseuse! You'd think, to read my plaintive cry, that I never had a ride on my daddy's shoulder, or a close hug from Nella, or a smile of approval by Betsy. I had all those things. My father was a wonderful man, nothing at all like the stereotype New Englander. He, mindful of our loss, gave up his career as an eye surgeon, and spent his time in bringing us up. His attention was always ours. We were his

Refinements of Love

focus and his fancy. More than many women of our class, he took care of us, never shunting us off into the care of servants—for none of us ever counted Betsy as "hired help." My father thought of us with joy and we returned every spark. My sister and brother were very close to me, though we never confused the fact that each of us was unique. Even today, I can write them without fearing they will misunderstand.

So how can I say that I was frozen, that for me winter was the year round? The ice floe, the wall of ice, the glacier moat that so encircled my life seemed to me to be around us all, as though we lived together in a family igloo, where the warmth of the sun couldn't penetrate.

When I fell in love with Henry, I thought he was the sun, come to thaw me and release me into the warmth of the world. I can remember that warmth as if it were an hour ago instead of thirteen years ago. Where did it begin? On the top of my head, the crown? That's the usual place for the sun to bask. On my hands, at his touch, when he took my hand as we went into dinner in his father's ministry residence in London? No, the warmth began, I remember clearly, a day when we were riding in Cambridge. By that time, he was a professor, actually an assistant professor, at Harvard, and I was quite enchanted with his worldly ways, his classical knowledge, and, I often suspect, with his quick sharp tongue. As I said, we were riding, and when we came to a lovely spot, a promontory overlooking the sea, we stopped, without, I think, a word of decision, but rather an unspoken, mutual agreement. He was off his horse first and he came over to help me down. As my feet touched ground, his lips brushed against my cheek almost as though by accident, so lightly he could have denied the effrontery. Suddenly I felt warm, very warm, like a taper lighting an oven or the heat when the door is opened on a glass furnace. I knew that he brought me warmth. He was my sun, and I would grow in his light and blossom and bear fruit.

∞

Much later, I looked up from my journal, and said out loud, to myself, "Bosh! Why must sensitivity and sentiment always write like sentimentality? How is it possible to express feelings in words without sounding like the penny dreadfuls the parlor maids read? It's all truth yet it reads like drivel!"

I felt even more foolish when I heard, "Madame, may I light up?" The upstairs maid at the door probably heard my lecture to myself. I answered with a politer than usual, "Just a minute, please." I put away my diary in its safe and secret place. Closed it all up, and went over and unlocked the door. "Come in, thank you." The maid lit the gas wall sconces, we agreed that winter would soon be along. I asked that my repast be sent up on a tray—only a thin piece of the chicken white meat, a bit of the bread, a slice of cheese, and a glass of milk.

I poured a glass of sherry from the cut glass decanter. I stretched out on the lounge until another knock on the door again interrupted my meditations.

"Clover?" asked Henry's New/Old England voice, rather like East Indian tea, unfortunately diluted by lemon.

"Yes?" I replied in a noncommittal tone, neither cream nor lemon.

"To perdition with it," said Henry, opening the door and shutting it behind him. I hadn't relocked the door—that measure is reserved to ensure my privacy when writing. "I'm jolly well tired of being polite. What's the matter with you? Why are you hiding up here?"

He stood awkwardly. Henry was never a very impressive figure, bald and small. I teased him that he wore his head upside down, for he sported a beard and a full mustache, both quite tidy and well-trimmed. Henry tended toward dapper, and tried, not always with success, to see that I was equally so. Usually his self-confidence enabled him to rise above his stature. But now he shifted from one foot to the other, in the manner of professors standing in classrooms, lecturers at Chautauquas, or preachers on salvation circuits. I had no intention of helping him this evening. He could jolly well come to the point if he had something to say.

"May I sit down?" he asked, looking around for a place to do so. I suppose my boudoir has become increasingly unfamiliar to him. My suite includes a sitting room which is my equivalent of his study, and a bedroom and dressing room beyond it, adjoining his own bedroom and dressing room. The boudoir is not furnished for company. Unlike Mrs. Cameron I do not receive in my private chambers. So I haven't felt the need to put in a chair to receive visitors. Finally, Henry settled on the desk chair, the only possibility, and sat down on it backward, his feet in front, his legs spread wide (and just barely making it) around the back of the chair. He folded his arms and leaned against the curving top.

"I need to know what's the matter. I'm concerned about you. The servants come to me and ask if there's anything they can do. They don't understand why you sometimes—for instance, today—don't come to meals or leave your rooms, much less the house. Are you avoiding me? Are you angry with me? What have I done? I don't know. I've searched my conscience and find nothing I have done to offend you. Tell me what is the matter!"

I looked at Henry, wondering what he was really thinking. Why had it become so imperative to him to know that he had brought himself to ask, nay to order me to tell him? Henry, like

all Adamses, has an ego in inverse proportion to his size. I sometimes think I can see his ego, standing on Henry's shoulders,
towering above him, the head of the ego rubbing its crown against
the ceiling. I wondered if it felt heavy on his shoulders: did it
weigh him down? He twisted in his chair, kicked his foot at the
rose design in the carpet, and looked in general as uncomfortable
as it was possible for an Adams to look.

"Clover, are you still mourning your father? Is that why
you're off your feed?"

He preferred to ignore any problem I might have with him and
think I was still preoccupied with my father's death. He knew from
the beginning how close my father and I were. People would often say that we were very alike, that it was "ridiculous that any man
and woman should be so like one another" as my father and I.

Perhaps my father indulged me the most by granting me
status as a grown-up person, with full license rightly or wrongly
to decide my own fate, change my views, be happy or sad, but
above all be my own self. Not many people and hardly any parents
grant such autonomy to another being. Certainly not an Adams.

So there sat My Adams, wanting me not to talk about my
sorrow, but to get on with it, at least to suppress that sadness so
it didn't inconvenience Henry Adams. And he had a certain justification there.

Still, what could I do more for my father than mourn him?
Yet Robert Hooper would not have thanked me for a black dress
and veil. Not for us the heavy crepe veil, the black arm band, or
the black worsted dress that felt, I thought, the way a hair shirt
sounded. I was not Mrs. Lincoln, who ordered her black mourning
dress and her widow's veil a month before her husband was
assassinated. By the standards of 1885, my family did not observe
mourning—at least not the ostentatious outward signs of mourn-

ing. We went about our business. We attended what dinners and
parties we chose.

Even so, we should be permitted to practice our ritual of
mourning—to keep the dead alive in our memories. What right
did Henry have, asking me, for his sake, to forget my father, so
that my husband would not be discommoded by my grief? I could
do that. I could keep my sorrow locked up in my diary, or in
letters to my sister or brother. But why should a husband not be
willing to console a wife's sorrow? One should marry to share woe
as well as joy.

"Yes, I miss him, Henry. How could I not? But he was happy
right up to the last minute, even with the pain and the expectation
of death. You saw him, you know what I mean. But I rejoice in
his life more than I mourn his death. Thinking about him makes
me happy, not sad. He was the best of fathers, and he thought us
the best of children. Not many people are so fortunate in their
views of each other."

Henry, not appeased, grumpily replied, "Well, if it isn't Dr.
Hooper, what is the matter with you?"

"Why do you ask?"

"Have you forgotten?"

"What?"

"What day this is. You know! Why aren't you dressed? Are
you sulking? You know we are having people to tea. We have
always celebrated this day. It's a historic day, not just for us, but
for Washington. How could you forget?"

Of course I remembered. This was the sacred Adams anniversary. Today, eighty-five years ago, at 1:00 P.M. on November
1, 1800, his great-grandfather John Adams became the first president to move into the White House. The day will live in glory
in the heads of the Adams family forever as recompense for their

expulsion as personae non gratae from the Garden of Eden. On this, the eighty-fifth anniversary of that epic event, I salute Abigail Adams The First for putting up with John Adams, earlier and later.

Henry regards the White House with a proprietary air, an old home place. Well he might, though neither his great-grandfather nor his grandfather had more than single terms. The nation can take only so much of the Adams men.

Henry had some grandiose idea that we had come to Washington as to a court, that as the grandson of a ruler, he was a prince of the ancien régime, royalty with an inherited right to be a courtier and to have a seat just across La Fayette Square from the White House.

I persuaded Henry to go on down and await his guests. I struggled into an acceptable tea gown. When I came into the room, I could hear him give his lecture. I had heard him tell it on the first day of November every year we have been resident in Washington.

"The President's house was still far from finished when my great-grandfather rode into town on a Saturday—he'd been expected on the following Monday. Granny Abigail loved to tell stories about hanging the wash to dry in the great East Room and climbing ladders because the stairs were not finished."

I refrained from pointing out that John and Abigail Adams had only a few months in the house, for Thomas Jefferson became president in March.

Henry had assembled a small party, mostly legation people, I was relieved to see, in the hopes they might not have heard his November discourse too many times. British Minister Sir Lionel Sackville-West and vivacious Victoria, his daughter; Turkish Minister Aristarchi Bey and his wife; a Japanese couple whose names I can't spell, who spent the whole evening wafting airs of bemusement; a rather elderly man in Chinese scholar's black robes, who nodded at every sentence, from agreement or sleepiness, I couldn't tell which; and Imperial Russian Second Secretary Georgi Bakhmetev and his wife, Marie, Emily Beale McLean's sister— certainly they had heard Henry's harangue before. Certainly they were too polite to say.

I was very proud of myself for suppressing put-downs as his speech continued. I really didn't want to ruin his tea, and his pathetic little effort to aggrandize himself. I even went so far as to give him his cue: "Henry, perhaps our guests would be interested in one of the stories your grandfather told you when you spent your summers with him in Quincy."

The sun rose on Henry's face. "Well, he was a great man, even if he was my grandfather. When I was a small boy, he used to tell me instructive anecdotes about his four years in the White House and eighteen in the House of Representatives. My boyhood ended when the old man died in 1848. Sometime, if you like, I'll take you to the Capitol to see the very spot where, in mid-oration, John Quincy Adams yielded the floor to a stroke. He died two days later in the Speaker's office.

"Should I tell about Quincy Adams and the great Marquis de La Fayette's triumphant return dinner?"

I nodded yes; after all I wasn't permitted to escape the house anyway. But our guests, as quickly as they decently could, put down their cups, pleading to hear about La Fayette another time. They left almost in a body. The sun set on Henry's face, and by the time the last guest had gone through the door, his face was dark and angry. Knowing him, I also tried to leave for the upper regions, knowing his propensity for taking out his disappointments on me simply because I was close and his wife. I was not quick enough.

"They left early because you were late to tea." He started November 1, 1885 his tirade. "That was rude, not only to our guests, but to me. Perhaps that's what's it's all about, you were insulting me through my guests. You were very rude to La Dona Cameron last night. I hope you will make amends. What is the matter with you, Marian? Let's have it out right now."

I looked at Henry and wondered how I could explain why Mrs. Cameron's arch remarks and subsequent revelation upset me. I am sure, if he only would listen just once, many of my problems could be solved. I think, in the beginning, he did make the effort, at least politely to give the illusion of listening, no matter how duplicitous. However, every year, it seems as if the block in the section of his brain dealing with me thickens. So on this night I thought I wouldn't try; I'd try to pass my anguish off as a simple female frailty, a thesis he was prone to believe in anyway. His anger didn't make it likely that he'd pay much attention.

"I am sorry. I had no intention of making you angry. Young Mrs. Cameron was herself apologetic about being sick here last night. The sight made me equally queasy. I am sorry I couldn't come down to help you see them off. Surely Emily McLean was able to cope?"

Henry, slightly mollified by my reasonable tone but still feeling wronged, went on to exact further apologies from me. "Well, I went home with them in the carriage. I couldn't just let the two women go by themselves, and one so ill. She really looked as though she were poorly, but she's so beautiful even illness is becoming to her."

"Henry, you do know what caused her ailment?"

Henry said nothing in return.

"She's with child. She's expecting in the spring. Is that not wonderful for her—and Don?"

Henry said nothing at all.

"Henry?"

He stood still.

I went to him and put my arms around him. He felt as rigid and cold as Jackson's statue in the park. His chill cooled my own blood and bone. I dropped my arms, ran back to the sofa, and buried my face in the loose pillow.

I suppose he left the room. I did not look, nor hear. The room grew still and eerily empty as though I had left as well.

CHAPTER 3

November 2, 1885

Elizabeth Cameron's Tale of Her Wedding Night

∞

Butler Johnson's quiet knock on the door came like a message from another universe. I was not sure I was ready to receive it. I hastily shoved my journal under the pillow on my chaise, its emergency cache.

"Forgive me, Madame, but I have a note for you. I would not have disturbed you, but Mr. Adams requested I bring it. Would you like me to come in or slip it under the door? I am afraid it requires an answer."

"Oh, come in, Johnson, I won't bite you," I said, straightening my robe. The note was on La Dona Cameron's card.

"Dear Mrs. Adams, I am so sorry I made you ill night before last. Surely you are all right now? I hope so. Will you please come to call this afternoon at three? I'm not allowed to go out at all. Come and cheer me up."

I looked at Johnson, reached for my own card, and hastily wrote on it: "Dear Mrs. Cameron, I am still not well. I hope your indisposition has passed. I'll visit as soon as I feel able."

"Please ask her coachman to give this to Mrs. Cameron," I said as I tucked it into its tiny envelope and handed it over to him.

At that, Henry walked in the door. "Clover, when are you invited to Mrs. Cameron's? At three? I'll have the carriage ready or will you and the dogs walk over? Would you like me to go along with you? Say."

"I have said I shan't go. I do not make calls. Certainly not when I am summoned on such short notice. Surely Mrs. Cameron is aware that I plan my days more in advance than four hours."

When Henry and I first came to Washington, I discovered that the etiquette of calling, laxly observed in New England villages, here was rigidly followed, as closely as the bells for prayers in a religious order. With Henry's approval at the time, I quickly announced to all that I would not make calls, nor would I receive them. But we'd be happy enough to greet friends—even accompanied by their less boring acquaintances—at tea at five in the afternoon. And to that I have adhered, with an exception or two of a call at the White House.

Henry turned and looked at the waiting Johnson. "Ask Mrs. Cameron's driver to wait a few minutes for the answer."

With Johnson gone, Henry, with a look of sweet reasonableness on his face, looked me in the eye and said softly, "You must go. There is no choice. I shall cut some of the last roses for you to take with you. I'll tell Johnson to say you will be there at three." And without waiting for my assent, he walked out the door. I resisted the impulse to throw Mrs. Cameron's card—or better a vase—at him.

The next question is why did I resist? I fished out my journal and thought with my pen:

Elizabeth Cameron's suggestions of intimacy with Henry when she came for tea jolted me as if I had been riding a bucking horse. Henry has always treated women with the gallantry one would expect of his generation and education. I could never complain that he ever forgot to hold a door open for me, or preceded me through it. If his speech is sometimes abrupt, well, that's his sojourn in England. I've always thought he had a fascination with women—for instance, his lecture "The Primitive Rights of Women" at the Lowell Institute. But until Lizzie Cameron, his interests have always seemed to be diffuse, encompassing the entire sex, a generality rather than a specificity. It's as though he obeyed a museum injunction to look, not touch. I believed that if he were ever guilty of adultery, it would be of the mind, not the body. So I've always been confident that whatever he denied me in demonstrations of affection, he was not reserving to bestow on other women. Was I wrong?

I was able to reconcile myself to live with Henry without children—indeed as if we were children ourselves emotionally, brother and sister, chaste, with no need for bodily comforts—when I thought that he had no choice. But if he has been able to give Elizabeth Cameron a child after denying me, then our life of the last thirteen years has been based on lies, deceit, fraud—whatever else can I say? And why should I care? Because, as ridiculous as it sounds, whatever he does—or doesn't do—I love Henry. I want our child.

Henry's insistence that I call on that little chit makes me feel degraded, put down, stepped on, whipped into submission.

The Ruba'iya't of Omar Khayya'm (Fourth Edition, 1876) echoes in my mind:

> What! out of senseless Nothing to provoke
> A conscious Something to resent the yoke?

Or closer to La Fayette Square, Poe's:

> Can it be fancied that Deity ever vindictively
> Made in his image a mannikin merely to madden it?

All of my fierce feminist principles, inherited from my mother and aunts, and my own hurt and envy gave way before Henry's insistence. He laid down the law. Mine but to obey it. How had I given my rights away? How had he taken them? And in what a foolish waste would he squander them—to force me to make a call to a woman I did not want to see? And to violate what I had thought was a gold-bound agreement between the two of us.

So why have I agreed to make the visit? Why curiosity, pure curiosity. I want to hear what she says.

∞

I put my diary back in its hidey-hole, and at 3:00 P.M., done up in the mauve daytime Worth costume I had bought on our last trip to Paris, I walked down the street with Boojum. I told Henry adamantly (what a dreadful pun, and it happened without my volition—I must get a hold of myself) that I would not go if he insisted on coming along, and I scorned the carriage.

As I walked out the door, bowing three times in the direction of the White House, in the manner of Muslims to Mecca, I determinedly avoided the thought of Elizabeth Cameron by surveying the terrain of my walk. The city is moving to higher ground—those who can afford it. We will soon be left low and wet here with the president, just keeping his head above water in his swamp palace just above the river. The massive flood in February four years ago, came within three blocks of the President's House.

Worst yet, the sewage seeps through the canals and the streams and into the flats south of Pennsylvania Avenue. Malaria surely rises with the stench from this murk. No wonder I have perpetual sinus problems. Though it makes me feel like a fool, I should have tied a handkerchief over my nose, as I usually do when I walk along these open sewers and paths of incontinent horses. The stinking sewer along B street has only recently been filled in with a proper sewer pipe. Before then, crossing the street without totally ruining your shoes and the hem of your dress was quite an athletic endeavor.

In the Cameron hall, I hoped against hope that Madame was indisposed suddenly and the butler would say, "Madame is not receiving." My hopes were aroused when he asked: "Would Mrs. Adams be so kind as to wait only a few minutes until the doctor leaves?" But I was not to be spared. Mrs. Cameron was expecting me, he said, but she hoped I didn't mind, Madame's health was such that she was receiving in her bedroom.

I amused myself while waiting by jotting down in my small notebook the protocol for calls for you, dear reader a hundred years hence. I hereby record the etiquette as taught to me by my mentor, Mrs. George Bancroft. By your time surely, not only the practice but perhaps the memory of these indignities will have passed.

To the butler at the door, I, the caller, offered two of my husband's cards (one each for the Senator and Mrs. Cameron), one of mine, since currently La Dona is the only lady (if that is the right word) resident in the house. I would never leave a card for that oaf Cameron—even if it were the custom for women to leave cards on men. I presume the butler has eyes to see me and a tongue to report my presence, still, I follow the custom of indicating I was actually on the doorstep by turning down the corner of the card, though I don't go so far as to bend the card in the middle as the overly zealous do. A pristine, unmutilated card indicates that it came in an envelope with a driver. Some brave society women—despairing of being Flying Dutchmen forever floating around Washington circles—plead ill health, stay at home, and send only coachmen and cards out on the rounds to fill the silver trays of entrance halls. Of course, then you are trapped by those who call on you. One of these days women will rise up and end this foolish waste of their time.

Alas, now, in Washington, card carrying is a serious occupation, rigidly set to a schedule known and obeyed as if it were a Constitutional amendment.

The ladies of the Supreme Court, by which are meant the wives of the Justices, receive on Mondays; Congressional ladies on Tuesdays; Cabinet ladies on Wednesdays; Senatorial ladies on Thursdays; Diplomatic ladies on Fridays. Washington's own Cave Dwellers—entitled to the appellation by their descent from the founders of Maryland and Virginia from which the District of Columbia was carved—receive on Saturdays, or is it Sundays? I forget.

Initially, the newcomers call on the wives of their husband's seniors. Thus a Congressman's wife must call upon all the wives of Congressmen who were elected to the House before they were, as well as the wives of foreign envoys, senators, cabinet secretaries, justices of the Supreme Court, and of course, the first and second ladies of the land. One calls on the sick, one's dinner hostess (within three days following the occasion), and so forth.

When one is not received, one pencils in initials standing in for French phrases on the lower left-hand corner of calling cards. These souvenirs from the early republic's infatuation for the French doubtless date from the time Franklin, Adams, and Jefferson spent in France. Of course, the lingua franca of diplomacy is French. If you, kind Posterity, have need to know, here are the standard ones, translated in case French is forgotten by your day. (More likely no one will speak anything by then but a deeply corrupted lingua americana.)

p.r.—*pour remercier* [to express thanks]

p.f.—*pour feliciter* [to extend congratulations]

p.c.—*pour condoler* [to offer sympathy]

p.p.c.—*pour prendre congé* [to say good-bye, take leave, used when removing one's self more or less permanently from the locality]

I wish I had the fortitude to hand the butler a card inscribed "*p.p.c.*," and skip the country.

∞

Alas, I was soon summoned. The invalid was arranged like an odalisque on her chaise. She was beautiful, I would have to give her that—grudgingly. Today her color was returned, and obviously hers and/or her guests' appetite, because a table was pulled up between her chaise and a simpler side chair.

"You don't look indisposed at all, Mrs. Cameron. I am disposed to think that you are better."

"Oh dear, Mrs. Adams. How you must hate me for that evening. How dreadful of me to be so sick all over everything— and you didn't even know why. Emily said she wasn't a bit surprised that I made you so sick you wouldn't come down again. Are you better? You must be or Henry wouldn't have let you come. Are these roses from your own garden? So late! It must be all this mild weather." Lizzie Cameron, coy in mixed company or when confronted with an actual man, when dealing with women is a gregarious lot. "I'll wager you could've been knocked over with a feather, dear Mrs. Adams. You'd decided that like you, I wouldn't have any children. Well, it did look that way. Not that I minded particularly. Don's children are enough, if not too much, for any maternal instincts I may have been born with, though they have not acknowledged my maternal rights to them."

With plenty of time to think during Elizabeth Cameron's monologue, I debated the primary question about the pregnancy: By whom? Surely not by that churl Don.

"Don is so pleased. A young baby makes a man feel young, don't you think? Why, Don's been acting like a boy. Likes to show off his young wife and his prowess with her, you know."

Mrs. C. opened her box of salt water taffy and offered it. I refused with as little disdain as I could manage. She ate the awful chewy glop, licked her fingers and around her mouth with her preternaturally long tongue—I half expected her to preen her whiskers like the alley cat she is. Instead, she settled back against her cushions and bestowed a smile of smug self-satisfaction on me. I would've liked to stuff the box of taffy down her throat until she suffocated.

"Well, I was surprised. Though I'm sure a baby will add much to your marriage."

"I don't mind telling you, it took a lot of gumption for me

to decide to do it. It wasn't all that easy to grit my teeth and put up with Don's attentions. I never wanted to marry him—I'm sure you've been told that, everyone in town knows I was in love with someone else, a *young* man, my age, someone who was in love with me. But my family had already arranged that I was to marry Senator Cameron. They wanted his money. He wanted a young wife, one he hadn't worn out as he did his first one. So I was sold to the Senator. When Uncle General Sherman fought to free the slaves, he didn't mean his niece. The family thought it a grand marriage. To give them their due, I do believe they had no idea how awful he is. The joke on me is that they wouldn't let me marry the man I loved because they heard he drank. Drank! He only sipped in comparison with the Senator. The Senator! Not only does he have money—he's a Senator! You know what that means: status, influence, all the things my family wanted. Even on my wedding day, I said I wouldn't marry him. But you know what it's like. If you're a woman, you do what you're told."

November 2, 1885

I thought, my heaven, how horrible! In spite of myself, I felt sorry for her! I suppose I'd never really realized what it would be like to be beautiful and in straitened circumstances—and to have a family who wanted money enough to sell their prized possession.

I had not heard the worst.

"I had done very well at escaping all that—marital duties, you know. Most of the time, of course, he was simple enough to get rid of, because when he started to get ideas, I'd offer him another drink, and before long he couldn't remember what he had in mind.

"How Emily laughs at my stories about dodging Dangerous Don. I became quite agile. I should write 'One Young Wife's Guide: Escape Routes.' Let's see. You know about the sprained ankle ploy I used to postpone our wedding."

So that was put-on. Everyone said so at the time.

"And then I was the reluctant virgin, afraid, shy, uncertain of what is required of her. But that joke was on me, literally. Horrible, horrible. He violated me on our wedding night in his private railroad car. I fought him. He stripped off my clothes, tearing them to shreds, and he beat me. He took off his belt and beat me. Then he slammed me down on the bed and took me by force. But he was sorry, because I told him if he bothered me forever after, I'd tell my uncle, and he would call him out and kill him in Bladensburg on the dueling ground. And Uncle General Sherman would have, too, if he knew how that dreadful Don treated me.

"Afterward, he changed his tune and pleaded with me, entreated me. Bought me jewelry, took me abroad. But I would always toss my head and claim inconvenient times of the month, sinus headaches. I developed unpleasant colds, full of coughs, sneezes, and wet handkerchiefs. Later, separate rooms, locked doors. The how-dare-you look. When he became too angry at my flirtations with everyone but him, and threatened to send me home without a penny, I found the most effective defense—I keep him out dancing too late, feed him too much party food, and always keep his decanter and his pocket flask full of bourbon, as if part of a wife's duty."

I couldn't move, but sat in horrified amazement at Lizzie's revelations. I had never heard a woman speak so frankly. Indeed, sex was not a word often mentioned in New England upbringing.

"I couldn't see that I owed Don a child. After all, his first wife had six children—no wonder she died young. She must have been a nice woman—all six of the children hate their stepmother—not that I pay enough attention to them to get in

their way. The only way I pleased them was by not having any
children. They were absolutely livid when they found out I am in,
as they say, an interesting condition. They don't want to have to
share their father's affections, or rather, fortune, with a new baby.
At first, I don't think Don cared. After all, his ability to father
children couldn't be questioned—at least before alcohol replaced
sex as his obsession—unless Mrs. Mary McCormick Cameron was
remarkably unfaithful to him."

November 2, 1885

Ah, that was the second Mrs. Cameron's knife, thought
Clover.

Don was a proved stud.

Unlike Henry.

The expectant mother smiled that satisfied smug smile of
hers, as though replete after a night of love. "So you want to
know, do you, why after seven years, I finally gave in? Certainly
I couldn't get pregnant by myself. Perhaps you're to blame."

Unthinkable.

Impossible.

Other women have not been Henry's problem.

Until La Dona?

And suddenly I knew what she meant. During the Camerons'
recent trip to Europe, I wrote Mrs. Cameron to go to the Louvre's
Long Gallery. "Oh, you mean that I told you to say to Van Dyck's
lady with the young child that she haunts me, and so she does,
so she does. Did she haunt you, too?"

La Dona smiled the smile of one no longer haunted by
unfulfillment.

∞

When I returned from the Cameron house, Henry, unchar-
acteristically untidy with ink on a finger, was waiting at the door.

He looked anxious out of all proportion, as though his fate would be fixed forever by my word. What did he expect me to say when he asked, "How is she?"

I petted Possum who greeted me by rubbing up against the hem of my skirt and looking up at me in the hopes of reciprocation. This gave me a minute to compose my answer. I couldn't possibly repeat anything Mrs. Cameron had said—not to Henry, not to my sister, not to anyone but my journal. What could I say? That Mrs. Cameron was dead of love for Henry, gasping for him with her final breath? I could say the divine lady was up and about, dancing waltzes with the latest young Senatorial aide to bring her bonbons? I could say the city's beauty was fine when I arrived, devastated when I left. None would be true, but all would be more interesting and lead to conversation. Aha! I thought of the right word to describe my afternoon and serve Henry right for asking.

"She was confessional!" I said.

I made the turn on the stair with Possum at my heels and saw Henry's face. We are getting in the habit of looking at each other obliquely. Or have we always looked at one another, not straight on, but out of the corners of our eyes so we wouldn't see more than we wanted to know?

In my own bedroom, I rang the bell for the maid and ordered tea sent up to my room. I slipped off my outdoor clothes and wrapped myself in the challis robe I bought in England—not very warm but enough solace when I stretched out on the chaise longue by the comforting fire.

Considering it has been less than a year since my father's death, actually almost seven months, conventionally I should be spared all formal calls. Certainly the fact counted for something, a valid excuse even according to the rules of the Washington society, which I scorn.

However, I did go out this afternoon, and I learned much about Senator and Mrs. Cameron. If she does not speak falsely, I think that no matter what the deficiencies of our marriage, we surely have a better one. Her family should never have forced her to marry him. What a terrible indignity! I know such marriages are often arranged, but I still find it utterly unforgivable that a father should acquiesce in such a travesty. Cameron's attack on her was beyond forgiveness. He is a beast—I have even heard someone call them the Beauty and the Beast. I have always disliked the man intensely, because he is the definition of that adolescent girls' cliché: "rude, crude, and unattractive." Besides that, he is politically corrupt—of that I am very sure indeed. For some time, I have tried to persuade Henry to forgo inviting Cameron to the house. But Henry has said that besides the pleasure of Elizabeth's company, he finds Cameron useful, because he drinks too much and thereby talks too much.

November 2, 1885

Strange, isn't it, that Cameron and I should have something in common—that we both are married to spouses who have no desire for us. At least Henry does not drink to excess, patronize the camp followers left over from the War, wallow (as the Southerners say) in corruption, nor brutalize me. Indeed, the more I think of Henry's wit, his manners, and, indeed, his gentility, I think perhaps I should not complain.

But Elizabeth Cameron will have a child. And I will not.

✿

CHAPTER 4

November 4, 1885

The Pen as a Weapon

∞

Dear Posterity,

I have dismissed the phantom father of Elizabeth Cameron's expected infant from my mind. Far better to focus on my own concerns, Henry, of course, being the chief one. I went down to breakfast this morning in the hope of a kind word, though breakfast is not Henry's best time. I was amazed to find from Jane that he had asked his breakfast to be served on a tray in the study. When it was presented, he was seen crumpling up paper and throwing it into the wastebasket while emitting a rude word. Jane said she hurried out after making certain she had not caused his curse.

I took my time with my eggs and bacon—I suppose the Virginians so heavily salt their pork to preserve it in the heat of their unhealthy summers. Afterward, I thought a wife might be permitted a short peek at a husband who had not appeared at November 4, 1885 breakfast without offering an explanation.

So, with Marquis, Possum, and Boojum as my honor guard, I knocked on the closed door of his study—and admittedly entered without waiting.

"What do you want, Marian? Do you not understand that when a door is closed on a study it means that the occupant is pleading for peace and quiet?" As he spoke, he turned the sheet of paper over, and, as if I could see through the thick bond, put a book atop it. The effect, obviously, was to arouse my curiosity to the point of my having to clench my hands behind me to keep from snatching the paper from his desk. I decided to avail myself of a glance at his blotter at the earliest chance.

"Get those dogs out of here. Their eternal yip, yip, is like Chinese water torture in my brain. Close the door after yourself and tell Jane not to fetch the tray till I say." He swatted at the dogs with a rolled-up newspaper, sending them yipping indeed out of his way. I picked up two of them protectively.

I had no choice but to retreat with a murmur of apology, a look of repentance, a head full of questions, and armsful of spurned dogs.

In the safe haven of my own boudoir, I settled down to try, in my usual fashion, to analyze in writing Henry's morning mood.

I shook my Stylographic pen. The writing instrument seemed dry and scratchy, suiting *my* mood. With a wave of memory, I thought of the first time I'd seen such a pen, when we were embarked on the *Gallia*, from New York to Liverpool, our second trip to England. A dining table companion, a bright civil engineer from Brooklyn, demonstrated its marvels and boasted that it would hold two weeks of ink. I was so charmed by the pen, and, oddly enough, the engineer by me, that he gave it to me.

Pens are tools of contemplation to me. My poetess mother before me often said, "How do I know what I think until I've written it?" Long ago, I decided that life was more bearable if you organize it into words, sentences, paragraphs, novels.

Especially in a marriage such as I have, I need to keep something to myself.

I was born with the curse of seeing the world through a kaleidoscope, tragedy and comedy broken into pieces and tumbled together against the light. I know my satire often offends others, especially when I insist on seeing the silly side of sorrow. I must, for my thoughts are deep and black. If I could not turn the kaleidoscope to see black holes as light and ludicrous, I would not be able long to look life in the eye. If laughter is a two-edged sword, well, it is better than having no weapon for your defense. But I have two—laughter and my fine-pointed pen.

I take my text from George Sand, who wrote in one sentence of her twenty-volume biography: "Write your own history," for I understand well that no other knows my heart—certainly not the other Five of Hearts, that stupid and inappropriate name that only John Hay would, in an excess of romanticism, apply to Henry's inner circle. It should be called the Three Kings of Hearts—Henry, John—and Clarence King. Actually Mr. King should be called the emperor. When he is here, the other two bow down and serve him. And Clara Hay and I are strictly the jokers—or the discard cards.

Thinking back on it now, I realize that the accommodation that Henry and I had reached between what I expected of him and marriage, and what he expected of me and marriage, began to break down when he first read *Democracy*, before it was published five years ago.

I began writing it as something to do. I refuse to stuff myself

like a Christmas goose with food and gossip at all the stupid lunches
and coffees inflicted on the idle women of the town. Henry had
decided that my services were no longer needed in the drudgery
of copying out research for his histories. Ostensibly, I was fired
from the job because I refused to take lessons from him in penmanship. He contended that he was weary of trying to read my
writing, and he would hire someone else to do it, which he did.
Admittedly I write with a loose, loopity-loop hand far different
from Henry's careful penmanship. But I enjoyed working with him
very much. The research into the backways of history is intriguing,
and at least in Europe, I was able to open many doors of closely
held historical secrets.

Novem-
ber 4,
1885

After I was summarily sacked, most days he went to the
State Department archives, and I stayed at home, writing. Henry
culls official papers to write his histories. But I think such documents are but the mummy wrappings of the past. The real story
of the world comes from the people who live, if wounded, through
the wars, the losers as well as winners of the elections, the bank
failures, the brides and grooms of the weddings, and the lovers
who die of shattered hearts. I flatter myself that though Henry is
a historiographer, I am a chronicler, one who writes what the
French call "little history."

Democracy, my first book, was a roman à clef. I had no need
to invent any of the characters. My heroine is a widow who moves
to Washington, goes round in political circles, is courted by the
just and the unjust. Finally, disillusioned and distraught by the
people and the process, she leaves the country.

Henry vehemently opposed my "exposing yourself in public.
It's just as though you had stood in the middle of La Fayette
Square and disrobed. Everyone will recognize the people you wrote
about. We won't be able to live in this town. We'll be tarred and

feathered and ridden out of town on a rail. Not only that, none of my brothers or my parents will ever speak to you, or to me, again. They'll blame me for not stopping you from publishing. What you should do now," and he reached for the manuscript as he spoke, "is to burn it. Neither of us will be safe as long as it exists."

I thrust the bundle behind my back and for once stood him down. I recall my words, I don't think that I am embellishing them in my memory. No, no, that time I had my tongue in the right place.

"Don't you dare touch a corner of my book! Don't you dare! This is mine, not yours! I've put in my hours for your books, I've copied pages and pages of dates and facts. I've sneezed and wheezed over your dusty documents. But this one is mine. It's my life and my work. And I will have it! I have no child to guarantee my immortality. But by heaven, I have a book, a true book, and you will not take it from me unless you do so over my dead body."

Well, maybe I didn't say all that. But I didn't back down. And *Democracy* was published.

The book was a huge success! I was so proud of my accomplishment! Everyone in Washington read it! Everyone in London!

As a roman à clef it was a succès fou. Everyone in our circle talked about it, speculated on who wrote it. Four of the Five of Hearts were suspect: Clarence King, John Hay, Henry, myself— all except Clara Hay, the quiet, retiring, motherly one of our group. There were those who postulated that we collaborated on it, writing every day at teatime. One report had it that John Hay and Clarence King had each written a chapter—Mr. King the one mentioning Worth gowns, of course.

As I expected, Henry, who had belittled my efforts, wouldn't permit me to acknowledge the book. He wouldn't let me tell my

family, or the other Hearts, much less the public. But then he
thinks that only a male Adams has the right to a public name, if
only on the spine of a book, not a ballot.

Recently many people—Aunt Carrie Tappan and my father
chief among them—guessed the truth, though Henry made me
deny writing it.

Last year, after my second book, *Esther*, was published, my
father was sure. *Esther* did not sell out as *Democracy* did, but the book
in many ways is closer to my heart. The characters are less disguised.
The central character embodies many of my own concerns—the
contempt in which society holds women's creativity, the restric-
tions on women's freedoms, and the derision with which women's
philosophic views on religion and science are held. What greater
themes are there than sorting out your belief in yourself and your
belief in the gods? The episode in it about the death of the heroine's
father still chills me. It came uncomfortably close to the circumstances of my own father's death, not long after.

Yet Henry lied and denied vehemently that I had written
either *Democracy* or *Esther*.

I am amazed that anyone, even as a joke, would think a man
had written either. I especially resented Henry's denial to John Hay:
"My wife never wrote for publication in her life and could not write
if she tried." Yet Henry even pretended to believe that John Hay
had written *Democracy*. I saw the letter, I suspect left out especially
for me to read, as he often does when he wants me to know he
is criticizing me behind my back. Henry wrote: ". . . the book is
one of the least sufficient, for its subject, I ever read. Since it
came out we have had half a dozen dramas here that might reasonably convulse the world . . . your novel, if it was yours, is a
failure because it undertook to describe the workings of power in
this city, and spoiled a great tragic subject such as Aeschylus might

Novem-
ber 4,
1885

have made what it should be, but what it never in our time will be. The tragic element, if accepted as real, is bigger here than ever on this earth before. I hate to see it mangled à la Daudet in a tame-cat way. Men don't know tragedy when they see it. What a play of passion we have seen here within two years this day."

I have no money from the sale of *Democracy*. A fair sum came from Henry Holt, the publisher. But Henry would only let *Esther* be published under the ridiculous pseudonym of Frances Snow Compton. He insisted on what he called an "experiment"—the book was published without advertisement, either in print or by word of mouth. Holt said that it would have done well if it had been listed as being by the author of *Democracy*, with a few review copies sent judiciously here and there. As it was, my royalties from *Democracy* went to pay to publish *Esther*. But Henry was adamant that it fail so I would be able to publish no more books. Henry feared that my small talent might give me a minuscule measure of fame, of approval. I might, perish the thought, be widely read by the public. I might make a bit of money, an unsuitable occupation for an Adams, even for one by marriage.

Worst of all, from Henry's view, more people have already read my books than any of his histories. And my books tell more of the truth, about Washington, about New York, about women, and about love, than Henry Adams will ever know.

What would Henry do if I proclaimed myself as author?

∞

As I put down my pen, I heard pawing at the door become more and more urgent. Marquis, Possum, or Boojum? Boojum. Obviously in frantic need of having his ears scratched and his warm, wet but empty mouth filled with a biscuit, to make up for

Henry's early rejection. When I let him in, he raced in, almost
somersaulting with enthusiasm. Ah, that was why he was so
happy—he'd proudly brought me a gift to exchange for a biscuit.
A sheet of paper, held carefully in his mouth, the way he'd been
trained to bring in the newspaer, without taking nibbles from it.
Only this was not *The Washington Post.*

Oh, dear, I thought, I hope it's nothing important. Henry
will chastise us both if it's a manuscript page. As carefully as I
could, with Boojum's dancing around, I extracted the paper. I
cautiously looked at it to assay the damage. The paper looked to
be precrumpled. That was a good sign. Probably came out of
Henry's wastebasket. Well, maybe that wasn't as bad as it could
be. Though Henry was rather funny about trash from his desk.
He never left it for the servants to take out. Even in the height
of summer, he would always burn in the fireplace his discarded
versions, ink-blotched pages, and those he crumpled in anger when
the right word wouldn't come. I supposed it came from working
in a legation, where the servants were always suspected of being
spies in the pay of other governments. But then, Henry did have
a certain perpetual paranoia. I thought I'd best read the letter to
judge the gravity of Boojum's sin. The writing was certainly Henry's, precise, easy-to-read Palmer penmanship.

> My Dearest Love. I should have answered your letter before
> this, but I hardly knew how to reply. Yes, yes, I long, I
> yearn, I crave what you propose. So long a denial. So many
> years of deprivation. I am not sure that we could meet
> without Marian's knowledge. . . .

I heard Henry coming in the door. Boojum pricked up his
ears at the sound.

❧

CHAPTER 5

November 5, 1885

The House on La Fayette Square

∞

My dear Posterity,

Hearing Henry coming in yesterday, I thought fast. Three possibilities flashed quickly through my head. I could try to send Boojum back with the letter, lock my door, and pretend I had never seen it. I could take it down to the study another time and try to insinuate it into his wastebasket without his knowing. I could burn the letter thoroughly. That was the most easily accomplished, so I threw it in the fireplace and pulverized its charred ashes. I hoped Henry would empty his wastebasket without poking through it.

I rewarded Boojum with TWO biscuits, which earned me much credit in his hungry little heart, and he and I cuddled on the chaise while I rubbed behind his ears and he licked my face with enthusiasm and biscuit crumbs.

November 5, 1885

But even Boojum's ardor couldn't cushion me from the shock of Henry's letter. "My Dearest Love"—Who is his "dearest love?" The one person I know it isn't is me. Such an effusive salutation—even for this age when words are sometimes as elaborate as picture frames, all curlicues and gilt. Could Elizabeth Cameron be the Love? Likely. Since we met her in 1881, she has been an object of fascination to Henry. And now that she has promise of being The Mother and Child, the embodiment of the Madonna he talks about as the Goddess, she is no doubt even more enticing. In *Esther*, I patterned Catherine Brooke, the quintessential ingenue, after Mrs. Cameron. That was before I quite realized the solace for her husband's boorishness she found in Henry's gentility. True, this letter suggested they had not been together for a long time—though perhaps that was an exaggeration for effect.

Most disturbing are the phrases about "longing," "yearning," "craving," "deprivation." The letter certainly implied a romantic tryst. But why was the letter discarded? Perhaps he has had second thoughts. After all, he says he is unsure what to reply. Unsure— that's my situation in a word. What shall I do? Shall I frankly ask Henry to explain? Would he?

The evidence has gone up in smoke. Boojum has been duly rewarded for his gift.

Enough of lamentation. Clover, list the facts please, for Posterity, and maybe, who knows, you'll find, rising out of the data, an explanation.

∞

Our taking up residence at the capital for the second time has not been notably successful. We came here in 1877 when Henry, having tried and despaired of law, academia, and journalism, decided to settle on history. History took us back to Europe in 1879 so Henry could research the diplomatic archives for documents about Jefferson and Madison. On December 5, 1880, almost five years ago, we leased this house, at 1607 H Street, at $2,400 a year rent. Though not quite a tenth of our yearly income, it is not cheap, being dictated by the location and, I might add, our insistence on the addition of a plumbing wing. I do think that a house in the most prominent part of the capital of the United States of America should have indoor plumbing facilities.

Everyone comes to our house for five o'clock teas—Elizabeth Cameron, judged the most beautiful woman in Washington; of course, John and Clara Hay from Cleveland, Clarence King from everywhere; Henry Cabot Lodge, a former student of Henry's; Senator L. Q. C. Lamar, that rarity, an honest man; John La Farge, the stained glass artist who appears as the artist Wharton in *Esther*. And of course, when he is in town, Henry James, who, some say, has patterned a heroine or two after me. James is not always kind to Henry. He once said Henry preferred Washington to London, because here he is "somebody."

By 1880–1881, I had become the best known and chronicled salon keeper in the Capital. I poured the tea and sharpened my wits against the others, much like a cat sharpens her claws on the upholstery. John Hay brought us all the important men of the day, the politicians, the lobbyists, the financiers. Clara Hay was indispensable—for listening when everyone else talked at once. And King, brilliant, amusing, undependable, always in need of tea, beef sandwiches, $1,000, and condolences. And Henry, with his histories—those to which he was born, those which he was to write. Our game only lasted for a season. Then the Hays and King moved away, and the exhilaration of that high season began to fade like a debutante's looks after too many dances and champagne toasts.

What of Clara Hay? Could it be that she is Henry's correspondent? What a thought! No one would believe Clara Hay would have a liaison outside of marriage. Clara Hay, so quiet, so acquiescent, so like a nice plump hot cross bun, crossed with icing. A kindly, a useful woman. Efficacious, friendly, fecund. Not so much a person as a pedestal for her parents, husband, children to stand on and perform.

Could such a woman really interest Henry? She is as nearly my opposite in looks, personality, oh yes, certainly in wealth, as anyone could be. Henry does have a preoccupation, perhaps even an obsession, with the Mother Goddess—not Minerva but the Madonna, the nubile virgin who exists only to give birth. Is it possible that Clara actually fell in love with Henry and he with her? That would perhaps explain why Henry was so anxious to have John and Clara Hay come back to Washington and build a house attached to ours.

Why *did* Henry want to build on La Fayette Square?

Henry looks from our little white house to the big one across the way, and feels small and unfulfilled. Henry has been and continues to be a critic of the great events in the White House across the way, but he is no part of them. He has known those who have moved the mountain of legislation that either buries public policy or leaves a road to it. But his influence is as small as his own height. He—and I—exist only, as he is fond of saying, as spiders on the wall, our influence limited to occasionally entrapping the unwary buzz-around insect who is stupid enough to blunder into our web. Our house is the web.

Everyone already calls it the Hay-Adams house. The position of the names is correct. Hay's house is certainly more expensive, larger, grander, as befits the size of his family, his wife's income —especially since his father-in-law's death—and his august official offices. Life seems to do things backward. Mr. Hay as a young man served as assistant to Abraham Lincoln's secretary. More recently, he was assistant secretary of state. Still he turned down the position of secretary to President James Garfield. Mr. Hay says he cares nothing for political life but only serves in duty. Though I am sure he will again be persuaded. For now, Henry would give my right hand for a title and an office in the government. But no president will offer Henry so much as a janitor's job.

I am sorry we haven't been able to have a son, so Henry could at least think that his progeny had a chance to regain what the Adamses think of as the family mansion.

Unfortunately, Henry's desire for a son is not strong enough to bring forth a desire for me, though my desire for him has, perversely, remained. Is his unattainability an aphrodisiac? Passions are so perverse. I once thought if I tried very hard I could entice him into the necessary feeling—otherwise I would certainly not have married him. Many believe in this day, so much more re-pressive than the last century, that women have no need for physical expressions of love. I do not hold to that belief, though I am beginning to believe that certain men do not. Before we were married, Henry's gestures of affection were formal and minimal —but I believed that such restraint was part of his charming manners, part British, part Harvard, part Adams. I also felt that he didn't wish to hurry me, respecting my aging virginal innocence. That reluctance seemed rather sweet, thoughtful, and I gave him credit for not being brutish or overbearing—unlike Elizabeth Cam-

eron's Don. I could almost forgive her for her efforts to enmesh
Henry when I consider Don Cameron's obvious bestiality.

There I go again, back to the Camerons. But this is about
the house.

Strange that we should build a house. I had always said, after
we built the cottage at Beverly Farms, I wouldn't build a serious
house. But as we had no children, the house seemed to be the
only thing we could raise together. It has taken somewhat longer
to grow than a child, but then, perhaps it will, in the end, be
more satisfactory. Building a house is likely easier than building
character.

However, the presence of its architect seems rather more
intrusive than that of doctor or midwife. I had no say in the choice
of H. H. Richardson as the architect. Indeed, I have had to be
ever vigilant lest he replace both Henry and myself as clients, or
as parents (he's bigger than both of us). Had Henry given me a
choice, I would have chosen a thinner architect, one of less gargantuan presence and philosophies and with more prudence. Henry
and I are small people, and Richardson is huge, tall as well as
wide. I sometimes feel as though he's a great river steamboat about
to run aground over me.

Indeed, I often feel as though his influence with Henry is
greater than mine. He had been at Harvard with Henry, so of
course that carried much weight. So does Richardson—375
pounds, or so I'm told. One of his draughtsmen told us of a lark.
The master architect had left his vest, forgotten on the back of a
chair. Three of the apprentices put it on together—they said with
some space left over—and paraded around for the others to laugh.

I should be more charitable. Sadly, he suffers from a chronic
renal disease, which accounts in part for his size, though his great

appetites help. Saint-Gaudens once told me that every time he went to Richardson's house, his host would put a magnum of champagne and a huge cheese on the table—both proscribed by his doctors. And say: "S-S-Saint-Gaudens, ordinarily, I lead a life of a-abstinence, but tonight I am going to break my rule to celebrate your visit, you come so irregularly." Actually, Saint-Gaudens told me, Richardson brings a guest home every night to serve as an excuse for his indulgences.

His work is always massive. Those huge arches of his are sized so he won't bump when he goes through the door.

Richardson began by digging a great hole for our house, big enough for a pond, a sea, an ocean. Before I saw that great void dug to its depth, I thought of the hole as waiting for the planting of the house, like a large fat bulb, or even a good-sized tree to grow toward spring, with halls like branches and rooms like leaves and flowers. Thinking back on the hole's immensity, I realize it wasn't round, shaped for a tree or bulb, but rectangular, oblong, like a mass grave dug for the victims of a plague or a hurricane. Perhaps that was the reason I was not surprised when Richardson had a cross carved in the stone between the two great arched openings. Henry hates the cross and threatens to grow it over with ivy, or (horrible) obliterate it with a bas-relief of Elizabeth Cameron's face. Of the two, I'd rather have the cross.

The cross is like a grave marker. Good thing I haven't blurted out that thought to Hay or Henry. They are not fond of my funereal fantasies—though Henry himself often rattles more bones than I. He objects to graveyard jokes because they scare him, as though they are premonitions of disaster. Not that he admits it. Henry used to go further than I in hesitating to build a new house. Henry often said he held to only one superstition: "Never move into a new house"—what a laugh now. Actually, he has many occult, if not religious, beliefs. He even tried to call up the spirits of the dead—at Mrs. Piper's séances in Boston. I wouldn't go with him.

November 5, 1885

I wasn't so grave—ha!—when we bought the lots in 1883 with John and Clara Hay. In London, on our honeymoon, Henry and I had admired the "New Art" houses, the red brick houses à la Queen Anne—their red-tiled roofs and carved brick ornaments hung with wrought-iron balconies very much like the iron jewelry German women favored. On La Fayette Square with the prospect of our own house, we spent wonderful days and evenings, drinking endless cups of tea over Viollet-le-Duc's *Dictionnaire Raisonné*, planning castles and then scaling them down to the cottages we could afford. We built the house on paper, with cards and saltcellars, and in our minds. We walked through it in our imagination, furnished it down to the pictures over the green onyx mantelpiece. In my mind, I served tea in its library—we didn't want a fancy parlor. In my thoughts, I've gone to bed on its third floor many a time.

We finally decided we couldn't afford the cream-colored stone from Ohio, which Richardson insisted on at first, and settled on simple, and less costly, Washington brick. Many a night, instead of counting sheep leaping over turnstiles, I would count brick being laid, one on top of the other. But it wasn't a satisfactory sleeping potion because it was enthralling to watch the house take shape.

We sent Richardson our scale drawings in mid-January last year. He immediately wrote to Henry—I think he had little interest in my opinion—that he thought Viollet was "an archaeologist— a theorist—never an architect." Amazingly, we managed to agree on the drawings by March. But in June, even after we'd signed the contract, he wrote, "The depths to which you must have fallen in quoting Viollet as an authority on design is painful."

Richardson added that architectural plans are nothing. He made this revelation, of course, after we had struggled for weeks and months over his drawings, arguing not only with him but with each other. Only when blocks of stone or rows of brick are in place, the sun and shadows changing the color and the shape, softening lines, altering perspectives, elongating and shrinking rooms and aspects, does Richardson believe the building comes alive and tells him what it wants of its architect. Friends of ours in Boston say that Trinity Church's board approved one set of plans, and then he built something quite different. Richardson admitted to Henry, "I really don't see why the Trinity people liked them, or, if they liked them, why they let me do what I afterwards did."

From my fiercely possessive view as client—after all, much of the money was my dowry—Richardson is outrageous. He disparaged our importance to his career by telling us that "house building is not architecture in the noble sense of the word." He was more honest when he told our friend J. J. Glessner, "I'll plan anything from a cathedral to a chicken coop. That's the way I make my living." He's already spent enough of our money to build a cathedral. I have to say that he does work very hard on our houses. He is never very well, and often has to work in bed, with draughtsmen and clients paying him court as though he's Louis XIV. He wants every stone, every brick to go according to his own eye's view. I think we, of all his clients, have fought him the most to have a house to suit ourselves. His illness must be worse, or we could never have won on the small preferences we did. He's even gone through the city saying that the design of the Hay-Adams house can not be judged as representing his own inclinations.

Richardson is deeply disappointed—he says—at the lack of

modern conveniences we'll permit in the house. So far, we've been able to save ourselves from at least one futuristic frippery.

November 5, 1885

Since 1877, the "electric speaking telephone"—Alexander Graham Bell's invention (he married the Grosvenor daughter)—has been sending out its wires like the tentacles of the dreaded kudzu plant. By the next year, government offices had installed more than a hundred. Henry and I did talk on one at the State Department, and I have to say you could understand the other end, but it crackled and snapped a good bit. The new apartment buildings have telephones from the units to the public dining room, the janitor's room—and even the elevator, a good thing considering the notorious unreliability of that means of transport. Some people—notably Richardson—think that telephones will eventually connect all better houses. But as long as we have coachmen to take notes from here to there, who would need them? As for telephones in the house, well, the bell system has served to summon one's servants since medieval times and I see no reason to discontinue it.

Despite my protests, we *have* installed both gas and electricity in our new house—a duplication of effort, not to mention money, but Richardson persuaded Henry that electric light will illuminate the future. That's all very well, I said, but will it light us in the present? The President has yet to agree to the White House being wired for electricity. As of now, electricity still often fails in ice storms, wind, and so on. So we went the extra money to back up the new with the old.

The city will soon be tangled up and choked with unsightly wires, draping themselves from lamppost to lamppost to buildings. Four years ago, the first electric lights began to glare in our nights. Henry and I, of course, didn't go, but friends told us how excited they were when the lights came on at James A. Garfield's 1881 inauguration ball in the Smithsonian's new Arts and Industries Building. The lights, strung like streamers, made a glare that sliced the building into pieces, the way lightning reveals a distorted world when it strikes. Now, some effort is made in lighting fixtures to make them imitate candles or gaslight, but the color is different, harsh and cool compared with the gentleness of either gas or candle fire. I would like to try some photographs in electric light. Of course, we still have gaslight in this house—our landlord sees no reason to jump into expensive so-called improvements when we are so soon to move on.

The city fathers talk of electric streetcars, but I'm thankful to say they haven't been inflicted on us yet. I suppose we do need some transportation for working people. Not everyone has a coach or carriage. And many people live in cheaper outlying sections at a distance from their work.

The city has grown a great deal since the War, with all this migration from the South—both black and white. I looked up the figures to be exact: in 1870, the population was 131,700, and in 1880, the census reported 177,624—59,696 of them Negroes.

The older settlers tell me the colored population now is quite different from just before the War, when a fifth of the landowners here were free Negroes—some early settlers—industrious, often educated, some professional, prosperous. During the War, 3,000 Negroes joined the Union Army here. Many contrabands, farm laborers from tobacco and cotton plantations, had fled the South before and during the war. "Marse Lincum's" boys, as they called them, were mustered out in Washington and stayed, flooding the town, hoping for jobs.

They've settled in small communities: Vinegar Hill, Foggy Bottom, Hell's Bottom, Swampoodle, Cowtown, The Flats, and Barry Farms, among others. They need schools and jobs and medical

attention. The Washington freed colored people, led by Frederick
Douglass, have done what they could to help. The Freedmen's
Bureau does what it can—it has established Freedmen's Hospital,
Howard University, and so on. I contribute money to Nella's
education annex for women at Harvard, of course, and the art
school in Charleston (we must help our vanquished foe). But I
give more to the Negro schools here. I would like to do something
else. I think I would enjoy teaching, but Henry doesn't think my
health is up to it.

Washington now has a true apartment building—Paris has
nothing on us. The Portland Flats was built in 1880 by Edward
Weston of New York. The seven-story building is topped with a
tower. Two years ago, Richmond Flats was built not far from us
at 17th and H Streets. The new hydraulic elevators are what make
these tall buildings possible. Though I think the result is too dense
a population.

Pacific Circle has become DuPont Circle by the addition of
a statue in its middle of Admiral Samuel Francis DuPont. The city
is moving north, away from us here where it all began. Even so,
to me, La Fayette Square will always be the heart of Washington.

Because our new house will face south, across the square, as
our present one does, I had good light in last winter to photograph
the construction. Hay's, facing east, was at its most photogenic in
the morning. I'm up early. In warmer weather Henry and I ride
in the morning. Sometimes I even load the dogs and my camera
and tripod in the buggy, Brent driving, and go to photograph in
Rock Creek Park. But in the winter, I'm not often out before our
noon breakfast.

Still, I was very dutiful, taking photographs like a proud
parent. The day in November '84 that the great Richardson arch
hung in place without its answering support, we made a picture

to mail away to Hay. Somehow, the pictures of the arch were misplaced or forgotten. I do tire of the long hours in the darkroom, bending over noxious chemicals. Still, photography for me is a necessity—as is writing—a way of showing others what I see.

Last winter was long and dark, despite our south windows. The unfinished, unheated house is cold and its plaster dust makes me sneeze and cough. I could hardly stay in it long enough to fight with Richardson over his pretentious ideas.

Now the house is finished. Richardson says so. My husband says so. John Milton and Clara Hay have been told it is finished. But I am not so sure. It does not seem to fit me. I feel strange in it, lost, though I know every inch of it by heart. The house is Henry's. I wonder if he will live there without me.

I wonder if Henry will look like Ezekiel weeping over his dead wife in Blake's ink drawing. When Francis Palgrave gave it to Henry as a wedding present, I smelled the dank and moldy air of the grave clinging to it—an ill omen for a nuptial gift.

∞

I put down my pen, and looked up at the charming portrait of Princess Charlotte by Zoffany, George III's court painter. Henry had given it to me on our seventh wedding anniversary when I gave him the wee Turner watercolor, only five inches by three but very early. We like tiny works—they don't overwhelm our own physical scale.

At the window, I was happy to see Henry walking down the street, probably on his way to see the new house, but perhaps not. Anyway, I deemed it safe to go downstairs. First, I carefully locked my journal and put it away in my reticule, covered loosely with two handkerchiefs. I dropped the diary's tiny gold key into the little pocket on my camisole. Henry wouldn't look there.

In the parlor, I straightened the eight-by-six-foot Salamancan linen embroidery. As usual, I stopped for a moment to look at it again and saw the Spanish town coming out of the Middle Ages —born with all the drama of the chick from the egg. I was surprised to see that Henry hadn't yet removed the Chinese silk brocade from the Turner landscape. I slid it off, revealing the scene and entering into it, losing myself in climbing the hill, watching the river flow, figuring out just how the sheep and the women fitted into its world.

I felt a sudden overwhelming, menacing presence behind me.

I pulled as far away as I could. But not far enough. His hand grabbed mine, exerting enough pressure to turn me at least partially toward my tormentor. Considering that I am at least a foot shorter and possibly 250 pounds lighter, no wonder I had to grab onto a table to keep from being knocked down.

"Well, k-k-k-Clover, eh Mrs. Adams. I didn't realize I had such an effect on you. You look limp. S-s-s-swooning at my f-f-feet, eh. Well . . ." said the voice of the wolf. Huff and puff and blow my house down. My immediate thought was to stay in the Turner river world. The women and the sheep looked quiet and happy. Perhaps if I kept very silent, I could remain there, safe. I wondered for one awful, superstitious moment if by writing about him in my journal, I had summoned the ogre up.

I cleared my throat and tossed my head, trying to control the impulse to throw the hand back in the face of its owner. I said in as calm a voice as I could manage, "Mr. Richardson, do me the courtesy of letting me stand up for myself. You don't know your own strength, but I do."

Novem-
ber 5,
1885

"Do you take offense at a hearty American handshake? I came to ask you which of your possessions you will take with you to the new house."

"Why do you ask, Mr. Richardson? Surely by this time you know me and mine very well. No matter how you choose to design around my person and my property."

"I've done my best my ladyship. But k-k-Clover k-k-Clutter isn't a period I'd worked in before."

"Nor had I ever expected to live in a Richardson Rambunctious Residence," I said with no smile but as light a tone as I could manage.

"Hello! What's this? Are you manhandling my wife, Richardson?" said Henry, bounding through the door with the comic air of the Boston terrier challenging a Saint Bernard.

Richardson moved away from me to the mantelpiece, using it to hold himself up. "Thank you, Henry, for coming to my rescue," said I. "And now I will thankfully escape, my virtue intact, my reason secure."

"But Marian, Richardson and I have been waiting for you to come down. He's going to help us decide what's to go where. Let's all sit down, I'll ring for coffee and cake, and we'll go over our list. The chandelier will, of course, go over the dining table, though I wish I could be sure of always getting twenty nondripping tapers. I do hate wax in the pudding."

Henry, being considerably closer to down than Richardson —especially since the maroon leather chairs were small and low to fit Adamses—was already seated when it became obvious that I was walking out the door. He hastily stood back up and hurried over to me, catching me by the hand. "Now, Clover, you must tell us your views," and he waved his other hand at the English watercolor by the door. "Tell me, dining room or library? Which would you have it?"

"I think it an ideal d-d-dining picture," said Richardson, disregarding the fact that Henry had asked the question of me, not him. "You have enough of the genre surely to d-d-do the whole room with them. How pleasant! How peaceful. When the roast beef is late to be brought in, the guests can k-k-k-content themselves with bucolic scenes of old England. Ideal! We must have it that way! Surely you agree, M-M-Mrs. Adams?"

For the first time in the encounter, I stared him in the eye and said, "For myself, architect Richardson, I prefer to have the William Blake drawing of Nebuchadnezzar gamboling on all fours and eating grass. How appropriate! How in keeping with the green onyx tombstone from Mexico, which you have been so eager to foist upon the fireplace," I said, the battle joined.

Henry, for the nonce, ignored my tone, though even to me it sounded brittle, very much like that of a *glasharmonika*—crystal lightly struck with a wet finger to play a tune. I try hard to make my voice low and pleasing, a full mezzo note, but under stress, the string will pull tauter and raise the octave.

"I must have the little Rembrandt ink and wash by my desk," Henry said. "And surely one good Turner deserves another. The Rhone Valley watercolor you gave me can go on the easel by my chair and the other on the wall. Now Mr. and Mrs. Groves. Should they go from side by side in this library to the new one, in an orgy of Sir Joshua Reynolds's portraiture?

"Did I ever tell you how we came to get the Reynolds pictures? You must hear it.

"One day, Clover received an anonymous message, saying if we would be willing to come to a certain address on F Street, we would find objects to our interest: two portraits, an escritoire and an armoire. We stiffened our nerves against some sort of kidnap scheme and went anyway. Outside, the house looked as though no one had paid it any attention in some time. The shutters were closed, and inside even the curtains, full of dust and holes, were drawn shut. An African, so dark he could hardly be seen in the gloom, answered the door and showed us the furnishings for sale. All were crowded into a library, as though they were only passing through, not resident there. The prices were reasonable and indeed the furniture and the paintings handsome, though all much in need of cleaning and restoration.

"The whole thing seemed just too strange. For all we knew everything was stolen, or infected with the plague, or riddled with lice and mice. I looked around for evidence of the ownership as unobtrusively as I could, since the African had seemed disinclined to confidences. Good fortune turned up on my toss, and on the desk, I discovered a book inscribed with the name Th. Dwight. He's the State Department librarian—we knew him from my research on the histories. Thus reassured, I called on him and he explained the mystery.

"The owner was a friend of his, an impoverished lady whose father had been chargé d'affaires in Belgium. She needed the money, not the objects, since she could scarcely afford the rent for a place to hold them. So the sale was mutually agreeable. Actually, Dwight had suggested she offer them to us, knowing our tastes, but she hated to do it directly, lest it seem as though she were begging. Anyway, it worked well for both us and the lady, who had known fairer prospects. Clover has the armoire and escritoire in her room now."

Richardson, looking bored with Adams garrulousness, nod-

ded, and said noncommittally, "Reynolds portraits to the library.
I presume Mrs. Adams will have the Watteau, the girl with bare
feet lying asleep on a k-k-k-couch, and the B-B-Bonningtons in
her sitting room," boomed Richardson. "Those are very ladylike
works. Suitable for the tender sensibilities of the fairer s-s-s-sex.
That settles that. Now there's only the T-T-Tiepolo sketch in this
room that must be placed as we stand here. I've put in picture
railing as you asked. It should be finished today. Shall I come along
and help you hang the show? You know, Mrs. Adams, the jux-
taposition makes a great deal of difference. Not all art lives happily
together any more than all p-p-people."

Novem-
ber 5,
1885

"You surprise me, Mr. Richardson. I, a mere woman, bought
all these images out of my own feeble taste. I would find it upsetting
if the art all began to make raucous noises at each other—the
Turner shouting at the Watteau, the Reynolds yelling at the Italian
chalk drawings. How will they fight for place? Tell me, Mr. Richardson, will they fence? box? shoot? How strange! An art war!
Choose your weapons, artists—wash against pencil, ink against
oil. And let the drips land where they may. But I, sir, leave the
field to you. You and Henry marshall your forces, and, like Ulysses
S. Grant, fight it out on this line if it takes all night."

And with that, I made good my escape, closing the door
precisely but firmly behind me, not bothering to glance at their
faces before the door hid them. I knew that Henry had only been
making a show of consulting me. Unable to defend himself against
Richardson, in the absence of Clarence King, he was using me as
a shield. I wondered why I directed all my anger against Richardson
and none against Henry?

I suppose that over these years, I have come to turn my head,
stop my ears, speak the soft answer that turns away wrath. Oth-

erwise, I certainly couldn't live with Henry. And, despite his obvious deficiencies as a husband, I still love him, in some way I can't explain. Yet why should I not only have to put up with Henry Adams but Henry Hobson Richardson as well?

I conceded today's battle—until I could marshall my forces.

♣

CHAPTER 6

November 6, 1885

W. W. Corcoran's Child Bride

∞

The Skye terriers—or terrors as I call them—hearing my voice, came racing in from the kitchen, leads in their mouth, declaring their love for me and their enthusiasm for the walk with uproarious yelps, their toenails and leashes clicking against the floor.

I felt much better at this expression of support. I still brooded over yesterday's fencing match with Richardson. I wished for a moment that they were Newfoundlands—or any breed with the bulk to knock over Richardson. Being unable to accomplish this swap easily, I pulled on my hat and coat, harnessed my team, and thus escorted went out the door into the November day. We walked across the street to La Fayette Park, where the faintest strange smell must be followed up immediately as fast as short legs can take you.

I opened the gate with its eagle decorations, walked into La Fayette Park proper in the center of the Square, closed the gate behind me, and let the dogs loose. The dogs ran toward the Navy Yard Urns, on the Pennsylvania Avenue side, where they've learned to expect squirrels. Flocks of birds prudently took wing in the path of the dogs. "Beyond the Square the country begins," Henry often says.

I swept the fallen leaves off a bench to sit under the great bare chestnut tree, one of a collection of exotics W. W. Corcoran had caused to be brought from the far forests of the world to enhance the view from his house. The tree is said to have magical powers to grant wishes made under its shadow. Since I profess agnosticism, I can hardly then espouse magic, black or white, but I could've used a wish-granting tree at that moment. I wished Richardson, and Elizabeth Cameron, separately or together, I didn't care, to be transported to Timbuktu, then I rigidly put such foolishness out of my mind by contemplating the bronze statue of Major General Andrew Jackson. The seventh president has been here since 1852, before the park was landscaped and planted to the Andrew Jackson Downing Plan.

As a devoted horsewoman, I admire the way Clark Mills sculpted the horse, rearing up in a equestrian version of the General's hat-doffing salute to his men. Henry has a hereditary dislike of Jackson, a family nemesis, since the hero of the Battle of New Orleans deprived John Quincy of a second presidential term. Henry considers that the statue was put there solely to block the White House and its goings-on from his critical view. When Henry James comes to visit he always walks over to admire the old swashbuckler, "prancing and rocking through the ages."

The sun was warm, the sky was clear, and the air had a crackle to it that promised surprises but didn't guarantee good ones. This weather is not uncommon for Washington in November, where both deep fog and brilliant sun can alternate on the same day, as does happiness and sadness in the mind.

I looked back at our house. The brilliant sun sparkled off our windows—at Henry's study the windows showed two rings. What were they? Could it be that Henry was looking through his binoculars? At what? Surely he had little interest in my comings and goings. Even so, I turned on the bench so my back was to the house before I took out my manuscript book, its key, research notes, and pen from my reticule and began to add to my narrative.

Dear Posterity.

In your time, the shapes of places may be different. But when Pierre L'Enfant laid out Washington, he made circles to go around and squares to cross to give geometry to life. La Fayette Square and its Park are like a great stage set up for the White House to see what life is like outside its moat of privilege and security. And the Square is lined with houses, the stage sets of past comedies and dramas, used from time to time for new performances by my neighbors: the well-bred, the well-fed, and the well-read, as they were called in President Jackson's era.

I find it hard to concentrate today with the thoughts of Henry's letter to "My Dearest Love" infesting my brain the way the November mold afflicts my sinus. No doubt, there has been a change in Henry since I came back from my father's bedside. Why? Is Lizzie Cameron—or, almost unthinkably, Clara Hay—

the problem? Is he worried I might publicly claim my novels? Or is there a scheme with King to which I am not to be party?

Again? Why am I going over all of that again, round and round, the triangle makes me dizzy. Enough of that, I'll get me back to my writing:

Henry always credits John Quincy Adams for the Park being renamed. When the Marquis de La Fayette made his triumphant tour of the United States in 1824–1825 people slept all night in the Park to catch a glimpse of the Revolutionary Hero. Perhaps this began the tradition of the Square, the Hyde Park of the United States, as the country's shouting place of praise and epithets at their leader.

Benjamin Ogle Tayloe, an earlier chronicler of the Square, reputedly came to the square in 1828 when he was chased out of his father's house by ghostly bells and unearthly presences. Colonel John Tayloe's 1800 Octagon, a block from the White House, is said to be the second most haunted house in town, after, of course, the White House.

In 1868, Henry and his family came back from Europe and Henry set up in Washington as a free-lance journalist—and lobbyist.

I wonder what our lives would have been like if Henry and I had married earlier? We first met in London, when his parents had my father and me to dinner at the legation. Henry certainly paid little enough attention to me. He was far more interested in his father's diplomatic and political guests. I thought him, frankly, rather a prig, one of those self-conscious men who are only interested in what you think of them, and think of you not at all.

Of course, no matter how young we'd married I could never overcome the fact that he was born an Adams.

His family have never really liked me—with the exception

of his younger brother, Brooks. And I know they've made asper-
sions about my family. Henry's brother, Charles Francis, brought
up the suicide of my mother's sister as a reason for us not to
marry. What a thing to say! Especially since the Adams family has
certainly not been without its drunks, crazies, and suicides. But
then, what family who knows its history in detail could say all
members were perfect, in mind and body?

I'm never going to write *La Fayette Square* if I keep riding off
on these diversions. But my mind often feels as tight as a horse's
harness that's too small—the straps will burst if I don't let them
out.

To the west of the White House is A. B. Mullet's Second
Empire extravaganza, the new State, War, and Navy building, all
balconies and mansard roofs. A few more years of finishing by way
of icing and a bride and groom on top, and Mullet's masterpiece
would serve as a giant wedding cake. For President Cleveland
perhaps? When we came to Washington, the south wing for the
State Department had just been finished and the workers and
documents moved in.

Then I loved poking through the papers in State's library,
Henry and I sitting cozily on adjacent high chairs. Those were
happy days because we were working together. I looked at his
papers every day, editing, filing, annotating, researching. When
Henry told me he didn't need my help anymore, I felt as if our
marriage, and my life, had been left at a dead-end street without
a map.

Recently, he's been very secretive about his work. What is
he writing now? And why am I excluded from it? Could he be
writing about me as I am about him? Oddly enough, Henry, who
always has maintained a vigorous correspondence, seems to leave
fewer letters in the silver tray in the front hall for Johnson to mail.

Or has Henry taken to mailing his own letters, or handing them
directly to Johnson so I will not know his correspondents? If so,
why? This letter draft Boojum found makes me wonder.

∞

At first the shadow on my paper seemed right and proper
as a part of the mysterious past I'd been trying to penetrate with
my research. Then I heard the elegant speech, the soft voice which,
to my New England ears, always sounded like eggnog tastes—
smooth, creamy to lure you into yet another cupful until the spirit
of the Kentucky Gentleman bourbon hits you with a wallop.

I looked up and smiled at the sight of W. W. Corcoran,
swinging his gold-headed cane. At eighty-five (next month, eighty-
six) he isn't always well enough to betake himself under his own
transportation to the park.

"Mr. Corcoran, what a pleasure to see you on such a day.
You see me sitting under your tree, in your shadow, so to speak.
I hope I have your permission to enjoy your largess?"

"Heavens, Mrs. Adams, after such a Southern-style speech
—you are surely learning the local talk—I would willingly go
fetch any number of trees to make you happy. Though I suspect
that it would be my going, not my fetching, that would please
you. I am interrupting your writing of secrets better shielded from
eyes such as mine."

"Far from it, Mr. Corcoran. You are just the man I need. I
am writing secrets, or rather it's a secret that I am writing at all.
I need you to be my collaborator, my informer, my reference."

"Gladly, if I am able. What can I tell you that a learned lady
like yourself wants to know and doesn't already know?"

I looked straight at the aged gentleman, metaphors madly
whirring through my mind. As landlords go, he had much to

recommend him, providing a long-suffering estate manager to produce repairmen when needed or himself to serve as the *pièce de résistance* at dinner when invited, but politely absent in England when a known Southern sympathizer's presence would sprinkle too much pepper sauce on a boiled shirt New England dinner.

His fine figure of manhood was well padded in the manner of a sofa, over the years becoming more comfortable as it assumed the contour of its sitters. His great mane of snow white hair gave him the air of a Southern senator who might any minute deliver an oration on states' rights. Corcoran bought his house from Daniel Webster, whose constituents paid for it. I almost giggled at the thought that Webster might have left behind the hair and the manner, though certainly not the oration. New Hampshire Senator Webster had been bent on saving the Union. Corcoran, to the contrary, had supported, with all his financier wiles, what he called the War for Southern Independence, and what my Northern relatives knew as the War of the Southern Rebellion.

"Please do sit with me, if the day is not too chill, though you look well protected in your fine fur-lined coat."

"I would be honored," he said, using his cane to ease the passage from up to down. "Now what, madame, if I may ask, are you up to?"

As I told him of my interest in the history of the Square, he brightened up, for Corcoran loves his city and has festooned block after block with fine buildings. I was pleased at my success, and went on to say, "I am right, am I not, that your house, which you're kind enough to rent us, is a famous and historic house, and not just because Henry lives there. (I laughed.) Wasn't its first occupant a journalist, as both Henry and John Hay have been?"

"Right as always Mistress Adams. Thomas Ritchie came to Washington from Richmond, to edit President Polk's *Union*, the administration organ. I'd built the house, but he bought it from me and I bought it back after his death. Later, I rented it to John Slidell, a congressman from Louisiana. A fine man, indeed, though not of your political persuasion. He was the Confederate envoy to Paris and a major character in the *Trent* affair, a famous case. You may have heard of it since it happened in the Boston Harbor.

"Captain Charles Wilkes then lived over in the Dolley Madison house. Wilkes forcefully removed the diplomat from the *Trent*, a British mail steamer, and detained Mr. Slidell at Fort Warren, in Boston. The British were so incensed at this violation of their sovereignty, they almost came in the war on the Confederate side. Unfortunately, by the time the Louisianan made it to France in 1862, he was not able to do our, that is, his, cause much good.

"Poor man, the Reconstruction government never would let him come home. He died in Cowes on the Isle of Wight in 1871. I'm sure you know that my son-in-law, George Eustis, also a former congressman of Louisiana, was literally in the same boat. He was the secretary of the Paris Confederate legation. Though today that's perhaps best forgotten."

Without stopping to think of old hackles I might be raising, I went on, aroused with the historian's ardor. "And you spent the war in Paris with your daughter Louise and her family?"

"Of course I did. You know my wife only lived five years after we married. Lou and her children were all I had. I went over to see them, and then it didn't seem safe to come back till the war was over. Though you know I'm a patriotic citizen of the United States, and certainly of Washington."

I hastily changed the subject. "I have heard it said, sir, that your wife was beautiful and your courtship romantic."

"Oh, so you've heard of my scandalous pursuit have you? Well, it is a good story. I was born in Georgetown—my father was a banker. At a young age, seventeen to be exact, myself and my brothers set up in the auction and commission business. It failed in the panic of 1823, but I negotiated a settlement and my debt was discharged from the creditors. I'm proud to say that twenty years later, I was able to go back and pay the debts that had been excused by my bankruptcy. Actually, I calculated the interest and paid $47,700, double the original amount. But you don't care about these monetary matters. You, as do most ladies, want to hear the love story."

"I do, I do."

"I explain my finances because you have to know that in the years before we were married, I was not a rich man. My bankruptcy had given me a bad name. I was a failure, a ne'er-do-well. Not a suitable catch for the important Morris family.

"My family was not friends with the Morrises. We were trade, moneylenders, and, perhaps worse, from Limerick."

"Coming from Boston, I know how that prejudice works."

"And Louise's father was Commodore Morris, the hero of the fight of the *Constitution* against the *Guerrier*, a famous Revolutionary War naval battle. Louise Amory Morris, that was her name. Our daughter was named after her.

"Anyway, I was in my late teens the first time I saw Louise Amory, right here in her baby carriage, out for a ride, pushed by her mammy. She was just a few months old, but when I looked at that dear little face, framed by the frills of a pink bonnet, well, I fell in love with her right then and there—and I love her still.

"I'd see the little girl, walking in the park, skipping to school, holding fast to her mother. I would always take off my hat to her and speak. I'm not sure why, but she took a liking to me. Her beautiful eyes sparkled like a firecracker when she saw me coming. I admit to you, because I know you to be a woman of the world, that I did have a few close lady friends in those days. I've always been fond of the feminine face and all that goes with it. I didn't marry in my youth—I suspect because I enjoyed the large variety of ladies available and I couldn't decide which one. But they seemed old, a bit world-weary, before her young innocent face and untouched skin. I used to tease Louise, when I could catch her by herself, and tell her I was waiting for her to grow up and marry me.

"When Louise was in her mid-teens, and I in my mid-thirties, I heard she had joined a dancing class. I made haste to join too, though the dancing teacher wasn't sure how the mothers of the other students would like the idea of the class including a man twice the age of their children. Actually, I'll tell you now, I paid the teacher twice her usual fee, and that did the trick. Worth every penny it was to have my arms around her! I even took to going to her church, the one behind us there, St. John's. The Morrises had their own pew, so I couldn't sit by Louise, but I could see her come and go, and watch her face during the sermon.

"Eventually, she agreed to meet me, at the flower market it was, though she was far more beautiful than even the roses. I suspect that my interest in horticulture comes from those days trying to entertain her at the flower market. I'd read up so I could sound knowledgeable about the posies. She'd go horseback riding, and I would too, and we'd flirt in Rock Creek Park, stealing moments to be alone together, in its secret places.

"Then the Commodore cottoned on to the fact that I was courting her. By that time, I had myself on my feet. I was certainly not rich enough to tempt the Commodore as a son-in-law, but I was far from destitute and I had good prospects. He didn't care, he still forbade Louise to see me anymore. I couldn't stand that. And neither could she. So one midnight, by arrangement, I left my carriage a block or so from her house. Carrying her little shoes in her hand, she sneaked down the steps. She was as far as the porch, when her father, sword drawn, came charging out. He was brilliantly red in the face—I thought he was about to have a stroke. And he shouted to her to go back in the house before he ran both of us through. That brave girl, she didn't budge, but put her arm through mine and said to her father, 'Go ahead, if you hate me that much. I love him and I always will.'

"Well. It was some time before he was coherent. But he didn't actually kill us. At last he listened to what we had to say. Then he sent for a preacher and had us married at dawn, just as the rosy rays of the sun came into their parlor, to dress my love with heaven's blessing. And it was done!"

"You must have been very happy."

"Celestially. Though our first child died shortly after birth. My father-in-law claimed the death was the wages of sin. That loss was very hard on my wife. Then we had our daughter, Louise, so much like her mother. Sadly, the five years we had together was clouded by my wife's bad lungs. She had consumption, so she was never strong. This climate is bad for frail ladies. I should have taken her away to the West, where the climate is better. But I didn't have enough sense then to know.

"When she died, I threw myself into making money for our daughter. Daniel Webster became a friend. And when he was Secretary of the Treasury, George W. Riggs and I were given the chance to sell $5 million of government bonds. We sold them at a profit and bought the United States Bank at 15th Street and New York Avenue.

"After the war—a great tragedy that war—I endowed a refuge for the less fortunate of my daughter's lady friends and mine, the widows of the Confederate patriots, who had lost their husbands, their inheritances, everything because of their loyalties to their home states. In the charter, I wrote that the home is for 'destitute but refined and educated gentlewomen who have known brighter days and fairer prospects.' I named it the Louise Home in memory of both wife and daughter. I go there on my birthday every year and they give me a party. Makes me feel just a bit closer to my Louises."

"Oh yes, sir. The Louise Home has been kind enough to ask us several times to help celebrate your birthday, you'll remember."

"Of course, how could I forget? You and the folks at the Louise Home are very kind to an old man like me."

I had my mouth open to ask my next question when Mr. Corcoran said, "I think I am a bit chilled. When you're as old as I am, Mistress Adams, you'll find winter comes earlier than it does when you're young. I wish you well in your project. There's much of the Square's history that needs to be set to rights."

"Thank you very much, sir," I said. "Do come to tea when you have time from your busy life."

"I'd be happy to come, not only to see you and your erudite husband, you'll forgive me for saying, but your Turners. I admire your taste."

"As I do yours," I said. And with the formalities observed, William Wilson Corcoran retired from the field with due honor. His story had the delicate color and lingering fragrance of a rose pressed in a book. The version told me by Mrs. McLean—who has little delicacy and less veracity—was somewhat more lurid. She asserted that Miss Morris, when confronted by her father, looked him straight in the eye and demanded to know, "would you kill your grandbaby as well, to punish me?"

Despite the sad shortness of her life, I suspect that Mrs. Corcoran enjoyed it. Mr. Corcoran, from all reports, was an ardent lover in his prime. And she must have been a woman of passion and poetry herself. Perhaps it's better to die quickly in a grand gesture, like a limb torn off and lofted by the wind, rather than to hang on as a dried branch decaying on the tree.

November 6, 1885

I had backed off when I saw that Corcoran was still prickly about his Paris sojourn during the war. Corcoran's collusion with the Confederacy was still a topic when we first came to Washington. Henry's father and Henry went on to a great extent about Corcoran's defection to Paris with most of his portable assets at the coming of the War. His fixed assets were more trouble to protect.

Corcoran's own residence, 1611 H Street, on La Fayette Square, was just about to be taken over when Henry Mercier, the French minister—hastily entreated by Corcoran—went to the Secretary of State and said he had leased Mr. Corcoran's place. The Secretary asked if Mercier thought his French flag was big enough to cover the house. Apparently it was, for the house served as the French legation for the duration of the war. The French had provided the same protection for the Octagon, Tayloe's 1800 mansion, during the British invasion of the capital in 1814. In 1866, Louis Napoleon directed the next minister, the Marquis de Montholon, to establish his claim on the Corcoran mansion, by giving the "most magnificent ball ever given in the capital." General Grant attended, as did Annapolis officers conveyed to Washington by a French ship. Imagine! The British minister led the first cotillion at five in the morning, and the dancing only ended with the sunrise. After the bountiful breakfast, everyone went to work or to their calls still costumed in their ball finery.

Though only costumed in my outdoor clothes, I too should go about my business. I put up my book and pen when the dogs, wearying of squirrels, came up yelping, rolling, and jumping around my skirts. I put their leads back on them and started back across the park, just as I saw Henry and Richardson going back into the new house once again.

I once had a fantasy that the house was like the Promised Land—when we moved in everything would be all right. Henry would immediately be transformed into the sensitive, loving husband I desired, and as I entered the door I would be at once beautiful and talented. Ha! I fear I will be like Moses, only given a glimpse of the Promised Land. But then, has life ever kept its promises to me?

CHAPTER 7

November 7, 1885

Boojum's Further Discovery

∞

I woke with an unexpected pleasant sensation of expectation. Perhaps it's simply that all the imps of despair, as the story tells us, pushed and shoved each other in such a frenzy, to escape Pandora's box, that the imp of hope, being a quieter, politer type, declining to be rude, stayed behind and now is comforting me. All this moralizing was doubtless brought on by my encounter in the park yesterday afternoon. Anyway, I was not disappointed. Hardly was I dressed before his butler brought a note from Mr. Corcoran. Would Mr. and Mrs. Henry Adams come to dinner at his house Tuesday hence? They would indeed, I wrote on my card and sent it back without inquiring of Henry. No matter what his plans were, they should take second place to an invitation to the most elegant house in town.

I went downstairs to tell Henry we were invited, but he is apparently out. Mailing a letter? I started to take advantage of his absence with a peek at his desk. And found his study door was locked.

"You see, Marian," said Henry so close behind me, I couldn't help a small shake of surprise, "I was right to lock my door. You do look guilty. Have you acquired an insatiable craving for my stamps? My multicolored inks? My Webster's? Are you perhaps planning a ball and writing a hundred invitations? Or are you writing your sister of my multiple misdeeds? Come, tell me, what leads you to breach my drawbridge?"

I took a deep breath, but uncertain of what tone would come out of my throat when pushed by such stops, I said nothing. Fortunately I had brought Mr. Corcoran's invitation with me. I mutely handed it to Henry and went back up the stairs, making up my mind to be surer of his absence before I tried to go into his study again.

Even I, who was there when it happened, can hardly believe this next episode. After this morning's encounter, the dogs and I walked over to the White House to admire the late roses still blooming in the south garden. Miss Rose was out cutting a few for the house. She was kind enough to give me a bunch, all carefully wrapped so I wouldn't be pricked by the thorns.

Back in the house, no sign of Henry, I gave my coat to Johnson and took off the dogs' leads, enjoying squishing that soft fur and the warm, friendly bodies. Boojum, the first to be freed of the leash, raced up and down the hall, looking for Henry, I suppose. And then, heavens! if he didn't poke the door open to the study. Before I could stop the dog, he pulled another paper out of the trash!

The salutation was to "Dearest." The next line said, "A tribute from his subjects awaits His Majesty." I could read no more for then the top of Henry's hat sailed by on the sidewalk. Henry was under it. He would be here any minute, I was sure. I quickly left his study, leaving Boojum chewing on the paper as though it were a bone. I went to the cloak room, divested myself of my hat and boots, and busily washed my hands, combed my hair, and arranged my face to look as unexceptional as possible. I took a vase from the shelf and filled it with water for the roses. I heard Henry come in and Boojum's welcoming yelps. Did he drop the paper when he yelped? Did Henry rescue it? I preferred not to know.

"Hello, Henry!" I said as brightly as my jet would burn when I finally came out. "You should have come with us instead of missing the sunny day! Just smell these roses Miss Rose gave us. How appropriate!" With a honey mustard look, sweet but spicy, I sailed by him.

In my own haven, I thought I might as well write down this episode in my diary. Surely the paper could be to someone other than "My Dearest Love." I have seen letters Henry has written to John Hay with "My Dearest" as a salutation. Doubtless this is just another discussion about King's tangled finances. "Tribute" sounds indeed like another loan to King. Has Clara Hay refused to allow her husband to redeem King's IOUs any further? I don't deny I, too, have been captivated by King's charm, but I also am well aware his friendship comes with a high price tag. He is always either in debt or planning grandiose schemes sure to incur debt.

I took my journal out of my reticule and poked my hand into my camisole pocket for the key. Of all the obnoxious things!

I have lost the tiny gold key that locks my journal. I must ask the downstairs maid when she tidies before tea. She seems an honest enough girl, but I wonder? The key is, after all, fourteen-carat gold. Perhaps it dropped out of my camisole in the White House Park. I'll send Johnson back over my route. I especially hate losing it because my father gave me the diary not so long before he died. Fortunately, it came with two keys, the other one is in my secret drawer. I laughed and asked my father if one was for him, to read my innermost thoughts. And he smiled benevolently and said, "Every daughter, perhaps every woman, should keep some secrets to herself." My wise father! How I miss him!

What if I dropped the key just now in Henry's study? And Henry finds it! And reads my diary! What would he think of my keeping a journal? Worse than a novel—true chronicles about the people around the Square. Would he perhaps worry what I would write about him? And his friend John Hay? Oh, those Adamses. They only want the world to know them in Adams' words—certainly not in Eve's. I could write a volume about Henry Adams, I could indeed, if I but dared. He'll never believe I intend these writings only for you, dear Posterity.

I wonder what he would do to stop me.

CHAPTER 8

November 10, 1885

The Old Man's Love Slave

∞

Dear Posterity,

Tonight Henry and I strolled in the yellow gaslight next door to our landlord's house.

"Our landlord or no, I'm still a bit surprised that he and I meet over dinner at 8:00 P.M. instead of pistols at 8:00 A.M.," said Henry, in a rare conversational mood with me. "When my father was minister during the War, you'll remember the crisis *du jour* was the *Trent* affair, in which Corcoran's son-in-law, Eustis, was a principal player. I wrote articles about the *Trent*, and the Manchester cotton famine, which my brother Charles published in the Boston *Courier*—under, unfortunately, my name. The London *Times* waxed satirical at my journalistic efforts, though luckily the newspaper was not aware of my position as my father's confidential

Novem-
ber 10,
1885
secretary. That was when I gave up journalism, at least for the War."

I made polite tut-tut noises—not that Henry needed any response in his eternal monologue with himself. But it was pleasant, for a change, to have any remark addressed to me, even such stories, always told in the same words, having been perfected as set pieces years before. I could have written them down verbatim. Indeed I have.

The Corcoran house is more than a tad fancy for what I sometimes call my "chaste taste." The banker acquired his fondness for eclecticism during his sojourn in Paris during the War, when Henry and his father were in London, trying to undo what Corcoran was doing in Paris.

I don't agree with those who call the interior "garish." Overwrought, perhaps. Even a shade "tacky," as the town's Southerners say. But then, it could hardly be worse than the decorative arts in France during the period of his exile.

As we sauntered along the walk, stepping carefully, Henry, though the season was at an end, welcomed Mr. Corcoran's landscaping as a subject to talk about. The Corcoran mansion sits firmly on the edge of the H Street sidewalk. The part of its almost two acres of land left over from the house is landscaped in a romantic, picturesque mode—the "Andrew Jackson Downing Beautiful" movement.

Downing was married to Catherine Elizabeth DeWint, a cousin of Henry's—she was John Quincy's great niece. In 1852, they were traveling on the steamship *Henry Clay* when it caught fire. She was saved, but he drowned trying to rescue one who could swim less well than he. The older people here, who had such great hopes of his design for the Mall, still call him "the late lamented."

Early October, Washington's best month, was the last time we had been to a garden party at Corcoran's. Fountains, well placed to serve as focal points for garden party guests, splashed and flowed—serving the dual purpose of cooling the air and masking the street noises.

Mr. Corcoran's trees, now naked of their leaves, bow in the November wind. The vine stalks imprison the brownstone building like rusty shackles. The other day, walking past, I looked hard toward the orchard in the back, but I couldn't see any apples. Probably they've all been given to teachers.

With my moroseness hanging like a rotten apple on a branch above my head, I haven't recently availed myself of Mr. Corcoran's kind permission to wander through the fruit trees. Not to bruise my simile, in the years when pleasure occasionally blossomed, I enjoyed the way the orchard's pleasant smells cleaned the street air of its stink of horse droppings and people sweat.

Trying hard to engage Henry's interest, I picked up one of our old subjects: Could the Corcoran house rightly be called Italian Renaissance?

"No one in their right mind would say so."

"James Renwick says so."

"Well, my case stands," said Henry. "He doesn't care what part of Europe he takes his designs from after his free trip to Europe, courtesy of Corcoran. Look at Corcoran's Art Gallery, Renwick stole that roof directly from François Mansart. Anyway, it's a wonder Corcoran ever got the building back from the quartermaster supply depot after the Civil War. I'm surprised they let him come back from France. I suppose the Treasury likes his taxes."

"Not fair, Henry. Mr. Corcoran did give his gallery and its

art to the capital. Besides, he raised all that money for the Washington monument. I think he paid his dues."

"You mean he paid his fare back."

So much for my efforts at noncommittal conversation. I
pressed my lips tightly (I have given up biting my tongue, having
so little of it left after years of dutifully not answering Henry back)
as we entered the expansive portal. Greeting us, as always, was
George, Mr. Corcoran's aged Negro servant, freed a number of
years before the War. He never left his post, rejoicing in his status
as the major domo of the wealthiest man in town.

I gave my fur coat and hat into his keeping, holding fast to
my muff, which held emergency hairpins, handkerchiefs, notebook,
needle and thread, comb, smelling salts—I still carry those oddments Betsy thought necessary. Before we went in to join the
company, the door of the picture gallery to the left beckoned me
as if it were a siren summoning Ulysses. Mr. Corcoran hangs his
paintings one above the other like the buildings of an Italian hill
town.

"My dear Mrs. Adams," said our host, exerting himself to
welcome us in the hall despite the demands of his rheumatism
and the other guests, including the aforementioned Renwick.

"I am always amazed that you could give so many paintings
away and still have such a wealth on the walls."

"Would you like a little tour? I don't know that I have many
new ones since you were last here. But then, you don't come as
often as I would like," he said, taking my arm and slipping his
hand over mine, virtually ignoring Henry, who stood in the hall,
wondering whether he should go around to the tradesmen's entrance. I looked again, his face had turned as crimson as the Turkey
carpet on the floor.

Mercifully, Miss Lee, one of General Robert E. Lee's daughters, came in the door, and Henry quickly and pointedly became engrossed in conversation with her.

Mr. Corcoran gave them only a polite wave from the gallery as he concentrated his attention on displaying *Shakespeare and Friends*—the painting familiar from its steel engravings.

This lady was duly grateful for his attentions to me. No matter that Mr. Corcoran at eighty-seven could hardly be considered a serious threat to my marital vows. After Henry's indifference, almost any masculine attention is welcome. Even at his age, Corcoran has not lost the glint in his eye, nor the intimate touch of his hand. Despite his reputation as a rake, I feel confident that his Southern manners keep him from the sort of unwelcome advances I fear from even the oldest Italian, remembering as I do, Roman pinches.

Oh yes, I enjoyed his new pictures thoroughly. He tends perhaps to the ornate, in which oil seems to be used more as gravy, smothering rather than lubricating the line, but the pictures are pleasant and cheerful. And their frames! He must grow a gold leaf tree in his garden!

Our host, judging that he had kept me long enough to make the point of our mutual attraction, finally led me into the grand saloon across the hall. Its ornately carved woodwork, the gold leaf again encrusting the ornaments, glittered in the gaslights. The flames flickered a bit, like their candle precursors.

In the drawing room, Harriet Louise Eustis serving as hostess came to meet me, and firmly removed me from her grandfather's grasp. Her brothers, William Corcoran and George Peabody Eustis, were up from Virginia for the occasion. Clementina Eustis, sister-in-law of his late daughter, who runs the house, was more plainly dressed than Harriet Louise, and seemed absorbed in the mechanics of the dining room. In all there were twelve of us, a rather intimate

dinner for Mr. Corcoran's dining room. But I suspect that he shares
my growing feeling that too many guests exhaust the room's air,
and one's attentions. Postprandial weariness may well be in exact
proportion to the number of people who have occupied the adjacent space.

After the sherry (excellent, as one might expect of the worldly
Corcoran, perhaps a bit sweet for me, but dryness is a Northern
taste I have learned), the group paraded into the dining room with
its Tiffany chandeliers, carpets and curtains from A. T. Stewart
and J & B Orme in Philadelphia. As usual, I felt almost suffocated
by all the heavy drapery and thick carpeting—the amount of dust
they must hold, even with the best efforts of such a staff, is enough
to give me an attack of catarrh just thinking about them.

All that saved me was a determined look at the bay where
the flowers, all blooming from our host's hothouse, lightened the
lugubrious look of the decor—and my spirits—until I noticed
that the *Greek Slave* stood chaste and chained in the bay. I put my
hand on the collector's arm.

"I thought the Hiram Powers statue was in your gallery, in
that great round room designed for her?"

"I was lonesome for her. I thought, just for the evening, that
I would bring her home. Maybe, you know, she is sometimes lonely
for me when she stands in the middle of the rotunda with all
those people parading around her. I thought for an evening perhaps
she'd like to have admirers who understand her as the perfect
work of art she is."

I sat down, averting my eyes from her. In the Corcoran
Gallery, I'm very careful not to look at her as I go by. Tonight,
my karma had put me just where I had to look at her if I were
to speak at all to the partner on my left. For the first course, I
was all right, because I could chatter away with William Corcoran

November 10, 1885

Eustis, with my head turned away from the statue. But when I had to turn to talk to James Renwick, my other partner, it was all I could do to avoid seeing her, it.

"Why do you cast your eyes down so, Mrs. Adams?" Renwick asked. And with a strange sort of prescience, he asked me, "Don't you like the bay I designed for Mr. Corcoran?"

"It's charming," I said dutifully and washed down the understatement with my glass of wine.

"Surely a worldly woman like yourself, familiar with the classic antiquities, is not offended by such chaste nudity?"

I managed a knowing smile and asked him about the plan he's been doing for St. John's Church. That, as you might expect, worked well.

"No matter what you hear, dear Mrs. Adams, I don't want to ruin Latrobe's fine design. But I have been hired to enlarge the church, and of a necessity, there'll have to be changes. As no doubt you've been told, I recommended that the building committee have that stupid steeple removed. That protrusion was not Benjamin Latrobe's idea. Perhaps its builder expected the good Lord to use it like a finial on a teapot, as a handle to grasp while removing the roof in a storm."

"Perhaps it's for angels to stand on," I said, gently. While he jabbered on and on, I found myself moving my head to try to interpose his between me and the statue, but it didn't always work. I considered excusing myself and returning to Eustis, but I was afraid Renwick would never forgive me. Also, it would be so obvious, if I were the only one facing to the left, in defiance of the etiquette of "turning the table"—following your hostess in changing which dinner partner you converse with at each new course. So I finally resigned myself to having to face the slave.

I suppose it isn't unusual to feel uncomfortable looking at

the statue. Mr. Corcoran has said that during the 1840s and 50s when she was on public view, galleries had separate showings for men and women. She was heavily draped when Queen Victoria went through the American section of the Crystal Palace during the Great Exhibition. Actually, I'm not such a prude that the naked body would offend me. However, when I look at her, stripped of her pretensions, her people, her place, her prestige, her position, I feel that I am very much like her. Sometimes I feel as though I am inside her looking out, trapped not only by her chains but by her marble body. I can feel the cold of the stone chilling my flesh, hardening, stiffening the bones, turning my brains to stone, until I lose the ability to move or think or care. Perhaps I am her. Not that I am alone. I realize many women feel the same way. They become their husband's chattel. Their money becomes his. Their every hour is circumscribed by his wishes—and often his follies.

Worst of all, I think, is the theft of our time. Every day, I feel that Henry steals my hours and never pays me for them. I suppose that if we had a child, I would feel as though I had given up my time at least to receive other pleasures. As it is, I am neither, as is said, maid, nor mother, nor mistress, just his slave. Not that I think Hiram Powers carved the slave with such insight—no man would be able to understand women's feelings so well. I wondered about his model—who was she? What did the real woman think of her task? What were her duties other than posing? Did she bear her chains gladly for love? Was Powers in love with her? Or did he suffer from the Greek malady? Perhaps he simply put her upon a pedestal and ignored her, paying no more attention than he would to the apple, knife, and plate posing for a still life.

Surely not. He carved her with too much appreciation for her physical charms. Powers made her beautiful, sensual in her innocence, alluring in her chastity, and above all submissive, chained not only by the links around her hands, but in her acquiescence November 10, 1885 to her fate. I think he meant her to stand for woman as man's plaything. Her sidelong glance says, "Whatever you say, dear. My life is in your hands."

I believe men and women should be able to live together, take mutual pleasures in their minds and bodies, and yet maintain their equality.

From which you will be able to deduce that I did not overeat of Mr. Corcoran's delicacies, but you may well suspect that I drank a sufficiency of his excellent French wines. His wine cellar is the best in any house outside the French legation—far better than the White House. Especially in these days of the temperance movement. I have accused Mr. Corcoran, with some evidence, of having spent much of his years abroad during the War in tours and tastings in the vineyards.

The meal, as I suspected, was as heavy as the velvet curtains.

I will save for Posterity the menu written in French, in a gold-inked calligraphy, elaborately framed in flourishes, embellishments, and ornaments. Food is an art like any other, as I learned in lessons at the Palais de l'Industrie in Paris in 1873. Mr. Corcoran has a good chef who must own a fishing boat. We had Blue Point Oysters, Filet of Red Snapper, Caviar, and Terrapin, as well as Veal Cutlets and Chicken. The dessert, an orange soufflé, was beautifully presented, with bowls of fruits, fresh, candied, and dried.

I was finally able to refocus on Renwick when he asked how I liked the new stained glass window. Though I was distracted by the exercise of phrasing a vacillating remark, neither a lie nor an insult.

In the silence that followed his attempt to sort out exactly what I meant, we were entrapped by Sir Lionel Sackville-West. I had not seen him since Henry's November tea. Perhaps he still lived in dread of the story of John Quincy Adams and the Marquis de La Fayette. This night, he sat across the table and encouraged our host to tell why he acquired the statue.

"I believe, sir, that you were—perhaps I should say are—a Secessionist?"

"It's been a very long time ago—more than twenty years—when such labels were useful."

"Tell me, is the *Greek Slave* dear to you because of your Secessionist sympathies? Do you see in her a glorification of slavery? Do you justify black slaves by this reminder of white ones? Sir?"

"Forgive me. I realize, Sir Lionel, American history is little studied in Oxford or Cambridge. Still, some of your countrymen did make an effort to bring the British in on the side of the Southern states. However, if you'll excuse my saying so, I am not sure many people in Europe understood the position of the Southerner.

"The War was not about slavery, though that is the excuse that Northern politicians—you will excuse me, Mr. Adams—used to make it a holy war. Such a ploy enlisted humanists such as the Alcotts and the Emersons. Otherwise, they would not have willingly supported a war bent on abridging the sovereign right of the Southern states to withdraw from a Union not to their benefit. The Northern states with different needs, being industrial rather than agricultural, treated the Southern states as their colonies, their breadbasket, to be used and abused rather than sharing prosperity and progress.

"I, sir, am a businessman. I do not say I have an academic knowledge of economics, but I have sold $12 million in bonds, at 6 percent interest—twice. Once on half a day's notice, I went to Europe to sell United States bonds in order that the Mexican War

be financed. Through the example my sales established, the government was able to raise money to buy territories from Mexico
for $15 million."

Before Mr. Corcoran could continue, Henry said, "My father
always thought you also sold Confederate bonds in Europe. He
considered you a dangerous threat to the Northern chances of
victory.

"We were always glad you weren't assigned to Great Britain.
You could have been the nineteenth-century Benjamin Franklin,
persuading all before you."

I glared at Henry, but I was not near enough for him to feel
the full force, I suppose.

Mr. Corcoran looked at him and shook his head. "Charles
Francis Adams had no reason to fear me. And I am sure that you,
having been his secretary during those years, know well that he
was not so misinformed. I spent the War years in Europe, mostly
in Paris, because I wanted to enjoy my grandchildren's childhood.

"That said, I have to point out that economic war had already
threatened the way of life of the Southern states before a shot was
fired. To protect Northern industries, Northern politicians impoverished the entire South with high import duties on industrial
goods. They restricted Southern sales of their agricultural products
to England and other countries. And they levied discriminatory
freight rates against my region. When Southerners insisted on an
honorable attention to their constitutional rights, the North invaded the South and occupied it as a vanquished nation."

"I appreciate your views," said Sir Lionel. "We know from
our Civil War, our War of the Roses, and our conflicts with
Scotland, Wales and most of all, Ireland that it is not easy for
sovereign states—or states that believe they are sovereign—to
recognize and uphold each other's rights to their mutual satisfac-

tion. And I do understand why Southerners, whose land was invaded, whose cities were burned, and whose people were conquered, would be slow to forget."

Henry spoke up. "If General Sherman were here, I'm sure he would repeat his famous justification for his march through Georgia."

"What is that, Mr. Adams?"

"Well, Sir, I can't really quote him in the presence of the ladies here, but I will be pleased to whisper it in your ear, if you will remind me after supper."

Mr. Corcoran, whose face had become tinged with red—and I do not think from the wine—looked at me and slowly around the table at the other guests. His eyes stopped with Miss Lee. And he said, "You ladies will forgive my lack of good manners in quoting General Sherman's excuse for the devastation he wrought.

"Sherman, when charged with his war crimes against the people of the Confederacy, black, white, men, women and babies, said, flippantly, 'War is Hell.' And I say to you here tonight, that is true. And I add another truth. The people of Georgia, and the rest of the South learned full well that War is Hell—and Sherman is Satan."

At that, Miss Lee said quietly, "You speak the truth, Mr. Corcoran. And Quartermaster General Meigs is one of his devils. He filled my mother's rose garden, right outside Arlington House, with corpses, so my mother could never live there again. Not content, the Union marauders stole her great-grandmother's keepsakes. The ancestor was Martha Custis Washington."

With that, our hostess stood up and said with a brave attempt at a smile, "Shall we leave the gentlemen with their cigars and their port?" And I chalked up one more thing to the score I keep on male brutality—making us leave the table just when the con- versation becomes serious. The wrenching thought of Miss Lee's lost family place, no matter the justice of her father's cause, brought home the brutalities of that terrible conflict.

The minister spoke up before we had a chance to gather our skirts to stand. "Excuse me, sir, but if you will bear with me, I would still like to hear how you acquired the *Greek Slave* and, from your great knowledge, how you see her positioned in art history."

I hastily added, "Forgive me, dear Miss Eustis, but may I join in saying I would like very much to hear your grandfather's learned comments. My mother was a very great admirer of the statue when it first came to our country. Could we postpone coffee a bit longer?"

And Mr. Corcoran answered, without consultation: "Of course, Mrs. Adams. Your knowledge and enthusiasm for art always pleases me. Do sit down for a minute more, please ladies. George! More wine. Yes, I enjoy the Powers sculpture on many levels. First, of course, because it is very beautiful, perhaps the greatest work of art of our time. I first saw her when she was exhibited in New York in the late 1840s. I was absolutely transfixed. I stood for, oh, half an hour staring at her, walking around all sides. Such perfection! Such modesty! If I could have picked her up, I would have left with her right then, but she wasn't for sale. She had personal appearances to make—she toured the country for five or six years.

"As I recall, Promoter Kellog charged five cents for children, ten for ladies and twenty-five for gentleman. If I'm not mistaken, Powers and Kellog split twenty-three thousand dollars between them."

"How many copies, I suppose I should say, replicas, did Powers make?" I asked.

"Six in all. I am confident that mine is the original. Though Dudley Selden, my art agent in Paris—we met when he was in Congress—always made the point that the true original is the model of wax, clay, or plaster. Likely Hiram Powers himself only made the maquette. The carver actually cut the stone. If I remember rightly, Powers started molding the statue in his Florence studio in October, 1842. Captain John Grant of London bought one before it was finished and exhibited it at Graves in Pall Mall. Of course, she created a sensation. Parisians came across the channel to see the lady, and, surely, all of London."

"I am surprised that Mr. Powers was daring enough to make an unclothed female," said Miss Eustis. "Surely he was concerned that no one would buy his work for fear of being criticized. Was he not afraid everybody would be scandalized?"

"Indeed he was. I've talked to him on that very point. He said that was the reason he put together a fancy brochure to be printed up and sent along where she was exhibited. I've quoted it so many times, I know it by heart. He explained that as all knowledgeable people could plainly see, the statue represented: 'the fortitude and resignation of a Christian supported by her faith in the goodness of God, leaving no room for shame.' "

"That's about as pious an explanation for appearing in the altogether as I have heard," I couldn't resist saying.

Mr. Corcoran grinned at me, and winked before going on with his story. "Meantime, one of the copies, I think Grant's, was borrowed to save the American face in the great Crystal Palace Exposition. A good thing, too, since about all the U.S. had to show before was a cathedral window made of colored soap. She was a hit! By that time Powers was claiming that she'd been 'inspired by the heroic struggle of the Greek people to throw off the yoke of their Turkish masters in the war that had ended in 1830.'

"Anyway, my friend George Peabody wrote me that I should come to see the exposition. He'd tried to give them an American flag, but nobody wanted it. Anyway, I thought that it might be possible to buy one of the statues.

"Another banker, James Robb of New Orleans, had put down $2,000 toward a price of $4,000 for the traveling lady. But he was fed up with the tour being extended to show her at the first World's Fair in New York in 1853. And Powers got tired of Robb's drafts for payment being returned. After some negotiations, I was able to buy her.

"She finally arrived—in a box that looked like a coffin—in 1853, just in time for my annual Christmas party. I remember very well. I put her in the west wing, the gallery, then lit by skylight, with only slits instead of windows. Now I like this position flanked by the garden. I always think Renwick made the bay as an indoor Garden of Eden, is that right, James?"

"If you say so, my kind client."

"Anyway, she looks like Eve, standing amidst the greenery. We had a rather nice buffet, and then we brought everyone in to see her—ladies first. After they had become used to the sight, and got over their giggles, we brought in the men to join them. Anyone who was self-conscious could go back to the dining room and have a second helping. Worked rather well, I thought.

"In 1850, Elizabeth Barrett Browning even wrote a poem about the statue. She put the feeling the statue evokes rather well—something like 'thy divine face . . . By thunders of white silence overthrown.' "

With the "thunders of white silence" echoing in my ears, I went with Harriet Louise into the withdrawing room. I heard not a word more.

❧

CHAPTER 9

November 11, 1885

Goddess on a Pedestal

∞

Dear Posterity,

I had the strangest dream in the hours before the dawn.
Before I forget I will write it all down in my journal.

I believe the place is Greece—certainly the Mediterranean.
I am up on a hill overlooking the sea. The sky and sea are so blue,
I can not be sure which is up and which down. Where they met
no seam can be seen. I now understood that little difference exists
between birds and fish, flying and swimming. The world is wonderfully whole in a unification I never realized before.

The sun's rays lap me like a warm Mediterranean wave. I
am not outdoors, but in a templetto, with columns shaped like
women holding each other's hands above their head to form a
cornice. The caryatids are my sisters. I yearn to lift their burdens,

to set them to dance, to command the sun to fill up the temple with washes of warmth, to cover the mosaic floor with rose petals of a lustful purple red. If I were a goddess, I could wave my hand and make it so.

And then I see him, so beautiful, so graceful, I know without question that he *is* a god. His step is so light as he enters my temple that I am not sure that he walks. He floats, as if he were a bird, a fish. He comes to me without hesitation, as though following a well-defined path, cleared over many years or even centuries, and agreed to by all. Yet, he approaches slowly, as if to apply that greatest of aphrodisiacs—caresses and kisses fondling first the imagination. I can see the pink, soft tips of his fingers reaching out. His lips full, red, slightly open, pledge a demanding tongue inside. His body—sturdy, no, wiry, capable of war but given to the dance—promises the ecstasies of love. I exalt in the rush of sensation that tingles the tips of my breasts, swells my gates in welcome. I can plainly see that he, in his naked splendor, is ready to join his body with mine. He draws nearer and nearer. My body burns as though the sun's rays were intensified by a lens.

At last he reaches me and wraps himself around me, as though my own self rejoined. I wait for rapture to begin, to rise to climax in glory. And then, with the coldness of space beyond the sun, the darkness of the eternal night, the never thawing winter, I realize I can feel nothing.

For he has transmuted my body to stone, cold, cold stone. No heat could thaw me, no passion could reach me, no love could fulfill me. All my feelings, all my cravings, all my yearnings are imprisoned in this hard, impenetrable granite that is my skin. My life is only an illusion. I am not real at all, but only a statue.

❧

CHAPTER 10

November 14, 1885

Photo of Frances Benjamin Johnston

∞

At 4:45 P.M., I fastened the last button on my fifth best tea gown in preparation for our guest, the young photographer Frances Benjamin Johnston. I have just enough time to set down a few notes in my journal about my consuming interest in photography.

After Henry's objections to my writing novels, I had thought I would go back to photography to try and satisfy my need to create. Pictures are surely the other side of the page of writing.

I try to be as professional as possible about it. I keep careful records of times and chemicals in my little book with the marbled cover. I compose my subjects with as much care as a sculptor or an artist. Henry complained to Lizzie Cameron that I did nothing but take photographs at Beverly Farms.

One of my best pictures is of Henry, in a characteristic pose, pen to paper, inkwells open, leather-covered volumes to hand, eyes firmly on his words. I also did a neat one of Henry and Boojum on the steps of our house. I photographed John Hay with the French edition of my book *Démocratie*, while Henry was teasing him by accusing him of writing it. I admit my opinions of people often seem to show up very well in my photographs. My father looks very handsome and sweet, though far more serious than usual, in his picture in the garden at Beverly. But Henry's parents from their porch look down their noses with the disapproval that has always been part of their attitude toward me. I've quite a portfolio of famous people, La Farge with his cigar and book, Richardson with his slide rule and elevation drawings, and so on.

John Hay admired my portrait of Papa Bancroft extravagantly. Without saying a word to me or Henry, he wrote our friend R. W. Gilder, the editor of *Century*, about it. Who in turn wrote and asked to publish my photograph—and diplomatically—asked for a short essay by Henry about the ancient and inimitable historian. Henry indignantly turned down the offer for both, without consulting me, saying that all our "unphotographed friends" would be jealous. I didn't protest, but I was hurt, rather say annoyed. Maybe both. Knowing Henry, I realized that part of the reason for rejecting the offer was not just the Adams family's disinclination to have their name appear in the public press, but also because he would be sharing the glory with me. And Adams men do not share. And Adams women do not have their names on their works.

I heard the bell and our butler's informed answer, "Oh yes, Miss Johnston, Mrs. Adams is at home and expecting you. Do come to the drawing room and I'll tell her you're here."

I greeted Miss Johnston, a fellow student of Clifford Richardson at the Amateur Photographer's Club. She was not at all, thank heaven, of Mrs. John McLean or Mrs. Don Cameron's ilk of woman, made of pleats and parties. Miss Johnston had a different style, one that was just becoming accepted in advanced circles. She had a sturdy look to her, as though she would not blow away if they huffed and puffed at her. Henry, who walked in a few seconds after me, was so engrossed with the young woman's skirt length, short enough to show off a pair of slender, well-shaped ankles, that it took him a minute to respond to my introduction.

"Certainly, we are delighted to see you. Chemist Richardson speaks very highly of you. We call him chemist to keep him straight from our Architect Richardson. Do sit down. Clover, pour tea for our guest. It's a blend we order from Boston. You know Boston, ha! is famous for its tea parties, eh?"

I asked the polite questions.

"No, I haven't been back from Paris too long. Yes, I loved it. I studied at the Julian Academy, but actually, just walking the streets was education enough. You know it well, I'm convinced, but it was all new to me. The very air seemed so full of art and freedom from restraints. You know, Mrs. Adams, Paris is a very uncorseted town for a twenty-one-year-old woman."

Henry was taken aback at such a frank statement. I was amused at this new breed of woman. I suddenly realized, with crystals of ice forming again on my spine, that Miss Johnston was young enough, or conversely that I am old enough, to be mother and daughter. I thought I'd like to have a daughter like Frances Johnston, though I'll bet her parents find her a handful or two.

"I'm sure it is," said I, as tactfully as possible. "Unfortunately, I was already an old settled, married woman when we spent much time there. Tell me, why did you go to Paris other than to take your corsets off? (Henry averted his eyes to the teapot.) Are you an artist? Or a writer?"

"I hope so," said Miss Johnston. "Though it's hard to say, because I have only the inclination and not much to show for it."

"If you're not a writer by the time you're fourteen, you might as well give up," said Henry, getting his nerves back and becoming all the sterner for having been shocked by the modern Miss Johnston and her visible ankles.

"Well, of course, I write a little and draw a bit, and have since before I was fourteen, Mr. Adams. But I doubt that a professional such as yourself would count my scribbles and dabs worth talking about. But I like words and pictures, and if I can't make many that are worth it myself, at least Paris has permitted me to enjoy others."

"But you are a photographer. I've seen some pictures of yours that are quite good. The idea of photographing the Negro life in the alleys of Washington is unexpected—not to say courageous. Henry would never let me go into such areas. I admire your gumption."

"I'm fortunate—or unfortunate—depending on your view, not to have a husband to tell me where I can go or what I can do. As for my mother, well, she's too busy receiving her friends to be able to keep up with me. I find it better not to tell her truths that would upset her."

I laughed, and Henry again looked aghast.

"I'm afraid I'm of another generation," I said. "But I admire yours, though I like to remind your age that it's members aren't the first to need the right to be themselves. My mother died when I was five, but she was a poet, published in *The Dial*. You probably don't remember it as a Transcendentalist publication. Or my mother's friend, Margaret Fuller, the editor, a great fighter for women's rights."

"How did your father feel about his wife's beliefs, if you don't mind my asking, Mrs. Adams?"

"Well, actually, both my mother's family, Sturgis, and my father's, Hooper, were often called eccentric. We came over to this country long enough ago to feel as though we own the place and can do exactly what we see fit. Now the Adams family is much more proper and correct. Perhaps it comes of having their family's peccadillos perpetually chronicled on the front page of the Washington newspapers.

"Unlike the Adams family, we haven't often been motes in the public eye—except of course for King Hooper, my illustrious, if Tory, ancestor of Danvers and Marblehead, Massachusetts. In the mid-1700s, he wasn't afraid people would think him proud— he copied his coach after that of King George III. When his new regalia, drawn by four horses, was too big to make a turn, he bought the mansion across the street and cut off its corner to accommodate his coach. And so it stands today."

"I am certain that my revolutionary relatives would surely have condemned your royalist relations," said Henry with a curl of his lips. "And I doubt seriously if the Adams family could have been accused of lacking in courage or enterprise. Anyway, even if the Adams family tends to like their wives to be ladies, I think we consider that a lady could, without loss of status, take photographs, just as she can embroider pillows or do cross-stitch samplers."

Miss Johnston's back arched like a cat's and looked as though any minute she would hiss and grow long whiskers to spit through. But with an obvious tightening of her collar, she managed to keep quiet.

I laughed as though Henry had made a joke. In a wifely fashion I tried to smooth matters over. "I'm sorry if my husband

has offended you. But you know, my husband is a photographer
himself, though he classifies it as a minor ability. He thinks of
photography, at most, as a useful device for the inartistic to record
images—the Nile, the pyramids, people's visages, dog's faces, art
objects being considered for purchase for other people."

"Not fair, Clover. I'm fascinated by the scientific aspect: the
chemistry, the light measurements, the historical worth of the
subject," protested Henry.

"Ah, yes, Henry, but for me, photography is an art, a way
of seeing the truth beyond the limitations of human eyes. A photographer uses a camera as another type of artist uses a pencil, a
pen, a brush, or a painting knife. The effect is different, certainly,
but so are the results of other basic tools used with oil, ink,
watercolor, or gouache. Since they both see the world as two-
dimensional, a photographer is closer to a painter than a painter
is to a sculptor."

Miss Johnston agreed. "Photography is light. The photographer's skill is in recording it. Painters can but imitate the memory.
Photographers can capture light itself."

"Well, that much is true," said Henry, continuing didactically.
"I've started an article on the subject to send to *Century*." He went
to the secretary and extracted a manuscript from a leather folder.
Henry proceeded to lecture the audience of two, in a professional
manner that overrode all other discussion and allowed of no whispering amongst the students.

"In the middle of our century, the camera has changed from
an instrument of sorcery to science. In 1839, at a seminar of the
French Academy of Science and the Fine Arts, a Viennese, Andreas
von Ettingshausen, saw a demonstration of the awkward Daguer-
reotype. To him, it was as if Rembrandt had been boxed to paint
for the nineteenth century. He consulted with his friend, Josef

Max Petzval, and in 1840, the first lens was perfected for the camera."

"You mean the 'German lens'?" asked Miss Johnston. "The lens Voightlaender produces?"

Henry nodded, his dissertation rudely interrupted. I went on to say, "What you say is true, Henry. Certainly, photography depends on the advancement of science. But during the recent national Armageddon, the efforts of Matthew Brady's staff were not science, they were art. Miss Johnston, remind me to show you the Brady pictures I bought when we came to Washington to see the victory parade in 1865.

"You know, Miss Johnston, we are not the only women who use the camera in an effort to make some sense of life. My husband's friend, Mr. Gaskell, told us that in England, Princess Alexandra, and they do say Queen Victoria, like to take photographs. And of course, another Englishwoman, Julia Cameron, is a true professional."

"What kind of camera do you have, Mrs. Adams?" asked Miss Johnston.

"It's cherry wood with brass fittings and a gear-driven focusing adjustment—made for me in London, thanks to my father's generosity. You might think it too small, since it holds only a four-by-five-inch dry plate, but since I'm not so large myself, I find it easier to use than one that would hold an eight-by-ten-inch plate."

"Sounds just right to me. It's hard to keep up, there's a new device or a new process every day," Miss Johnston said.

"Oh yes," I sighed, "particularly the developing methods. Mr. Richardson has been very kind to be my mentor. He's encouraging, unlike Henry, who's often impatient with me, and likes to poke fun at my 'hobby.' About two years ago, Mr. Richardson kindly smuggled me into the National Museum—I was the only woman, no surprise! We spent three hours watching Siebert demonstrate his patented process of printing from negatives. I've paid Siebert a small sum for the right to use his method. And now I, too, can transmute light in the air into pictures on paper."

"You're off again, Clover," said Henry.

"Not so, Mr. Adams, I think she's very on. I know of the method she's describing. It's a wonder," said Miss Johnston. "I also do know it's time to go. I've drunk up all your tea and eaten all your cookies and used up your time and good nature. Thank you so much. I do appreciate your kindness in receiving me, Mrs. Adams. I don't want to presume, but do you think it would be possible for me to come sometime and see your darkroom? I would be so interested."

"Of course," I said. "If you have time, I'll show you now."

"Marian, I'm sure Miss Johnston has other engagements. It's getting quite late."

"I wouldn't want to press you to stay, Miss Johnston."

"Nor I you, Mrs. Adams. I have plenty of time and no one is expecting me, least of all my mother. But I wouldn't want to interrupt yours and Mr. Adams's evening plans."

"I haven't any. Come on and I'll show you." We left Henry, standing perfunctorily.

I was rather proud of my darkroom. Not many amateurs have one so well equipped as my small room originally intended as a mop closet. It has running water into a wooden sink, put in at just the right height for me, and shelves for my chemicals in glass bottles with glass stoppers to keep fumes in and oxidation out. Fortunately, my chemist friend well instructed me in the dangers of photographic chemicals. I'd heard all sorts of horror stories about the poisonous nature of a single drop of potassium cyanide. Its very vapors could kill you if you breathed them too deeply in an unventilated room. That's why I keep crystals, not solution. The glass of the room's single window is covered in red tissue. I open it and lay my plates, covered with sensitized paper, on the deep windowsill. The sun's light prints them.

"Somewhat better than developing everything by feel in a box you have to carry around wherever you are photographing."

"Do you mean you did wet plate processing?"

"That I did. But then I took up photography when we were married in June 1872. What a mess! The gelatin-coated glass plate is a great improvement. I'll bet Matthew Brady wished he'd had it in the War. Imagine mixing your chemicals, putting the collodion on the glass plate, and pouring silver nitrate over it, then putting the whole mess on the back of the poor camera, taking your picture, and then developing on the spot—all while there was a war going on all around you. I wonder they ever got anything. Of course, he did have a completely equipped wagon along with more helpers than some Confederate divisions had soldiers. Even so!"

She thanked me in the best style, one colleague to another. I almost felt as though I were a true professional. What a nice young woman to take me seriously!

"I look forward to our club's next exhibition. I'm sure you'll win another prize."

"If Henry lets me enter," I said, wryly, not all in fun.

After she left, I made haste to escape Henry, but I wasn't quick enough.

"I doubt Miss Johnston will be able to catch a husband with her knowledge of the platinum process," he said and walked away toward his study, shaking his head.

This evening, I left Henry to an interminable dinner with, of all people, Senator Don Cameron, that unscrupulous politician whose qualities and defects, Henry says, makes him one of the most useful members of the Senate. Everyone thinks I based Senator Silas Ratcliffe in *Democracy* on Senator James Blaine, but actually I put a great deal of Cameron in him. I protested heartily when Henry wanted to invite him to dinner—La Dona Cameron is sending him out as much as possible so she can get on with having her baby.

Knowing Mrs. Senator Cameron, I suspect she's told everyone in town the gory and grotesque tale she's told me. But I have no desire to add either to her notoriety or mine by retelling the story—certainly not to Henry. So since I wouldn't tell him why I wished to cut Cameron, I simply explained that I do not care for the member of Congress.

Henry said, "Who does? But he's very effective. Adams statesmen have always had to deal with these men of no scruples to get anything done."

"In that case," I said, "since you are willing to deal with him, and I am not, I leave you to dine with him *à deux*. Then you can fill the dining room with cigar smoke and smoldering intrigue. I will have the rest of the tea sandwiches in my room."

He made a face, but I think was pleased at having Cameron to himself without my digs.

I wondered if they would talk about La Dona Immobile.

So now I had several hours to do exactly as I pleased. And I pleased to work in my darkroom, all fired up by my encounter with Miss Johnston. A few days ago I had made a photograph of Henry, but hadn't had time to develop it.

I remembered to crack the window a bit for ventilation, lit my kerosene safelight lantern with its red shade, took the dry plate out of its dark plate holder, put it in the tray and poured developer over it. I hoped my developer wasn't too old; I mixed it up a while ago, but I haven't been doing much darkroom work recently. I checked to see how my cyanide supply is holding out. I rather worry about having such dangerous crystals in the house. But there's no help for it; if you're going to do laboratory work, you have to have laboratory chemicals. I do try to be as careful as I can, measuring ingredients precisely, wearing a mask against the fumes, and, above all, keeping the door locked. I wouldn't want the puppies to come prancing in someday and knock over noxious chemicals.

I approached the moment when the developer began its transmutation as I always did—with the feeling of the supplicant, quivering in expectation of the heavens opening and the miraculous goddess appearing. This transcendental experience is truly an ephemeral art, happening only once for each negative. Since my darkroom is small, I am able to jealously guard this moment to my private pleasure. Though I wish my mother were alive to compose a poem on this minute.

As the developer works its will on the plate, it caresses every inch, poking the particles of silver nitrate, delicately seeking out the ones exposed to the light that thereby can be enticed into darkening. Light is the lover. When light is captured by the lens, it pays no attention to empty air, passing on through. But when it reaches a person, or a tree or a dog, it excitedly goes all over it in almost an excess of desire. It fondles the chin's dimple, nuzzles the lips, awakens the eye with kisses of affection, and embraces the figure with snuggles and squeezes. The chemicals rub the surface of the plate until the unexposed skin flakes off.

I concentrated on the birth of the image. At first, I could see only the faintest outline, like a hesitant ectoplasm. A small round spot appeared—Henry's bald pate—the lightest part of the picture is the darkest part of the negative. I thought to myself how I longed to rub my wet lips over his bare head. I bravely tried it once, and found it wonderfully sensuous, but he shook off my lips and said with an exasperated tone, "You make scratchy noises in my brain." Those big ears of his. He hated his ears being touched most of all—by flesh or words. He wants to hear nothing that I say. He blocks them up so no message of mine will get through. I would have liked to whisper my secrets in those ears, touch my tongue to that enticing entrance into his head, nibble on those soft earlobes. What raptures that would bring! Even now, the feeling moves through my secret places, a warmth spreading like the sun on the tiles of a Spanish courtyard. His nose, wouldn't you know it, pokes itself into the picture. I would never dare even nuzzle Henry's nose, much less kiss it. That nose, that very nose in the air affected by all Adamses, looking down at the lesser breeds. Now the image is more complete, not just his mustache and beard, but the few hairs on the back of his head, the whiskers on his upper lip and chin, but all in reverse, white beard, white mustache, white hair on a black head. What fun to pull his beard and bring his lips close to mine! But I have been pushed away too often. Why won't he let me love him? Why won't he love me?

His full figure has materialized, his suit, his hands holding his pen against his manuscript on the table—I thought he looked very different, not so enticing, as in those first moments when he was dimly seen. Ah, he is like that. Through the cameras lens you see him in his full, unyielding rigidity, posed, arranged, a man of premeditation. All things change in the developer. As the apparition, the elusive spirit began to form out of the swirling clouds of the developer, I caught a glimpse of a witty, darling, adorable man full of light and warmth. And the picture deepened, darkened, developed into the Henry I know, who knows me not, who loves me not.

Tomorrow morning I will put the plate and the paper in the sun to print.

CHAPTER 11

November 15, 1885

Night of the Destroyer

∞

I was awakened by the feeling that my feet were unaccountably cold. When I heard Boojum and Possum barking at the door, I realized I'd lost my furry foot warmers. They barked at the door as though every cat and mouse in the world were taunting them from behind it. In between their yelps, I heard the noise that had set them off—shattering glass, hammering, banging. I pulled on my peignoir and followed the noise with my escorts. I thought later that was very dumb of me. I could have encountered a burglar or worse.

I can't say when I realized the racket came from my darkroom. The dogs, their little feet a blur as they ran, made it to the room before I did. By then, the noise had subsided. The terriers stopped at the sight of Henry, standing just inside the door, looking at the ruin.

"Don't come any further," he said. I wasn't sure whether he meant me or the dogs. Of course, I wouldn't stop, but kept on. Henry, red-faced, moved to stand under the hall's gaslight so he could see to wind around his hand the handkerchief from his dressing gown. The handkerchief was already soaked with blood.

I put my hand on his arm to try to see his hand.

"Henry, how terrible! Let me see! How badly are you hurt?"

He pulled his arm away from me as if my hand were a red-hot skillet just off the fire.

"Don't touch me!" He shouted. I moved away from him, muttering something about only wanting to help. He turned and went down the hall.

I looked in at my darkroom. The room was indeed dark. I picked up a candle from the hall table, lit it with a long match, and saw its rays bounce about the room.

The floor, the counter, the sink were covered with hundreds of splinters of glass, as though someone had found a cave of icicles at the end of the world and assaulted them with both ends of an ice pick, turning them into sharp, piercing glass fencing foils, attacking, defending, darting here and there in mad combat— *seconde, tierce, carte septime.* The myriad of reflections in the candlelight were strangely, devastatingly beautiful.

Here and there I recognized a still intact bottle stopper or a thick glass flask bottom. My sinus difficulties had pretty well robbed me of my sense of smell as well as taste. But judging that we were still alive, I presumed the potassium cyanide solution I had left over from my darkroom work last night must not have been splashed about the room—I didn't see the small, glass-stoppered bottle. My glass measuring beakers must have been thrown against the wall and ricocheted back to break against the sink. But most of the fragments, as far as I could judge, were my precious glass negatives. My boxes of glass slides, my years of work, all overturned, most hammered into crystals. Careless of the peril of being cut, as Henry was, I picked up one of the few larger pieces and saw a ghostly image on it of Henry's disembodied hand. I recognized it as all that was left of the negative I had developed last night. Now it would never be printed. I dropped the piece of glass as if it were something obscene. Which it was.

The line that held the photographic prints for drying was pulled down, and each photograph had been torn into shreds.

I had to grab the door to keep from sinking into this quick sand, the smashed smithereens of my work. I leaned against the door for what seemed one unending night. I almost fell again, for the door needed as much support as I. Not only was it barely hanging by hinges virtually pulled out from their moorings, but the door itself, like my negatives, had been battered, shattered, splintered, reducing the solid oak into slivers along its edge. I pulled it more or less shut, as best I could, so the dogs wouldn't be tempted to go in. Their dear little feet would be cut to bits.

The dogs, almost flip-flopping with get-em enthusiasm, went yelping after footsteps in the hall, I was relieved they were down the way from danger—for the moment.

"Sir," said Brent. "Are you all right? What can I do?" And I realized the coachman must be talking to Henry. He must be standing in his bedroom doorway.

In a hard voice, like one of the sharp slivers, Henry said, "Some vandal has wrecked my wife's darkroom. Go for the police. And tell Johnson to come and search the house to see if the miscreant is still in the house. Away with you, man! Didn't you hear me? Go!"

Novem-
ber 15,
1885

I couldn't stand to look at the destruction of my pitiful little refuge, where I had practiced my small, insignificant talent. With what vengeance the vandal had deprived me of its products and even means! I waved the candle around for one sickening, despairing last look at the wasted years.

Only then did I feel the cold November wind coming in from the window and realized it was open. I turned and ran for my room, in terror of that icy air.

Before I could close my room against the horror, Brent brought in the policeman on our beat, the friendly face quinine yellow in the street's gaslight. He looked rather pale as Brent brought him through the front door before coming into the light. I closed my door, leaving just a crack so I could hear what was being said.

"Whooee! What a mess! What in tarnation was he after?"

Henry, in his driest, most official voice, made short shrift of the story: the open window, the ingress, the egress of the destroyer; the extensive damage; the high cost of these unusual oddments, so foreign to the policeman's experience; Henry's feeling of outrage at having his house so ransacked; his indignation at such effrontery; his scorn for a so-called police force that would allow such an atrocity to take place. The policeman audibly took it all down; I could hear his pencil scrunching against the paper.

"Yes, sir, very bad indeed, such a shame, and your good lady very upset I'm sure. Such a nice lady with the dogs. She often speaks kindly to me when they walk in the park.

"Harumph. Would you please tell me, sir, if you can, was everything broken or was something stolen?"

"Obviously, officer," Henry said in a tone of exasperation, "I have not been able to inventory the damage. That will have to wait for light and the morrow. Since it is a darkroom, there is no gaslight in it. Understand? A candle is not satisfactory for assessing the loss. Yet I have not seen my camera and lens. Since these are objects of great expense, I presume the assailant left with them, though carrying that awkward camera must have been difficult. I did not hear a carriage or a wagon, but I am at a loss to imagine how else it could be removed, if it were indeed."

November 15, 1885

"My camera" indeed! Even in this extremity, Henry couldn't bear to say, "My wife is a photographer. She does serious work. She has expensive equipment. She has an occupation in life other than me."

I almost bolted out my door to protest, peignoir and all.

"Thank you, Mr. Adams. I'll be by again in the morning. Don't be troubled. We'll catch him. Maybe even get your camera back." I heard the outside door close and the dogs scampering back. They whimpered, then barked outside my door. I opened it just enough to let them in. They scampered in, nuzzling my ankles, wagging their tails, trying hard to console me. If anything could have, their affection would have come close. I waited a few moments on my chaise in case Henry would come to commiserate with me. He didn't.

I was devastated. I couldn't imagine he wouldn't have the human kindness to at least knock on the door and say, "Sorry, we'll build you a new one and buy you a better camera." I would have gone to him to see how his injury is. I was really upset to see the blood. But he pushed me away so rudely, I wouldn't dare intrude on him. What can I do?

I can close my door firmly, turn the key, go back to bed. The dogs, with happy noises, went back to being furry hot water bottles.

The next day, I kept to my suite, seeing only the maid who came now and then to bring a minimal meal, or open the curtains, or change the bed. She reported that Brent and Johnson had cleaned up the debris that had been my darkroom and Henry had left immediately after breakfast for the State Department archives, saying he would lunch at the Cosmos Club and perhaps take tea there as well.

The hours merged into one another like a soggy rain, soaking layers of earth. To keep myself from thinking about the demolition of my hopes, I read through my La Fayette Square notes. I'm still not sure if it will be a contemporary history, a novel, or mulch for the roses.

In the afternoon, some dam against despair burst and spilled over my mind, flooding all the defenses I had built up. And I raged, cried, protested, and screamed against the unfeeling universe but silently, as is my wont, in the manner of a proper New Englander, with pen instead of voice, in my journal.

The extirpation of my work left me feeling as though a child had been "untimely ripped" from me. Photography was beginning to take the place in my life left empty from my childlessness. I knew I couldn't claim a body of work, but until now it had been growing every day. I thought eventually I might have a creditable *oeuvre* to show for my days. I would have liked to be good enough so that it could be said of me that I was a journeyman photographer, if not a master. I don't know now whether I will ever have the courage to begin again.

When my eyes were drier, my mind saner, I began to wonder why. The event was very strange. I can not understand it. Surely there are people in Washington to whom I do not bow, and who do not bow to me. But none I know who would be driven to such lengths. I am sure I arouse scorn, perhaps envy, amusement, disapproval. But none of those, with the exception, perhaps, of envy,

are a reason strong enough to cause someone to come in the
middle of the night and lay havoc to my fragile occupation.

To begin, who would know of my darkroom? Not that many
people. A number, though not large, know I am a photographer
of sorts. My name has been in the paper as winning a small prize
in the photograph contest. However, who would know, other than
our intimate friends, chemist Richardson, Frances Benjamin Johnston, and our staff, past and present, where the darkroom is in
our house?

Oh yes, workmen. I remember vividly the German plasterer
when we first came to Washington and were supervising the repair
work on the house. I suppose Henry did give him a hard time.
Henry can be quite a perfectionist. Henry came into the room
every few minutes—checking on him, making suggestions, changing what he wanted. Finally the Teuton yelled at Henry in German.
I heard him and came in to see him waving the putty knife at
Henry. I spoke to the man, in my most fluent workingman Deutsch,
and gradually, I thought, calmed him. I was wrong.

That afternoon, the contractor came by to say the plasterer
had stolen the company's best putty knife and stuck it in his own
wife. Henry and I were fortunate the workman had been able to
contain himself for two hours.

The plasterer cannot be considered a possibility—having long
gone to his punishment. But I am sure there are multitudinous
workmen—from this house and the next—who have good reason
to want to shatter any reflection of the Adams couple.

As for our own servants, I have had no trouble. Betsy Wade,
who brought us up, gave me a goodly and kindly training in
managing a staff. The best way to get dinner on the table when
you want it: hire the right people—colored or white, American

or foreign—and give them the appropriate tools, time, and trust.

Some ladies of the house in Washington fancy themselves as chatelaines indeed, going around all day with large metal circles dangling with keys. They measure out the flour, the milk, the butter, and so on for the day's meals, leaving nothing to the chance that the servants will, as they say here, "tote" your supplies to their home at night. I pay my servants well. I don't begrudge them their meals. I give them what surplus we have. And we are well served in this house.

This said, I have to add that the odds are that the damage was done by someone with easy access to the house. Most astonishing of all is the fact that the destroyer was so willing to make so much noise as to draw attention to himself. And then he escaped so quickly. The motive? Well, the seller of a rare camera rig like mine would be apprehended immediately. I suppose we'll have to wait and see. But if he doesn't sell the camera, we may never know who hated me so much that they destroyed my last year's work.

Still another loss: if the thief had not taken my camera, what an amazing, abstract photograph the devastated darkroom would have made.

So now comes the question: am I up to re-equipping myself? Thanks to the generous bequeath from my dear Pater, the cost is not a consideration. But what is at doubt is whether I have the energy or the enthusiasm to begin again. A year ago, I would not have doubted my vigor and dedication. Today, I'm not so sure. Inertia is perhaps the most debilitating of all diseases. Try again? Not till I get my courage up.

❧

CHAPTER 12

November 17, 1885

Refinements of Love

∞

Dear Posterity,

The destruction of my darkroom, the theft of my treasured camera, the shattering of my negatives and my hopes set me to thinking again about picture taking and its place in my life.

In the beginning, Henry thought there was enough photography, as well as history, and chocolate eclairs for both himself and me. On our honeymoon trip photography had been all that had kept me from going mad, especially after. . . .

From my secret compartment, I took out the box of my letters to my father and admired the photographs I took of Henry aboard the *Isis* on our trip up the Nile. Not bad. At least we sailed smoothly, unlike the voyage to England. Here's the sketch I sent my father, July 13, 1872. Looking at it now, I am afraid it told

more than I hoped he would ever know. It shows Henry and me,
separated into our respective bunks, Henry with a nightcap, myself
swaddled in bedclothes, both of us staring fixedly at the ceiling.
We could be in separate coffins, prepared to be buried at sea. I
wrote my father that the drawing showed us as bedridden with
seasickness. Would this were our only ailment! I wrote no one of
our problem. I was tempted now and then to discuss it with my
sister Nella, who is also childless. But though she has always been
a confidant, the delicacy of the difficulty, and the principle of one
never, never seriously criticizing one's husband, even to one's sister,
has held me back. So now, for the first time, I shall write it all
down for myself, oh yes, and you, Miss Posterity, may read over
my shoulder. I suspect even in your distant time you will be
shocked.

On our wedding night, Henry was very polite, very considerate of my maidenly modesty. With an odd air, which could have
passed for embarrassment had he not been Henry Adams, he
changed clothes in the dressing room. And seemed pointedly un-
interested in my gorgeous peignoir, layers of chiffon, the top one
white, the innermost a rather nude peach. Nor was he interested
in the me inside the gown.

Oh, but Henry made an effort. He read me poetry—unfortunately in German, with its growls and grunts, an infelicitous
choice for a honeymoon. Just before he blew out the candle, he
kissed me chastely on the forehead. I thought, oh well, he's tired
and he thinks I am too.

I thought surely our life together would begin when we
embarked on the *Siberia*—what an ominous name for a ship. I
always thought oceans very romantic, primeval—back to the beginning, "for the earth was without form and void."

But Henry was seasick on the boat, and he made it clear I

couldn't possibly expect to be made love to by anyone who was seasick. The ship was very dirty, the food bad. Frank Parkman, the historian, a friend of Henry's, took our second stateroom, his own was so bad. The saloon was so nasty and dark only the commercial travelers could sit in it. Henry wrote my father in our joint shipboard letter: "Worse than ever. Deadly sick and a calm sea."

November 17, 1885

In England, we went down to Chester, putting up in a medieval hotel with Mr. Parkman and another bachelor friend of Henry's, John Holmes. Certainly, I had not considered spending my first weeks of marriage competing for my husband's attentions. But Mr. Parkman and Mr. Holmes were very agreeable and I tried to be as well.

We left them to stay with Mr. Charles Milnes Gaskell, a very dear friend of Henry's, at his country seat, Wenlock Abbey, Shropshire. The abbey is ruined, but the abbot's house, where we stayed, is very grand with gargoyles and thirty-five-foot-high ceilings and walls as thick as the crust of the earth. Henry and I were assigned an apartment in the Norman wing, eight hundred years old. Each room had an immense fireplace putting out warmth in inverse proportion to its size and a huge old bed, each big enough for ten the size of us. That night, after dinner, when we came up to the boudoir between our bedrooms, I thought now at last, within these thick stone walls, we have privacy. When we shut the great oak doors, we are in our own island, nay, our continent. We might be the only two alive in the world.

I went to Henry and lifted up my head to be kissed. He managed a perfunctory effort and then excused himself, said good night, and went into his own room. At least, in that old stone pile, no one heard me weeping in that great lonely bed. The next morning, very early, before we were brought tea, I heard the door

open and Henry go out. At breakfast, he and Mr. Gaskell said how
much they had enjoyed the early hour exercise.

That night, Henry looked as though he should say something,
or explain something, or at least make an attempt. He actually
came to me and kissed me on the mouth. I was so shocked, I
could hardly respond. By then, I felt as though I were fastened
inside an iron maiden machine in someone's medieval torture
dungeon. Again, I slept alone in the bed so large I felt as if I had
been abandoned to float alone in the sea.

Since Mr. Gaskell and Henry spent most of their days in long
walks, which they assured me would be "too much for a lady," I
had to find other pastimes. Mr. Gaskell encouraged me to poke
through the house at my pleasure. Obviously, for a compulsive
reader such as myself, the library, with books dating back to the
early days of movable type, was the most fascinating place in the
house. I only wish I had world enough and time to read every
one. There was a librarian, an impecunious cousin, I suspect. He
was quite helpful and friendly, climbing up on the tall ladder to
get books from the tippee-top.

I had turned back, with only a cursory look, Blake's 1790–
93 *Marriage of Heaven and Hell*. I thought the title far too applicable
to my own status. But I gratefully accepted the opportunity to
examine a fine 1794 volume of Blake's *Songs of Experience*. I settled
down to read it in a deep leather chair while librarian Peabody
wandered off to some unexplained duty.

I cannot to this day excuse what I did. I am sure you, Miss
Posterity, and all right thinking women will be horrified at my
transgression, but I also doubt if anyone could have resisted. Because there in the book was a letter, unfolded, flattened out. I
could not help but see that it was Henry's distinctive writing,
written on February 8, just before he asked me to marry him. So

I had to read it. The subject was Boston women, in the context of a luncheon party he had given for a group of young ladies, to which I was not invited. To this day, I can remember every word of one paragraph:

"In this Arcadian society sexual passions seem to be abolished . . . I suspect both men and women are cold, and love only with great refinement. How they ever reconcile themselves to the brutalities of marriage, I don't know."

From England we went everywhere, as though we were fleeing the police: Antwerp, Geneva, Bern, Nuremberg, Dresden, Florence. Henry seemed determined to make up the deficiencies he saw in my education. I think he found me an apt student. He would talk of medieval history, a pleasant accompaniment to the cathedrals and fortified castles, and at night I would dutifully—actually with pleasure—read the books we carried from town to town like an ancient scholar's prized traveling library. Every night we read out loud from Schiller's *Die Geschichte des Dreissigjahrigen Krieges*. It did improve my German, though I fear the vocabulary I learned from it, being rather militant and out of date, did me little good in the shops. I preferred Schiller's *Sturm und Drang* plays, really very enlightening on social problems. In Berlin, at the time, my cousin by marriage, George Bancroft, was the American minister. He gave two marvelous dinner parties for us, with a remarkable collection of great scholars. I was very glad of my studies in Greek when I sat beside Ernst Curtius, the archeologist and historian of classical Greece. (I try to find a small bit of time everyday to keep up with my Greek; I'm now reading the *Iliad*— I wonder what it would be like to be Helen—or perhaps better Achilles. Henry doesn't read Greek, but he's good at medieval Latin.)

Always, Henry was and is unfailingly polite, gentlemanly,

solicitous. He tried hard to please—at two arms' distance. At Lake Como, he rented a boat and rowed me for hours around islands and in inlets, by great stone villas guarded by marble saints and popes, here a cave, there a waterfall. An island covered with roses appeared magically.

I had hopes as high as a small pyramid when we began our trip up the Nile on the *Isis*—a *dahabeah*, as the Egyptians call this sort of river houseboat. I hoped that after four months he would be over his hesitancy, his shyness—or whatever. Why did he marry me if he didn't want me? Finally, one night, he brought in a bag of a white powder. I suppose he'd bought it from one of the crew. I asked him what it was. What do you do with it? And he said, "I'll show you." He proceeded to cut it into lines, slide it onto a piece of parchment—and sniff it. "Cocaine," he finally explained.

Afterward, he did at first manage some semblance of what I had been led to expect. Though his encounter with evidence of my virginity soon ended his interest. He spent what seemed hours washing off my blood. I found the experience painful certainly, that I had expected, but his revulsion was worse than his previous obliviousness of me.

The next night with a grim, do-or-die look, he took more of the cocaine—but collapsed into a state of supreme indifference to the reality outside his interior cocaine-induced florid fantasies. After two weeks of either a studied distance from me or a few futile, half-hearted, limp sexual approaches, I finally realized that Henry not only had no desire but perhaps no ability for the customary marital practices. For a few weeks, I hoped that the solitary attempt would be enough at least to give me one child. When I realized that I was not pregnant—nor ever likely to be —the prospect of a life of barrenness overwhelmed me. For a time, I found myself unable to write letters, hardly able to converse

in public. Those six hundred miles from Karnak to Memphis
projected before me as though I were being forever transported
on an Egyptian funeral barge.

Henry did make an effort to distract me. We went to the
Alexandria bazaar and he bought me a handsome Bedouin necklace,
though a rather startling one for my style. Too massive to be easy
for me to wear, but I loved it as an expression of affection.

As my wedding gift to him, Henry'd bought a camera in
Germany, expensive, the latest thing—with the idea of photographing the remains of ancient Egypt. As a way to change the
subject, he taught me what he knew about photography. Cameras
are amazingly bulky, not easy for anyone our size to manage. But
with the help of the stewards and the tour staff, we managed to
lug it along.

Photography focused on an entire new art form for me. Of
course, I had the mandatory drawing classes, watercolors and oil
as a young woman. But my eye was very much better than my
hand. So I contented myself with looking at, not making, pictures.
Photography gave me the technique to create. At first, Henry
seemed to enjoy teaching and then working with me taking pictures. I suppose it must be my fault that soon he left the picture
taking to me while he became an expert on Egyptian death rituals.
I am afraid the thought of being entombed for eternity in a pyramid
was rather more chilling than exciting to me.

At last the voyage was over, and we had to work our way
back across Europe. Most nights, Henry slept as far away from me
as possible, in another room if two were available, in a second bed
if it were not. Occasionally, when there was only one bed in
someone's house or hotel, he would not object if for a moment I
lay close to his back. But only a few minutes. He would move so
far away, I would listen for him to fall off the bed.

And so it went. I began to accept things as they were. I rarely had to complain of Henry's attentions. He was unvaryingly helpful, considerate, amusing—and brotherly. He would not discuss the subject of marital relations nor barrenness.

When we were buying books and pictures in Europe, we spent an evening wondering to whom to leave them. With the tacit acknowledgment that we would have no children to bestow them upon, we decided that if we died of Naples fever, we would leave our collection to Harvard, which of course we would endow. We drew a thrilling plan. I wrote my father in fun that "if the president of Harvard, [then Mr. Charles William Eliot] had even a squint at it, he would at once dispatch emissaries abroad with prussic acid to slay us. So beware this rumor does not reach him."

But all that was more than a decade ago. Since then, nothing has changed, except that he seems increasingly less interested in me except as the lady of the house. He no longer pontificates by the hour for my education. Henry, as I have written, won't permit me to help him with his research, though I know I did it well.

And, of course, we have separate rooms. I satisfy myself with nightly lovers—though only in my dreams.

So with this background, Miss Posterity, you can understand my shock when Elizabeth Cameron made so many flirtatious illusions to Henry—and then pointedly, even tauntingly, revealed her pregnancy. I could not help but wonder if, having spurned my inadequate offerings, he had found her charms a miraculous elixir. From what surreptitious reading I have been able to do in my father's medical library, I gather men, whose major sexual equipment is their mind, are sometimes not aroused by women who are their social—much less intellectual—equals.

We have long heard Clarence King discourse on the delights of primitive women. Though I've tried many times to provide an

agreeable feminine presence to amuse Mr. King, he seems only
interested in the unavailable or unsuitable. For King a proper
woman would be too reminiscent of his mother, raising incest
prohibitions.

For a while, though, I thought, true, Mrs. Cameron is of our
own class, but she is rather a reckless type—and Henry is surely
taken with her. Even so, I know she has many other admirers who
would be happy to supply her husband's deficiencies.

The more I ponder all of this, the more I suspect that Henry's
interest in Mrs. Cameron, and indeed in Mrs. McLean et al., is
desire for the romance of love without the actuality of sex. He's
fond of women only as subject for adoration, not as sexual beings
or indeed as equals.

Perhaps he thought I felt the same way about men. He looked
at my face and thought, "she's plain, not a pretty woman who has
been the object of masculine attentions. She won't know what she's
missing. She'll be grateful for my courtesies. And she's a bluestocking. No woman who even fancies herself as an intellectual—
learning Greek, indeed—could possibly have erotic fancies."

He may have even believed that as a properly brought up
woman, I would not make unseemly demands upon him. Proper
women, even in this, the last quarter of the nineteenth century,
are viewed by many as without sexual needs. Henry may have
thought that being married would keep him from being importuned
by improper women with serious sexual intent, and would give
him an aura of settled respectability so he would not be required
to give chase, and certainly not capture an ardent creature of
passion.

Perhaps so, but it isn't only the lack of husbandly affection
I miss. The greatest difficulty has been Henry's refusal to talk with
me. I could reconcile myself, reluctantly, to a sexless life if I had

a child, even an adopted one. At least I deserve some reason for being, some useful occupation, a career such as Rose Cleveland's professorship, or George Sand's authorship, or best as an equal intellectual partner in a lifetime companionship, a collaborator in writing a joint autobiography in time. But Henry's pride—if that is what it is—keeps me in bondage.

∞

When I finished writing, I hid my journal with my father's letters in a new place, in my cedar chest, wrapped in my bathing costume. I worry about what happened to its key. The parlor maid and the butler both looked for it, in the house and in the park. But it hasn't turned up yet. I certainly hope Henry has not found it and put it to use. Surely he wouldn't do such a thing? Still, Henry has been acting differently, well, at least a bit. That episode the other night, when I was trying the door of his study! Wonder if Boojum ate all the letter, or Henry caught him at it? Does he think I'm spying on him—or, more correctly, setting Boojum in place?

CHAPTER 13

November 20, 1885

The President and the Prostitute

∞

Dear Posterity,

When I went to get my journal this morning, I was puzzled. I always put the journal in with the top end toward H Street, south, that is. I must be losing my mind as well as my key. This morning, the journal was in sideways, the top end pointing east. That's odd. It's such an established habit with me to put it in the same way each time. Accidental? Or is someone reading my diary? Or am I becoming hysterical?

For the last few days, following the demolition of my darkroom, I have had little conversation with Henry—not even one of his panegyrics of Mrs. Cameron. He has no cause to berate me. I can hardly talk to him about her difficulties with her husband. Henry is unwilling to discuss my despair over my losses. I can't

understand why he doesn't want to talk about this vandalism. I
have tried several times to bring up the subject—to ask if the
police have any leads, or to discuss ordering a new camera and
darkroom equipment. I suppose with the new house so soon to
be finished there's no use in asking to reinstall one here. But Henry
is either silent or changes the subject to something of no importance, or to some fancied misdeed of mine. I do not, do not know
what is the matter with him. Henry keeps his tea parties, goes out
to the Cosmos Club and the occasional dance, and spends the rest
of his days writing in his study, the maid reports when she brings
my tea. I spend the hours of quiet writing on my chaise.

This evening, I had to put myself together. I was barely up
to it, although I had been looking forward—as much as I could
with the present uncertain truce with Henry—to the evening:
dinner at Bancrofts' house, close neighbors at 1621 H Street.

By the time you read this, dear Posterity, doubtless not only
such annual plants as myself will be forgotten, but perhaps even
such great evergreen trees as George Bancroft. So I will tell you
who he and his wife are, as well as our oldest (in more than one
way) friends on the square.

I justified my existence to Henry, at least for a time, by
arranging for him to meet Dr. Bancroft, the dean not only of
American diplomats, but of American historians.

Minister, Doctor, so many honorifics, it is difficult to decide
which to call him, so most of his dear friends (a thousand for each
of his years?) call him Papa Bancroft. He served Lincoln, Andrew
Johnson, and Grant, and knew every president from James Monroe.
Henry first met him at the Berlin legation, where the great man
had served as minister since 1867. Minister Bancroft invited Henry
to lunch with the proviso that he go to the hotel and bring back
his wife. I was in my wrapper when Henry came to fetch me.

I was particularly concerned to dress properly for the Bancrofts, because when my mother died, Cousin (third) Elizabeth Davis Bancroft stepped in to advise Dr. Hooper on what clothes to buy the two motherless daughters, how to deal with seamstresses, and to expound on such arcane subjects as the number of petticoats necessary for respectability.

Thus for her sake—and their guests, the President and Miss Cleveland—tonight's occasion, though a small dinner, rated the old gold brocade, the next to best dinner dress of my eight Worth gowns, bought on our last trip to Europe. Its large lace collar and cuffs give it a certain distinction.

When I came back from seeing my father off on his eternal journey, I had a long conversation with Cousin Bancroft as to whether I should accede to my father's request that we not wear mourning for him. He was very explicit, and cited the injunctions of my grandfather William Sturgis, followed by his children and grandchildren. He disdained conventional, outward signs of mourning, especially crepe veils. He said we should not mourn but rejoice in the lives of those who had passed on. Though I have eschewed strict all-black mourning, I have worn subdued costume—much gray or mauve in the daytime, no jewelry. Still, tonight I wore a single strand of pearls my father had given to me. I pinned on a camellia from a flower woman who came to the door. I hid the tremors of my heart under my Pingat evening cape, and declared myself ready at the appointed hour.

"I always enjoy the Bancrofts," Henry said in a conciliatory tone, as though he were offering around the scones. And then as we settled in the carriage, "After all those years abroad, changing history, George Bancroft now joins me as stable companions to the mighty. We can offer advice or stand on our heads, but no one notices. You'd think Grover Cleveland could find some use for our services. But so far he has not even uttered the polite Southern formula I had from Lamar: 'Of course Mr. Adams knows that anything in my power is at his service.' Southerners do know how to formulate courteous forms for discharging perceived debts. It was Lamar's place, after being a habitué of my house and ideas for years, to make me the offer. And it was my place, as a moral man, disinterested in collecting payments for nebulous debts, to decline and thus free him from any obligation. So Lamar's honor and mine were both satisfied."

I gratefully accepted Henry's more agreeable mood, which he seemed to put on with his dinner dress, along with the proper tie and cufflinks. I wondered idly where he kept his formal agreeable mood when we weren't going out. Did he have his valet fold it neatly and put it in his stud box? Or did he have it smoothed carefully out and hung in his closet?

At the Bancroft house, we came into the wide central hallway dominated at the end by the huge portrait of Wilhelm I, Emperor of Germany. Large bowls of roses stood everywhere. In the drawing room, the great man himself sat easily in his big overstuffed chair, a piece of German *moebel* he had brought home with him in 1874 at the end of his seven years heading the United States legation in Berlin.

He waved but didn't get up as we came in the room. "Henry, Clover, so good to see you," Papa Bancroft said. "I'm sorry not to get up, but you know how it is with me. I promise you, though, I'll make it to the dinner table. We've been promised *echte Wiener Schnitzel* and I don't care what Dr. Hagner says about the digestibility of the *Deutsche Kuche*, I intend to enjoy it."

"If I know you," said Henry, "you'll stuff us with it so we'll get fat and yourself eat only a morsel. Dinner with you is only a spectator sport."

At his Methuselahan age, Papa Bancroft has decided he can November 20, 1885 dispense with shaving. The white hair on his head is sufficient for cover against the cold, but straight and stern compared with the exuberance of his fine white beard, curling, as if each twist is an aide-mémoire to an idea for a book to startle the world. Cousin Bancroft, by contrast, with her own full white hair parted in the middle and pulled back in the manner of the fashions, looks more like a basic text, though with wonderful ruffled shawls and bows at her neck as footnotes.

In their eighties, the Bancrofts keep their grasp securely onto history—the world's and their own. At a time of life when most people would be wrapped in flannel and constrained by nurses, the Bancrofts keep their friends, their work, their cook, their interests and enthusiasms. Both husband and wife are—were— favorite subjects of my camera.

"Papa Bancroft," said I with a gesture toward a huge vase of roses, "how gorgeous your roses are, far superior to my paltry efforts. How many species are you growing now in Newport? But then you have John Brady—the English gardener is, I'm afraid, superior to ours."

"We will share him with you, dear Clover, we'll share. I counted fifty species of roses when we were up at Roseclyffe. Did I tell you we have some varieties from Bismarck's own garden? Next summer, I'll bring you some cuttings for your new garden."

"How wonderful you are! I'm glad to see you sitting down tonight. Every time I go by, you're either out working in your garden or riding in the park. I'm amazed you ride so often."

"I can ride when I can't walk," he said. "And I still get up at dawn. I write until lunch—you know it takes two secretaries to keep up with me. In the afternoon, when I ride in the park and tend my roses, I think about what I'll write the next day.

Come sit by me, Clover. Tell me, dear, are you keeping up your German? Do you read it every day? Out loud? Your accent is so much better than Henry's."

Henry made a face. "It's because she spent so much money while we were in Germany. Nothing like shopping to help your command of a language, I say."

"I don't know about that," said Bancroft. "I always thought the best way to learn a language is to conduct a courtship in it."

Mrs. Bancroft frowned, shook her head at her husband, and said reprovingly, "I was far too ill in Berlin to spend a mark, much less flirt—that terrible climate. The dark skies never lightened during our entire tour, even in that spa on the outskirts of Baden where, as you know, I stayed much of the time. I didn't care too much. After all, Berlin is not Paris, and the shops are not the temptation. I can't imagine what I would have done had you not sent me all the volumes of George Sand's *Histoire de ma vie*, Clover."

"Are you taking her advice: Escape oblivion. Write your own history, all of you who have understood your life and sounded your heart. Did you decide whether to go on to editing your Berlin letters? How are you getting on?"

"I'm still pondering. The London letters, 1846–49 are far more interesting. I haven't had as much time to work on them as I would like because we are working night and day on my husband's biography of Martin Van Buren. But there's no rest for the wicked. When he finishes this one in three or four years, he wants to start on a life of James Knox Polk. I thought his *History of the United States* and its revision was long enough to be the history of the world, if not the cosmos."

"It's an expensive hobby, this writing of history, as I warned Hay when he started his Lincoln biography." said Henry. "I've calculated that over the ten years I worked on them, my two

Madison and Jefferson volumes have cost me rather more than supporting a racing stable. On the other hand, I suspect I have had more fun from riding the hobbyhorse of history than racing nags."

"Which reminds me, Henry, you haven't sent back the proofs George asked you to criticize. We do need them back soon, you know how publishers are. They take so long to do their own work—you'd think they were making the paper by hand in the Coptic manner—that they must constantly harass the authors. But enough about dusty manuscripts, what about your concerns, Clover?"

"Oh, as well as can be expected for one of my temperament. You know what I'm like, the sun goes under a cloud and I think it's an eclipse."

"What about your photographs? You're becoming quite the professional. Clover, do talk to Henry again about that wonderful photograph you made of George last year. I so wish when Richard Gilder asked for it for the *Century*, Henry had allowed the picture to be published. Perhaps when George's history comes out?"

Had it not been for the destruction of my darkroom, I would have soaked in the unaccustomed praise for my work. I sometimes feel as though I go looking for affection, a hungry child begging in other people's houses for crusts and scraps.

In the circumstance, I wasn't sure how much to say. That my darkroom had been smashed to bits? That the plate on which Papa's photograph lived had been ground to crystal? Why not? These are my friends and they are concerned about me. They will sympathize and their gentle words will help console me, I thought. So I began, "We had a dreadful . . ." And before I could go on, Henry looked at me with such sharpness, I felt as though his eyes had fired some of the glass fragments into mine.

"Marian isn't up to that sort of thing," he said, daring me to dispute his words. "She's been rather upset recently over nothing. I think just a bit of November melancholia."

My words trailed off. I wonder now why I didn't stand up for my rights, to explain that I had every cause to complain. That my unhappiness had good reason and was not the result of cloudy days or imagined slights. But before I'd got my nerve up, the Bancrofts, not wanting, no doubt, to interfere in a husband-wife dispute, changed the subject.

"I'm not sure if the President and his sister are coming this evening," said Mrs. Bancroft. "That's the trouble with inviting the White House—you can't count on them. They promised to come if he could finish his papers in time. I count it as a mark of favor that they would even try to come. Miss Rose said they liked the thought of an intimate party. They do get so tired of the big squeezes. We like Miss Rose Cleveland so much—and I know you do. We don't know him as well, of course, but he's an unusual man."

"Did you see that Grover Cleveland interviewed himself in *The Washington Post* today?" asked Papa B., and without waiting to see if we had or had not, continued, "Richard Weightman was to interview him in two or three days or so. But President Cleveland is an impatient man. He wouldn't wait for Weightman."

Papa B. grinned at me in acknowledgment of his pun. He knew I caught it. "Our President sat down at his desk with a pile of yellow paper and wrote not only his answers but the questions and sent the article over to the *Post*. After it was set in type, he even corrected the galleys. So it was very much his own scoop— on the subject of civil service reform. So far he hasn't said he misquoted himself. Ha!"

"I suppose we'll have to become used to a number of changes

with a Democrat in the White House," observed Henry, leaning over me to shoot his volley at closer range to Bancroft. "A friend of mine got a letter from President Cleveland saying he was on his way to preside over a state dinner, but he'd rather eat a pickled herring, a piece of Swiss cheese, and a chop at Louis' instead of the French stuff the White House chef would give him."

"I've heard he plans to run off Chef Cupplinger and bring down the cook from the New York governor's mansion," said Mrs. Bancroft. "Cupplinger does too many sauces for his simple palate, he says."

"He'd better keep Cupplinger through the season," I warned.

"Miss Rose Cleveland," announced Jacob Starnes, the Bancrofts' butler.

The chatelaine of the White House obviously enjoyed the looks of consternation on our faces, as we realized she'd overheard our conversation—but didn't know how much. Indeed Mrs. Bancroft, I, and even Henry were as abashed as small girls caught with their fingers in the cake batter. Only Papa Bancroft remained majestically serene. We metaphorically wiped the batter off our hands and tried to look welcoming.

Miss Rose, as she was called, gave her brother's excuses, though leaving the possibility he might still turn up if his secretaries didn't push more papers at him. Then she picked up where we had stopped, since she'd gathered we considered the chef's passage a delicious tidbit.

"Chef Cupplinger's a small loss, for all his fancy French sauces. We became used to Cook Eliza when Grover was governor of New York. We'll do much better with her good, plain, New York cooking. But the day Grover takes the social office away from Pruden and Young is the day I pack my bag and leave as well! The two of them are magicians at producing formal affairs out of

a hat. You know I'm not much for Mrs. Grant's sort of frivolity
—rose teas, nautical breakfasts, and so on are, I'm happy to say,
passé."

"They are charming, but a shade—casual—not really suitable
for the White House, do you think? I do prefer gilt-edged for-
mality," said Mrs. Bancroft. "The White House should have the
dignity of tradition. Will the President keep on Sinclair as his
steward?"

"He will keep the title of steward," said Miss Cleveland.
"Frankly, and please don't say it outside this room, he's been
Grover's valet since Grover went to Albany. Grover knew Sinclair's
father before him—he was the steward at the City Club in Bal-
timore. But Bill's not a manager. Besides, it still is not too easy in
Washington to bring our New York arrangements into effect. Since
Bill is a mulatto and the doormen are white, it doesn't make for
a smooth running household. So the way I have it working, is that
Bill keeps the title 'steward,' but we've raised one of the doormen
to be the manager, with the title Chief Usher, at the same salary
as the steward. And Grover has hired Chef Segar for the season.
If we just have to have galas out of season, well, Washington has
lots of caterers.

"I need all the help I can get—what with the card receptions,
the small dinners of fifteen to twenty-five, not to mention the big
public levees for several thousand three times a season—what was
called genteel squeezes in Dolley Madison's day. Anyway, I hope
you four have received our invitation and will be kind enough to
favor us by coming to dinner on November 25, our preseason
dinner for the cabinet. Our Congressional dinner, actually the
season opener, will be on December 1, as usual. But we thought
you four would rather come to the smaller party, where the crush
won't be so bad. We'll see what Segar can do."

"Yes, thank you. I've already sent in our acceptance. Henry and I would be honored to come. How good of you to ask us," I said, and Henry switched his face to delighted. The Bancrofts made the proper noises. That settled, I went on to comment, "I've never understood why the Washington season begins on December 1. It would make so much more sense to begin after Congress comes back from the Christmas recess. Though I certainly understand why the season ends with spring. And in summer, the heat turns this swampy land into a boiling cauldron. Here on the line where both northern and southern trees flourish, we have twice the variety of pollen. Spring rains are more mold and pollen than water. If one kind doesn't get you, another will."

"What I don't understand, Miss Rose," said Mrs. Bancroft, "is how you manage all of this with your career. Being a professor at Houghton Institute is quite enough to worry about on its own. Buffalo, after all, isn't that near, and you lecture all over the place."

"I manage, though, I admit, I think it's long past the time when Grover should have a wife to take over all this sort of thing. I'm already weary of it and he hasn't been in office a year. My sister—you know Mary Hoyt, don't you, Mrs. Adams?—helped me the first month, but she has her own family to tend."

"But you have your own books to worry about, surely that's as important," said Mrs. B. "Clover and I, as we wrote you, were delighted with *George Eliot's Poetry and Other Studies*. A very scholarly work. It's good for our young women to have a serious student like yourself to set an example."

"Not to mention how wonderful you look when you make calls from your landau wearing your ostrich hat," teased Henry, interrupting the ladies lest we go off onto the forbidden subject of women's rights. "I've never seen a landau painted green, black, and purple before. Did you paint it to match the hat?"

Fortunately for Henry, dinner was announced before Miss Rose demolished him, as she was quite prepared to do. Henry was not really accustomed to dealing with as strong and outspoken a woman. We went into the paneled room, brilliantly lit by a gilded baroque chandelier. I told Mrs. Bancroft how much I admired the fixture.

"From Prague, as you might suspect. Not that it's comparable to the one that illuminates your dining table. I dislike auctions very much, but I mean to go to yours after you die, Clover."

The company laughed. I'm not sure why, but fingers of cold stroked my back. I shivered involuntarily.

As we reached our chairs, the butler announced, "The President of the United States." The company, caught with bended knees on our way to sit, stopped and straightened up to stand at attention as best we could.

The twenty-second President of the United States is a pudgy man, with a face rather like a well-fed buffalo, the animal for which his previous city of residence was named. The hair on his head is close cropped, but his mustache has escaped the scissors to swoop enthusiastically around his voluptuous lips. Like Richardson, he rather overwhelms me. I have the awkward feeling that if I don't step smartly, Cleveland might bump into me, no matter where I stand. His manner of speaking rather bumps and jumps over words and ideas as well. He seemed not so much dressed as upholstered, befitting so generous a figure of a man. However, he was neatly and correctly turned out, and presented such an impressive sight that he would have been hard to overlook in any company. The Bancrofts were indeed honored that he would come to their house.

Miss Rose sat on Minister Bancroft's distinguished, if slightly rickety, right hand; the President, of course, on our hostess's right;

leaving Henry and me respectively to the left of our hosts. The
company was so small that conversation was general. Mrs. Bancroft
didn't bother to turn the table; she started right in with a general
question to the Clevelands.

November 20, 1885

"Does Hawkins suit you as a driver?" Mrs. Bancroft asked,
following the general rule amongst ladies accustomed to running
large houses to fill in the cracks of the conversation with talk
about the servants.

"Hawkins is fine, but his stories are not as good as Jerry
Smith's. Perhaps you know Smith was a stable boy when the Grants
came to the White House, but Mrs. Grant trained him for the
house. Now he's a footman, but he's also the spook sayer. Colonel
Lamont and Grover are too grand to hear his ghost stories, naturally, but every time I find Smith in the butler's pantry polishing
the silver, I have to hear about his latest apparitions."

"And you a fine agnostic," I said, with a small laugh. "Whom
does he see?"

"Everybody," said Miss Cleveland. "Smith wasn't in the
White House when Lincoln was, but he says he heard strange
stories from Noah Brooks, Lincoln's secretary, and Marshall Ward
Lamon, who slept in front of Lincoln's door. Smith tells remarkable
stories about Lincoln's haunting himself."

"What do you mean?"

"Oh, I thought surely you would have heard the story by
this time."

"I have heard something from Hay," Henry admitted, with
the air of one knowledgeable but bound to secrecy. "He's very
discreet, of course, about his years as Lincoln's secretary. I suppose
he and John Nicolay want us to wait for their biography. How
does Smith tell it?"

"Everyone knows," said Miss Cleveland, with an air of settling in for the evening, "that the Lincolns were quite superstitious. Not religious people, but believers in spirits. Of course they weren't alone. You'll excuse me, dear Adams, but I've heard there were forty thousand spiritualists in Boston in the sixties. The Lincolns, if my informant can be believed, held eight séances in the White House itself after their young son died. Indeed, they thought they'd spoken to Willie. During Lincoln's last term, his own preoccupation with the occult began to be an obsession. He would dream of riding a barge to a distant shore on the nights before important battles were fought.

"One night, he woke in the middle of the night and heard sobs and feet shuffling and stomping. He followed the sounds to the East Room. In the middle of the room, he saw a bier draped in black. 'Who died?' he asked a woman covered with black draperies like the catafalque. 'The President,' she said. 'Abraham Lincoln, dead by an assassin's bullet.' It was not a week before he was shot by Booth at Ford's Theatre."

With such a story, everyone had to have another round of wine before we women were willing to leave the men at the table with their port, their cigars, their views on civil service reform, immigration, and Congress's constant preoccupations with private bills for veterans.

In the drawing room, Mrs. Bancroft poured coffee in wonderful gilt-and-cobalt-edged demitasses. As we started to sip, we heard a commotion on the street. We went to the front windows, pulling the curtains back just enough so we wouldn't be exposed. Across the street, a woman dressed in finery, fancier than refined, stood on the sidewalk. Her companion, a rather well-dressed man, had his arm around her. They looked startled. From the porch of the house above them, a man shouted at the couple, "Go away, you slut. Go away. This is honest folks' territory. I'll not have you

sullying my street." And considerably worse language. Miss Rose,
Mrs. Bancroft, and I avoided looking at each other.

"Why, that's William Nicholson. Why is he carrying on so?" asked Mrs. B.

"Then why are you here if it's Honest Street?" shouted the woman back to her berater. "I've as much right as you do to be on public property. If you don't like my looks, go back inside and close your door."

With that, the man holding onto her whispered something in her ear, tipped his hat toward Nicholson, and walked hastily away.

Nicholson yelled after him, "See that you keep better company next time. You dandies go whoring around, you'll catch something and serve you right." He came determinedly down the steps, taking off his belt as he did.

The woman turned quickly and started to walk away, but her assailant was too quick for her. As we watched mesmerized, he kicked her in her breast, knocking her down, and began to beat her with his belt. Her companion, hearing her scream, turned, came back, and helped her get up. Dodging Nicholson's belt as best they could, they ran to a house just at the edge of our sight. Nicholson ran after them, and just as she started up the steps of her own door, he kicked her in the mouth. The street was strewn with her teeth and blood. Her companion abandoned her and ran as she made it up the stairs, trying to stay ahead of Nicholson's foot.

"Heavens! She's Katie Cusick!" said Mrs. Bancroft. "George, send Starnes for the police. Right this minute." Not waiting for Minister Bancroft, she began to ring her bell, energetically calling, "Starnes, Starnes." He appeared, bottle and towel in his hand.

"Yes, ma'am."

"Summon the police! Get a doctor!"

Such was the force of Mrs. Bancroft's orders, Starnes did put down the bottle, but he ran out the door still holding the towel.

Mrs. Bancroft went to find her maid to send over to that poor woman's house to see if she could help her until the doctor came.

Finally hearing the disturbance, President Cleveland, Henry, and Papa Bancroft came in from their port, demanding to know what all the fuss was about.

"Elizabeth, what on earth are you sending Starnes to do?"

"To get someone to arrest that dastardly dolt!" said Mrs. Bancroft. "If I were not an old lady, I would have gone after him with a broomstick. I never could stand Nicholson. He's nothing better than an assassin. After all, Katie Cusick has every right to be on the street. She lives around here, too. Even if she didn't, he's got no right to assault her." We all took up the story, all interrupting each other.

By the time a puzzled-looking policeman approached the Bancrofts' house, Nicholson had gone home and Mrs. Cusick's light was off. "Grover, do something about this," said his sister. "See that Nicholson is charged with assault and battery. He had no cause to attack that poor woman. There was no evidence that she was soliciting. But even if she had been, he had no right to molest her! It's unbelievable what violence men are permitted to unleash against women without fear of legal retribution. When we have the vote, we'll do something to punish such thugs."

The President turned at his sister's tongue lashing and went to the door. The policeman drew back when he saw who stood there.

"Officer," said Cleveland, "I think you should go down to that Nicholson's house and arrest him for disturbing the peace."

And he explained. The awed officer saluted and headed down to Nicholson's house.

November 20, 1885

"The women in this town have a hard time," said Miss Rose. "Washington has a remarkable number of employed women, clerks, shop girls, and, of course, teachers. They should be able to walk down the streets without being accused of being Ladies of the Night. The very idea!

"No one seems to worry about the status of the women who are not in society here. I've decided to do a little thing—something to give a little pleasure to these young women who come from all over to work as clerks here. Perhaps I'll have receptions or teas on a day of the week, I suppose Saturday, when working women can come."

It's a measure of our standards that both Mrs. Bancroft and I thought Rose Cleveland had made a useful suggestion.

The President, who'd continued his conversation with Henry and Papa Bancroft, stood up about then, shook hands, and paid compliments, with a careful look around to see if he'd counted wrong and overlooked a baby needing to be kissed. He excused himself from staying later, pleading the tyranny of the official papers.

Henry hastily protested: "But surely, sir, you won't deprive us of the pleasure of Miss Rose's company? My wife and I will be pleased to see her home ourselves, though I fear our carriage is not as colorful as hers." As the President assented, Henry, saving Bancroft from having to move his old bones, saw Cleveland to his carriage.

On the other side of the room, I appreciated the other two women's indignation over the evening's events, as well as their free-spirited views in general. Growing up, I'd known many women who believed in their own rights—Mrs. Bancroft and my mother had been original members of one of Margaret Fuller's "Conversations" circles. Henry once acknowledged that he thought Mrs. Bancroft was "the most intelligent woman in Washington." However, his remark suggested there were not that many, and he didn't include me in the number.

"After the Negro men were given their suffrage," Mrs. Bancroft said, in an oft expressed complaint, "I thought surely women would be next. But here we are today, injustices everywhere and no recourse at the ballot box. Did you hear about Frederick Douglass's speech on behalf of women's rights? You'd think he'd make white men ashamed."

"Not an Adams."

"You must have come as a surprise to the Adams men," said Miss Rose.

"Oh yes, they think I'm a strange one, unwomanly because I talk so much and have views, and of course, because I'm barren. Adams men think that women exist only to produce more Adams men." I realized I had said too much. I looked away, too late disassociating myself from the bitter remark.

Miss Rose and Mrs. Bancroft both glanced at me quickly and then turned to discussing roses. I am sure they wondered exactly what had persuaded me to give this unaccustomed harsh account of Henry's family. I work hard at making my conversation bright and smart, but I have avoided criticism of my husband and my husband's family as if I stood in danger of immolation on the funeral pyre of their reputation.

After my faux pas, there was nothing for me to do but to brazen it out, go all the way: "I think we'd better go home. I've obviously had too much of your port and your kindness and honesty, Mrs. B., and too lavish a helping of your belief in women's intellectual worth, Miss C. I had best go home and sleep it off, before I think myself worthy of walking hand in hand with my husband at an equal stride. Such a thing would never be permitted in this year of 1885. After all, the Constitution isn't even a hundred years old yet, why should we think the American male would get around to admitting that women are people and citizens? We'll need at least another hundred years. I'm off, before I fully disgrace myself. Henry?" I raised my voice to my husband, who fortunately was engaged in animated conversation with Papa Bancroft. "We must go."

"Oh, must we?" he said with an air of disappointment. "We had almost all the problems of history solved. I'll see you home and then come back."

I was saved by Mrs. Bancroft, who looked Henry in the eye and said firmly, "Why, Henry, by the time you escort Miss Cleveland home and then tuck Clover in, I'm afraid George and I will be, as they say around here, plum tuckered out. You know, since we've been 'eightied' we're not up to as many all-night talks as we used to be. Good night, dear hearts."

Henry, crestfallen at the admonishment, somewhat abruptly shepherded us out to the carriage. After Miss Rose had been duly deposited at the White House's north portico, Henry turned to me and said, "Marian, for heaven's sake, why did you egg on Miss Rose and Mrs. Bancroft? You forced the President to embarrass himself for that dollymop. You and Miss Cleveland make yourselves ridiculous with your ladies' causes."

I did not trust myself to speak.

❧

CHAPTER 14

November 23, 1885

Hay, While the Sun Shines

∞

Dear Posterity,

While I dressed for tea I heard an unusual bustle going on downstairs. I had foregone breakfast, Henry's appellation for the noon meal, in favor of tea and biscuits in my room. I had gone over plans for Thanksgiving, only three days away, with Cook, checked the condition of the festive table linens with Maggie, discussed with Johnson the necessity of dipping the Skyes in a flea-exterminating solution, and written Cousin Bancroft a thank-you note to be taken over with the morning's batch of banana bread. I wouldn't dare send them roses—mine are nothing to compare with theirs. All of this kept me from hearing further from Henry on my misdeeds at the Bancrofts.

For once, I am in good spirits because Henry James is to

arrive in time for Thanksgiving and the White House dinner. Henry November 23, 1885 James is assuredly someone to be thankful for. I adore and admire our famous novelist, as much for his dear self as for his sensitive novels.

When I went to the drawing room, Henry was already there, with, to my surprise, John Hay, his arm around the back of Henry's chair, the two of them with heads close, talking softly.

"You must be surprised to see me," Hay said, removing his arm from the chair and reaching out to me.

With as much enthusiasm as I could muster, I said, "The only surprise is your waiting so long between visits to see your palace a-building. Will we be able to be thankful for you Thursday?"

"No, but both my wife and I will be at the White House with you on the night before. I'm sorry I can't be with you for Thanksgiving—I enjoy your cook's Southern feasts."

"I'm sorry, too. Cook used to work at Berkeley Plantation in Virginia—you know, the Benjamin Harrison place. She has told me a wonderful heresy to twit my orthodox Bostonian husband at the autumn feast. She says the Harrison family assert the Virginia settlers actually celebrated the first Thanksgiving—not those Johnny-come-lately Massachusetts Pilgrims. The Virginians claim to have held the first Thanksgiving ceremony in a ship just off Jamestown in 1607 and then the first feast on the Berkeley Plantation in 1619. That, you'll notice, is before the 1620 Plymouth landing."

"Twaddle," said Henry with a vehemence all out of proportion to my mild twitting of, after all, our mutual ancestors. "Marian, you spend far too much time listening to the servant's tales. You give their fancies far more credence than my careful research."

I thought it better to change the subject again. "Where's your wife, Mr. Hay? Why didn't you bring her with you?"

"My wife's with her mother. Mrs. Stone's health is not reliable, as you know. I had meetings with John George Nicolay about our Lincoln biography. We'll be able to work so much easier, I've told my wife, when we can move into our new house. She's coming in time for the White House dinner and then we'll have to leave after it to make it home for a late Thanksgiving. I thought it too short a trip to bring the children."

"Is it now?"

Henry looked straight ahead as though disassociating himself from my existence. In search of a distraction, I went to the cupboard in search of the tea set, babbling as I went.

"Henry, why aren't you using the Five of Hearts tea set Clarence King gave us? Don't you think the three of us constitute a quorum? I wonder if we'll ever be the Five of Hearts again?" I took out of the cupboard and set down the quaint tea set, each piece shaped like a heart, decorated with roses and a clock face set at five. "Indeed, how like King—I wonder from whom he borrowed the money to buy it?"

"What a horrid thing to say," said Henry. "You know well that if either of us had a last dime and King wanted it, we would give it to him instantly, even if he intended to throw it down one of those silver mines of his—which he seems to be doing with some regularity with all his money these days. No matter, his own dear presence is gold enough."

"True," said John, with what I thought was rather a rueful look. "Did I tell you that he wrote not long ago to say he couldn't pay me for a bit he'd borrowed, and he signed it 'unremittingly yours.' I wish he'd give up on all his get-rich-instantly schemes and settle down at some good university. Harvard, I'm sure, would

be grateful to have the surveyor of the Fortieth Parallel, the founder
of the United States Geological Survey, as professor of geology."

"He'll never give up on his hidden mines and buried treasures,
John," said Henry. "It's a good thing he's an honest man. When
King's eyes light up and he starts to talk about all the riches he
will dig up, I'd fall for it any day."

"He certainly saved Rothschild a lot of money."

"That he did, that he did."

"What do you mean?" I asked.

"Have you never heard the story, Clover?"

"Of course not, you've never told me."

"I'm surprised, it's been years ago. Someone, I forget just
where, was selling stock in a gem mine. Oh, they had a pile of
gemstones—a mixture, amethyst, diamond, sapphire—I don't
know what else. And King broke up the scam by pointing out
(and here Hay did his famous Western imitation), 'Why, suh, you
just don't ever find a mixture of gemstones in one place like that.
Gems are no better than humans in learning to be neighbors.'
Then he showed one of the gems was not only far from freshly
found, it had even been faceted.

"Rothschild was about to invest in the mine, and King's
discovery saved him a great deal of money. King's always had the
ability to make money, though more often for other people than
himself—but managing money is a different problem for him."

"John, you have to admit that his mother and what is it, ten
relatives? are like a flight of Transylvanian vampires returning every
night to suck his blood."

"Henry! At tea?"

John Hay had another cup of tea and another croissant,
commenting, "This is the only house in Washington, I suspect the
only one outside mine in the United States, where you can drink

a decent cup of tea. And these marzipan croissants are wonderful!"

"Mrs. Beale sent them over with the recipe this morning," said Henry, helping himself to the last one.

Henry couldn't prevail upon our Cleveland colleague to stay with us. Well, Wormley's Hotel is devoid of Congressmen until the session begins December 1. As usual, they never come to Washington until just before Congress convenes.

Wormley's Hotel, run by a mulatto family, is a pleasant place to stay. We lived there for a time when we first came to Washington. As often as possible, we put up our visitors there. It's only at Fifteenth and H Streets, a block away.

While I was ruminating in such a fashion, the two, their chairs abutting each other, had their heads together, Mr. Hay's hand on Henry's shoulder, talking with great animation. I thought they looked rather like their new houses, fitting so close to each other, two parts of the same whole.

As I recall, Henry met the Westerner when both were in Washington in 1860, during the second term in Congress of Charles Francis Adams. At twenty-two, they were both secretaries—the apprentice career of young men with expectations too large to think they had to earn a proper living and educations too pretentious to be drawing room dogs. Henry served his father, and with somewhat more enterprise, Hay had been apprenticed to his uncle's law firm, in which, happily, Abraham Lincoln was a partner. John Hay, with all the idealism of his youth and abolition sentiments, was a captain in Lincoln's election campaign. And the assistant secretaryship to the great man was his reward.

Men need men more than women do their own sex. They are born into a sort of club. They have a language and interests that they jealously guard against women. They see us as an alien species. Birds to sing. But other men as companions.

Close companions they are. Henry once said, "Certain men November 23, 1885 with common tastes were bound to come together." For Henry, the "certain men" were John Hay, H. H. Richardson, Clarence King, John La Farge, and Augustus Saint-Gaudens.

I was recalled to the present by Henry's interjection: "I'll show you!" They both stood up—John Hay is my height, five-feet-two, two inches shorter than Henry. How small they will look in Richardson's great arches. They went out the door to see their houses-to-be, I presume to check on some point of disagreement. Henry passed by me without comment, but John Hay waved from the door.

In some ways, it will be easier for me when John Hay moves here. I have given up trying to explain to Henry how I feel about his attentions to Elizabeth Cameron and Emily McLean. Well, those ladies—if that's the word for them—will soon find out, as I have, that John Hay is powerful competition for Henry's attention.

But what of Henry's mysterious letter? Does it have anything to do with John Hay's visit? Why did Clara Hay not come? You'd think she'd be anxious to see her new house. Could the letter, as eventually rewritten and sent, warn her not to come? I still have difficulty thinking of Henry and Clara carrying on an *affaire de coeur*.

I need to go on with my own work, *Letters to Posterity from La Fayette Square*. I have to send to London to have Louis Gandolfi make me a new camera. What if I illustrate my epistolary work with my photographs? But Henry would never allow it. Before emancipation, some slaves actually earned the price of their freedom by working for money during their off-hours. I wish Henry would grant me the same privilege.

Before I could decide to go upstairs to write, they were back again. "Too dark?" I enquired. Henry gave me a brusque nod.

"Have you read this new book yet, Clover?" John Hay said, holding up a copy of my *Esther*.

"What did you think of it? I'm surprised you have it. I haven't seen a copy in the bookstores."

"It was sent to me. However I came by it, I found it a pleasant but sad book. I sat right down and read it, thinking it was some friend who was testing the market. But so far no one has owned up to it. Do you know who, Clover?"

"Someone who prefers to remain anonymous, I suppose. The world these days is full of people who write books but don't have the courage to put their names on them. When you read the trash that's in them you understand why."

"I had thought you would be more sympathetic to *Esther*, Clover. She reminds me very much of you. Her inability to accept a religious belief, for instance, and her effort toward—not a career because for a woman that's not really proper, they have too many other responsibilities—but a hobby, an avocation, I should say. I did find it inexplicable that she wouldn't accept this perfectly charming man, who was offering her his hand and his protection. And I surely couldn't see where she was going from there. Throw herself into Niagara Falls, I suppose."

"But then, my dear Hay, you are not a woman, and have no idea of the enormous resources we bring to life. As for denying the possibilities of a woman having a career, well, I should remind you of Miss Cleveland's scholastic and literary occupation. I think a time will come when all well-educated women will find something better to do than leave cards on each other and go to crushes, those rightly named gatherings. Even in our benighted century there are already women who do—though it takes an extraordinary talent and willpower."

"Ridiculous," said Henry. "The rigors of literary endeavors

are far too arduous for delicate women. You have quite enough
to do in support of your husband's work. Though I must say, John,
that the wild abandon of Clover's handwriting is not much help
in trying to read one's research, and she often has to be coaxed
to pour tea. Isn't that so, Clover? Well, if you won't ring for more
tea for us, I think I for one will peel off these exterior wrappings
and settle down for the evening. What about you, John?"

November 23, 1885

"I suggest that I take you and the beautiful and agreeable
Mrs. Adams to Wormley's for dinner. Surely whatever has been
prepared in the kitchen could be tucked away for the morrow."

"And have Cook quit? Heavens! My dear friend, while I
appreciate the kindness of your thought, I assure you that your
wife would be scandalized if she knew you'd made the suggestion
and I had acquiesced."

"Now, now, Clover, he was just trying to entertain us. John,
I'll tell you what we'll do. We'll go have supper as soon as the
cook can put it on the table, then you and I will go have some
liquid sustenance at the Cosmos Club, and Clover can enjoy the
peace and quiet of the house without us."

"Ideal!"

So my fine supper of duck, orange rice, mushrooms, carrots,
lamb, potatoes, pecan pie, and so on was quickly downed by the
two of them, hardly finishing one course before beginning on
another in their haste to get out of the house.

Finally, after gulping down my coffee, I excused myself and
left them to their cigars, port, and secrets not fit for feminine ears.
I came up here to write down these thoughts. I was especially
interested in Mr. Hay's remarks about *Esther*.

I heard the door slam as they went out. From my window
I saw them arm and arm walking down the steps, down the
sidewalk, toward the Cosmos Club in the middle of Madison Place.

The knock on the door startled me—of a sudden, I couldn't imagine who it might be. Only Jane, come to bring my hot chocolate and put me to bed. Indeed, despite my afternoon nap and coffee at dinner, I felt tired beyond all reason. In my peignoir, I drank the chocolate—it tasted somehow different. But delicious.

"Do you like the chocolate, ma'am?" asked Jane. "Mr. Hay brought it especially for you. He said Mr. King gave it to him for you. From Mexico, it is. Mr. Adams said I was to fix it for you."

Jane was hardly out of the room before I was asleep.

Whatever the epicurean quality of John Hay's hot chocolate, it was not as efficacious as Mr. Corcoran's potables in bringing on erotic dreams. I dreamed instead that Henry and John Hay came into my room and looked at me. One whispered: "What is to be done?" And the other: "I'll think of something."

The strangest of my night's dreams began, I think, shortly after, though who is to say how dream time is reckoned? Dreams come like the wind, blowing in strange fantasies, shaking your mind as though it were a tree, and leaving an eerie sense of bare branches, fallen leaves, and emptiness behind them.

The dream began not in the mind's eye, but its ears. I could hear metallic screeches and thumps, whining and low voices. I dreamed I went to the window to look for the cause of these disturbing sounds. I could see very little, but it was clear the noise came from east of the window, from our house-to-be.

I went out my boudoir door, not bothering to change from my peignoir; down the hall, my open-heeled shoes flapping as they went; down the stairs, floating rather than stepping; out the front door and onto the sidewalk, turning left toward the new house; heedless of my negligee, almost tripping in its long skirts, I ran next door. The clamor increased with every inch. By the time I faced the house and the tidal waves of sound, what I saw was no surprise. Only the enormity of the destruction startled me.

November 23, 1885

The house was being wrecked. Huge machines such as I had never seen were beating great metal balls against our windows, bashing the bricks, battering the structure, playing a mad cacophony, like some water organ powered by a Niagara. What had taken so long to put together was coming down like the House of Usher, crumbling back into splintered wood, clay, crystallized sand, marble and slate stones, into an organic pile, a ruin. Our house! Our house! Gone! Gone! Gone!

I lost all feeling, the locks on my joints dissolved, and I collapsed, as devastated as our house.

CHAPTER 15

November 24, 1885

King Comes

∞

Dear Posterity,

I woke up, saw that no light peeped from the top of the curtain, and determined that there was not enough day there for me. My brain felt fuzzy, as though it were wearing a fur hat. I amused myself for a time with the thought of a hat worn inside instead of outside your head, but all my ideas were woolly. I lay there, trying to focus on a single thought: why did I feel so peculiar?

All sorts of strange images floated by my blurry mind's eye. John Hay's arm moving away from Henry. Henry's eyes dilating when he spoke of Clarence King. My lover in the temple, his touch turning me to stone. Mr. Richardson's hand on my shoulder. The yawning archway of the new house. My father's voice saying good-bye. My horse Prince's hoofs striking the path. The maid's hand giving me the cup of hot chocolate. The dogs barking at my door. Emily Beale McLean and La Dona Cameron dancing together with Henry. All these images floated in a circle. I opened my eyes with great difficulty, like the hatch on a boat in a windstorm. The people had vanished, presumably washed down the maelstrom. But the room was going round and round. I held on tightly, trying to hold onto the bed, my equilibrium, and my sanity. Just as I was about to descend into this vortex, I was able, by a supreme effort, to raise my head up and slide the extra pillow under its mate. The tornado began to die down. The room slowed, as though my boat dragged against a reef.

November 24, 1885

When I finally came to rest, I was so exhausted by my whirl that I fell asleep, waking to darkness again. Jane's tentative knock brought me more or less to life.

I asked her if it were raining outside.

"No, ma'am. It's just the way it be in November."

"What time is it?"

"Four-thirty."

"Why did you let me sleep the day through? You know I am always up by eight. What's the matter with you? What's the matter with me?"

"I don't rightly know, ma'am, but Mr. Henry and Mr. Hay told me not to bother you. They said you hadn't been feeling well, and a good long sleep would set you up."

"Set me down, rather. Here, take the tea and help me get dressed."

John Hay and Henry, standing together, looked surprised at the sight of me.

"We weren't expecting you," said Henry.

"You weren't?"

"I was hoping you'd come!" said a voice behind me.

"Clarence King! How come you are here?"

"I am your boomerang. Throw me away and I come back to you always," he said, taking my hands.

"When did you arrive?"

"Last night when you were well asleep. And your night has turned into a sleepy day. How are you? Are you rested? I am very glad to see you!"

The three soon ignored me, allowing me to sit back and review my thoughts about the players of the Five of Hearts. I wasn't sure how I felt about the return from exile of the King. His majesty. The one to whom these knights errant gave their fealty. And Henry's hero.

Henry's overwrought devotion to him I often thought excessive. I suspect as jealous as I was over Henry's homage to King, that Clara Hay had even more reason. John Hay once said that his "true country, my real home" is in King's presence, wherever that might be. Heaven knows how much of his wife's money John Hay has poured into King's crackbrain schemes. Fortunately, our $25,000 a year doesn't allow Henry to lavish money to equal his affection on King—and my father to some extent safeguarded my inheritance, paltry compared to Clara Hay's, against a husband's capriciousness.

Never before my first year of marriage did I realized that such fanatic adoration as Henry and John Hay give to King could exist in this age. Henry was fond of telling people, "When the Lord might have made other men like him, why the D. didn't he? Women are jealous of the power King has over men; but women are many and King is one."

King is the tallest of our Five of Hearts—five feet, six inches, four inches taller than me, not that this qualifies as towering. He has more muscle than John Hay and Henry would have if both were flattened out and rolled together like gingerbread men. His face is the color of a saddle, from his years riding in one all over the West. Beside him, John Hay and Henry look weak, wan, and wispy, as if they are pictures cut from a book and only King is real. In the last few years, his beard has grown thicker and grayer, like moss on a rock, though the top of his head is becoming Bald Mountain.

King does the deeds that John Hay and Henry wish they could—had they his courage, energy, and that remarkable driving quality of his that keeps him going. Perhaps that's the real reason the two of them admire the outdoor man so much.

With all King's undeniable muscle—both in body and mind—he lacks two attributes: luck and health. Unlike Midas, everything King touches turns to dross. I had not heard the gem story they told last night—I can't imagine why. But I am not surprised. If the gems had been natural to the Ali Baba cave where they were found, they would have turned to glass at King's touch. He is one of the truly unlucky people of the world. His father's fortune was lost at sea. His stepfather's businesses died with him. His mother chased away his fiancée. And so on.

As for health—he is constantly ill with unusual fevers, debilitating diseases, and grandiose schemes that lay waste his cash and his career. Were it not for the money and influence lent him by John Hay, and to a lesser extent Henry, I doubt he would have been with us on that day. Though you never could tell where King would rise up. I sometimes thought him capable of transmigration from one hemisphere to another without using physical means of travel. He would appear and disappear unheralded, unexcused, unexplained. That was true of most things about King—as close friends as we were, he remained a multifarious and mysterious figure.

King's taste for women who are either married or unmarriageable is well-known. Since I fell into the first category (sometimes I felt as though I were in the latter one), King and I had always been friends. He made a great show of swashbuckling masculinity (such as the time he aimed a gun at a Washington drawing room chandelier. When a nervous woman asked if it were loaded, he offered to do so). Still, he is decidedly an aesthete. I often found conversation with King rather like visiting with a close woman friend. We chattered away about clothes, collections, and decorations. We gossiped about our friends.

One of the stranger conversations—about peignoirs, of all things—I had with King touched on both his ambiguity about women and his interest in their fripperies. He went on at length about the degree of transparency desirable in the fabric, the extent to which the front should be fastened or allowed to fall open "accidentally," the way the shape and embroidery design of the collar should frame the face and receive the hair, the most effective color for both morning sunlight and evening gaslight, the proper length to flirtingly display the ankle—a hundred details. After I thought he had exhausted the subject for all time, he described the peignoir—perhaps I could call it the "working uniform"—of a courtesan he had once employed on the Orient Express. King said he was sorry he had not been able to find one like it for his mother. Since then, he told me, he had many times looked at his mother and envisioned her wearing the peignoir!

King has often alluded to the time in his youth when his

mother broke off his engagement to a thoroughly suitable young woman. He has supported his mother, past her remarriage and into her widowhood, to the detriment of his own comfort. I, too, have always been close to and concerned with my father's welfare—but I never imagined him posturing in dishabille.

My reverie was interrupted by the King himself. "My dear Mrs. Adams, you know I could not stay away from you for long. I am here in Washington only for the purpose of kissing your hand and listening to your charming satirical stories of the capital. Tell me one immediately!"

Before I was made to comply, dinner was announced and we went in to eat Cook Margery Talbot's Virginia ham, cooked in the Southern way with mustard and brown sugar. The men went off into a farcical discussion of the first time King and Henry had met.

"You'll remember, King, I had come West in 1871 to see exactly what you were up to in your geodesic survey. Following my mule's nose in Estes Park looking for the camp, I found the cabin and you. I was so enchanted. I knew you instantly! I suspect we were friends in Greece, in classic times. King, were you Alcibiades or Alexander?"

"I was whichever one you weren't. But of that time in Estes Park, what a night that was, as though we had indeed known each other always but had been briefly out of touch and had to catch up."

"King, you remember there was only one room and one bed to share. But who cared? We didn't sleep until dawn! Think of that buggy ride back! There was never a time when all four wheels of the buggy were on that mule path at once."

"Gentlemen!" I interrupted. "Before you get to the part

where King dresses formally for dinner in the middle of the wil-
derness, please pour me a bit of wine and have another slice of
ham and a spoonful or two of sweet potatoes."

"King, I'll never forget your touring outfit in Europe, in—
let me think now—1882," said John Hay. "That green velvet suit
and artist's beret, the silk stockings and those amazing yellow
shoes."

"The toes were so pointy, I could have fenced with them."

"You gentlemen would have looked pale and poverty-stricken
beside Henry in his gilt-edged diplomatic uniform. The glitter
almost put my eyes out the first time we met in London, when
my father and I were invited to dinner at the legation. He wore
a navy blue coat, topped with a high stand-up collar. I say it was
blue, but so thickly embroidered with gold thread on the cuffs,
collar, and lapels that the base color was almost in doubt. The
buttons were embossed with patriotic gold eagles—they are still
in my sewing box. The chapeau ornament, knee buckles, and shoe
buckles were vermeil. His vest was a virgin-pure white Kerseymere
with matching breeches, followed by white silk stockings, accompanied by white gloves—and of course, an eagle-headed sword,
vermeil as well. It's a wonder he could carry it all around."

Everyone laughed, though Henry's seemed perfunctory, as
though he thought I was making fun of him.

And so the evening went on. Finally, I could stay awake no
longer, excused myself, leaving them to their cigars, port, and
gratefulness for my departure.

My maid soon came in to help me undress and serve me the
remarkable hot chocolate King had sent. I drank it with pleasure,
along with reading my book. But hardly had I read the first word
than I was fast asleep.

I drifted through nimbus clouds, shining with light. I could feel their soft, sensuous, wet warmth rubbing up against my body. It was so peaceful up there in the mist, I felt it soak into my body, making insulating pillows for my nerves. Once I almost drifted down from my private stratosphere at the sound of wild laughter, but then a breeze lifted me and gently floated me onto another luminous cloud.

November 24, 1885

CHAPTER 16

November 25, 1885

RSVP The White House

∞

Dear Posterity,

A few notes in my journal about White House parties before we go:

The night of our White House dinner engagement is frosty and foggy. However, according to Washington etiquette, we must appear at this command performance—your own funeral is the only excuse for missing a White House dinner.

Anyway, we have to go, for the sake of our houseguest, who just arrived this morning. Henry James was invited while he was still in England, he said. But then Miss Rose is literary. I was not surprised to hear that John and Clara Hay were asked—even though they were fervent John-Blaine-for-President supporters.

They have enough money and influence to ensure them White House invitations in perpetuity, no matter the party. I did not, however, expect Clarence King to be on the guest list, since he was also a Blaine supporter and has no money to excuse it. Perhaps the President invited him to make Hay happy. The invitation to Henry and me, Cleveland supporters, not to mention Henry's ancestral right to the premises, is to be expected.

Speaking of White House etiquette reminds me of when Mrs. Senator Blaine accepted a White House dinner invitation tendered by President Rutherford B. Hayes but refused all food or drink to show her disapproval of his administration. My favorite visit with Mrs. Hayes in that overstuffed warehouse was for tea: we sat and rocked in front of a cheery wood fire.

I put on the soft burgundy velvet my father sent me from Boston last December. I wear it with an overlay of Louis XIV lace that Henry bought me in France. I added a gold locket with miniature paintings of the eyes (one each) of my mother and father. When they were young, ocular portraits were popular, to add mystery to romance.

∞

Now I take up my journal again to relate the events of the dinner:

Henry and Mr. James were already downstairs, resplendent in formal dress, when I came down. The Hays—Mrs. Hay arrived this morning—and King are staying at Wormley's Hotel and will arrive independently.

We might have strolled across the park had it been October. But this was a night for carriages and fur robes. The chill made my nose twitch and my mind wonder if I had enough handkerchiefs. The carriages were lined up on the circular drive leading through Jefferson's portico. When our turn came we went up the steps and into the entry hall, whereupon each man was handed an envelope with a diagram of the table, marked with his name and seat number and that of the lady he was to escort. Henry was awarded Mrs. General Miles, Mrs. Senator Cameron's sister. I suppose she's here to see how La Dona is getting along with the baby. Our lady novelist, Frances Hodgson Burnett, whose children's books are wildly successful, was properly thrilled to find she'd been drawn by the famous expatriate author Mr. James. Mrs. Madison's great-nephew, Mr. Cutts, came over to say he'd won me in the raffle.

While most guests turned this way and that to inventory the company, I was more interested to see again the great Tiffany glass screen—I believe it's Louis Comfort's largest work. Henry prefers John La Farge's stained glass—he and Richardson talked John Hay into ordering a window for his house, but I was able to talk him out of it for ours. It would have been pretentious and ridiculous. But I do think Chester Arthur spent his $15,000 wisely on the Tiffany redecoration.

Much is left to do in the furnishing of the White House, though I agree that Arthur was well advised to auction off the peculiar flotsam and jetsam of things left behind by various administrations—including, according to legend, the trap that caught the rat that ate the hat of President Lincoln. We were too clever to go, but it is said that more than 5,000 came to bid on the twenty-four wagonloads.

We moved through the cross hall into the East Room. The beams and columns were added when the ceiling began to sag in Grant's administration, so I've been told. I always have an uncomfortable feeling it may fall on me. The room is rather eerie anyway. Too much has happened in here.

November 25, 1885

After the guests were assembled in the East Room, the Empire clock on the mantel, one of two ordered by Monroe from France, began to strike eight o'clock. I am always amused by the figure of Hannibal standing guard over the clock. I wait for the time when he'll strike the hour and start his march across the Alps. I wondered where the Clevelands were? Usually they come down the steps exactly on the hour—Miss Rose's schoolmarm insistence on punctuality, I would suspect.

Henry saw the Hays and King standing by the south fireplace, so we went over to ask them why the delay?

"Oh, greetings, Henry, Mrs. Adams. And Mr. James. Washington must be coming up in society if you are honoring us."

"Do you think the President has overslept his afternoon nap? Asleep at the switch, eh?"

"Hadn't you heard, Henry? The vice president died earlier this evening."

"No!" I exclaimed. "What a shame, Tom Hendricks is a nice man. I hadn't realized he was ill." I had a sudden, awful thought. "Not assassinated? I hope! How dreadful that would be! The country isn't over President Garfield's assassination yet."

"No, no, calm your fears, Mrs. Adams. I haven't heard the cause of death yet, but surely someone would have said if he'd met with foul play. I do know President Cleveland just got the message and called the cabinet together to announce it. Fortunately, since this dinner is in their honor, they were all assembled here."

I had some awful minutes there, remembering the James Garfield murder. Henry and I had a friend, Dr. Folsom, one of the medical experts who arranged for us to have a seat at the trial of the assassin Charles J. Guiteau. Much of the expert testimony was to the point of whether insanity is hereditary—and whether he might be not guilty by virtue of being of unsound mind. Both

Henry and I have had relatives who perhaps were adjudged beyond eccentric, so we were more than ordinarily interested—not to say relieved when the experts pretty well smashed the theory.

After the hearing, we went with Dr. Folsom to the jail. A man who I supposed to be the jailer stood up and courteously greeted us. I shook hands and then suddenly realized I had shaken hands with Guiteau! I wrote my father about it and warned him not to tell, because for sure my in-laws would write Henry and say they "were sorry to hear that your wife had asked Guiteau to tea."

By the time I'd composed myself and come back to the present, the Marine Band struck up "Hail to the Chief."

Miss Rose and the President came down the great stair and swept into the East Room. Their procession was not a bad show. Though Cleveland's figure is not up to his clock's. The cabinet followed down the stair with less ceremony. They all assembled on the stage at the north end. President Cleveland raised his hand for attention.

"Dear friends, I am sorry to have to tell you that our good friend and great public servant, Thomas A. Hendricks, died an hour or so ago at his home. He was fine yesterday, went to a party, seemed very cheerful and anxious to come to Washington to join us here tonight. But this morning, he sent word he wouldn't be able to come to our dinner. About six tonight, his wife went downstairs to receive a visitor. When she went back to his room, he was dead. His doctor called the cause neuralgia of the heart.

"Now we all know the vice president would have wanted us to go on with our dinner, just as planned. I want to dedicate this evening as a memorial to him, and recommend that we talk about his manifold gifts. Now let us all bow our heads in silent prayer."

With that, the obsequies were done. And the occasion began. November 25, 1885 Each guest was announced by Marshall McMichael. Senator Perry Belmont was there (I wrote him into *Democracy*, but I think I was far too hard on him) escorting his mother, Mrs. August Belmont. Papa Bancroft, I was delighted to see, had made it, leaning on his lion's head walking stick—I think he had it from Budapest. He told me his wife was bedridden; I must go to see her after Thanksgiving. I am sorry Henry James is leaving after the dinner tomorrow. Mrs. Bancroft would love to see him. I didn't see Mr. Corcoran. I hope he's not ill.

Mark Twain and his wife came down from New York for the event. He is a wonderful-looking man with all that bushy white hair, mustache, and beard. "Mr. Clemens," said I, "I greatly admire *Huckleberry Finn*. I believe you have written the great American novel, sir!"

He grinned at me and took my hand. "Why, Mrs. Adams, I am delighted to hear you say so. I wasn't so sure that a proper speaker such as yourself would be able to wade through all my different dialects along the Mississippi. Nor a lady of your refinement willing to meet my traveling actors, lynch mobs, faded gentility, and such."

"It is certainly a part of the United States with which I am not familiar, and I am grateful to you for letting me meet such people and their picaresque adventures—at a safe remove."

"Hey, Mr. Hay," Twain said to that worthy. "Have you written any more ballads? I'll always be fond of 'Jim Bludso of the Prairie Belle.' I have to complain that at times those last two lines—

> 'And Christ ain't a-going to be too hard
> On a man that died for men.'

run through my head like a freight train on a circular route around a mountain. Keeps coming back again till I have a wreck in my train of thought."

I laughed and then turned at a touch from Henry James who had come up behind me.

"I'm moving into your territory soon, Mr. James," said Mr. Clemens, "we're on our way to look over Europe, to see if there's a novel there you may have overlooked."

"Happy hunting," replied the expatriate. His acquired English accent reminded me that someone once said, "He's the nicest Englishman I ever knew."

I saw Emily Beale McLean go by and whisper to him that she thinks he was mean to Daisy Miller.

I told Mr. Clemens Mr. James came to visit us to listen to the debates at the Capitol and to attend this dinner. I doubt he will stay in this country long. America is too real for Henry James—he'd rather live in a world he makes for himself where everyone speaks properly and not through their noses.

Professor Sousa's band struck up so I could hear no more conversation. My ear problem, exacerbated by the foggy, foggy dew, makes it harder and harder for me to hear in crowds—unfortunately, it still allows me to hear Sousa's cacophony. I waved to Cheng Tsao, the Chinese minister, senators Thom Ross and Mack Carry; and Henry's former pupil, Henry Cabot Lodge, due to tea any day now.

The East Room closely resembled what I've heard of the Guatemalan jungle. I expected a jaguar or a margay cat to come snarling out of a corner. Palms and other exotica stood in every corner and cranny. The chandeliers—draped and festooned with smilax—sparkled like the planets reflected in swamp water. The mantels and the windowsills were full of potted plants and ferns in gilded basket pots. Miss Rose was another bit of greenery in her hunter-hued velvet, appropriate to the holiday season—a good color with her short blonde hair. Her bodice was ornamented with a fichu of Irish point lace. She carried a bouquet of Christmas red hothouse roses. Her brother's face was about the same color— the heat of all those bodies in the room or too much pre-reception claret, I'm not sure which. The President was chastely put together in proper evening dress, with his only jewelry tasteful gold studs. He is said to have a big hand and a heavy foot politically, but he's big and heavy all over physically as well.

I am told, though I certainly couldn't hear Miss Rose myself with Sousa and the Marine Band tooting and banging away, that she has something to say—often a personal remark—for everyone in the line. At any rate, when we went through, she smiled and asked when I was coming to photograph the White House! I thought: What a wonderful idea! I might do it one day. She is a nice woman! And then I remembered, I had no camera, no dark-room. Henry made a grimace at me. I do wonder why we have not had a police report on the matter. I must ask.

We went into dinner at 9:00 P.M., through the cross hall, with its poinsettia plants brave in the niches. In the State Dining Room, the long table was set with white wax ornaments defining the ends. White swans about to take off held jellied pâté de foie gras. At the other end, eagles had a more militant air, as though they would swoop at us if we dared to rob them of the pâté. Silver compotes sailed down the middle of the table carrying cargos of conserves, chocolate candies, peppermint drops, and smoked salted almonds. The china was that hilarious joke of the Hayes administration. It isn't so upsetting to eat oysters off a porcelain plate made to look like oyster shells, but ice cream from an Indian snowshoe?

"Isn't it hilarious, Mrs. Adams?" said a voice to my left.

"Why, Clarence King! You didn't tell me you were my partner. I didn't have a chance to look at the seating chart. What a happy circumstance!"

Following custom, I turned my attention first to Mr. Cutts on my right and we went through the polite regrets over Mr. Hendricks's death, though he was not well-known to either of us. I remembered, fortunately, that my dinner partner is the grandson of Anna Payne Cutts, who often helped her sister, Dolley Madison, entertain in the President's House.

"I've always heard that before the War of 1812 Mrs. Madison's entertaining was by far the most elegant ever held in this house," I said, more in politeness than to elicit information for my *La Fayette Square Letters*. Mr. Cutts immediately picked up his cue along with his oyster fork, and in between bites regaled me on and on with stories about President and Mrs. Madison, beginning with the verity that she was the first to give dinner parties in this room.

"Didn't she replace Jefferson's pell-mell with protocol, and his all-male gatherings with her Wednesday night levees—for women as well as men?"

" 'Drawing rooms,' she called the receptions, if you'll excuse me, Mrs. Adams," he said. "The Adamses gave 'levees,' which smacks of royalty. Anyway, Aunt Dolley's most famous hospitality, surely you've heard, was the dinner over which she did not preside. If you'll permit me, I'll tell the story."

I wondered what he'd say if I announced firmly, "I would not permit it."

I did not forbear to brag, "My husband has studied the period thoroughly in preparation for his *History of the United States During the Administrations of Thomas Jefferson and James Madison*. John Quincy

Adams, my husband's grandfather, was a Congressman in 1844. November 25, 1885
That session, the House voted unanimously that 'whenever it shall
be (Mrs. Madison's) pleasure to visit the House, she be requested
to take a seat within the hall.' Wasn't that a remarkable honor
since women had no acknowledged place in the government of
the land? Then and now."

"Oh, really?" said Mr. Cutts.

The oyster and soup courses were removed, and by custom
I turned my attention to Mr. King, and Mr. Cutts to his other
partner.

"You look ravishing tonight, Mrs. Adams."

"Though you don't speak the truth, I am grateful."

"I have been looking forward to the opportunity to ask if
you have read Gaston Paris's treatise on *Lancelot?*"

"No, we don't get all the French periodicals."

"He has coined the phrase, 'amour courtois' to describe the
twelfth-century ideal of love everlasting, forever unfulfilled."

"He may well claim it, Mr. King, but the idea of 'courtly
love' goes back far beyond Monsieur Paris—before King Arthur's
Court. Indeed, I believe the whole Camelot story invaded England
from Provence."

"I find it very romantic," he said, as much to the caviar
canapé as to the subject.

"I find it very tragic," I said. "Think of the loneliness, the
yearning of star-crossed lovers."

"True, but all beauty has a sadness to it because eventually
it will grow old and wither away. Courtly love tries to surmount
desire and lift it to adoration."

"To what use?"

"Well, for instance, I could become your troubadour. You
are married, and I love your husband as well as yourself. In honor,

I could not ask or expect favors of the flesh. So instead, I will write you poems, sing you songs, bring you a chambered nautilus from a far place."

"But what will you have gained for your devotion?"

"Ah, that's the whole point. To dedicate yourself to an ennobling love, transcending earthly pleasures, is to become a saint, a god. Aspiration is all. Attainment is nothing."

"So you think it better for Lancelot and Guinevere to never touch, never comfort each other, to live their lives in denial?"

"Think what standard of purity they maintained by denying the cravings of the beast within!"

"To me it sounds like choosing death rather than life."

"Martyrdom is certainly part of it. To die for one's love is the ultimate sacrifice."

"But by dying you ask the object of your affection to sacrifice the pleasure of your affection. Publius Ovidius Naso encourages such fatal idolization in a few of his love elegies. And certainly Spenser's *Faerie Queene* glorifies knightly danger to defend and aggrandize their royal icon. But it is still a sad, unsatisfying kind of love."

"I don't have to tell you of the events of August 24, 1814," Mr. Cutts interrupted, claiming again the turn of the table, though I had not seen Miss Rose switch conversation partners, I was so absorbed, or perhaps horrified is the better word, in King's discourse.

I took this opportunity to enjoy the salmon with a sauce Hollandaise. Mr. Cutts, unlike Mr. King, did not need a Greek chorus.

"A year earlier, in May 1813, that cur, British Rear Admiral

November 25, 1885

Sir George Cockburn, sent a threat to Mrs. Madison saying that he would 'soon make his bow at her drawing room.' On August 24, a year later, you'll remember, the British marched to the 'Bladensburg Races.' The battle was so called because of the town's history as a place of horse races. The heat, the hideous sort that even today drives residents out of Washington, must have been hard on the invaders—despite what they say about mad dogs and Englishmen."

The waiter refilled my wineglass, for which I was grateful. The dissertation of Mr. Cutts made my mouth dry.

"Did your husband write about the volunteers who flocked to Bladensburg?"

I was permitted a quick nod.

"What fops! The volunteers, largely Maryland and Virginia gentlemen of condition, came in brilliant uniforms: white trousers, plumed leather helmets, big thick cross belts, not very convenient at the time of night alarms. Oh, excuse me, Mrs. Adams. The fashionable high boots caused feet unused to marching to swell. They brought all sorts of useless objects in their knapsacks, from overcoats and smallclothes to even dancing pumps. They presumed, you see, that after the victory they would dance in celebration at the President's palace."

I had to laugh at the pumps. Certainly Henry had missed a salient fact! However, Mr. Cutts was not finished.

"There was no celebration, no victory. For many there was only death. At the White House, Mrs. Madison was still under orders predicated on victory. She expected to feed forty courageous victors. She had the servants put the plates to warm on the fire, roast meats on the spit, lay out knives and forks, put the wine in the coolers."

It was obvious to me that this story is Mr. Cutts's stock in trade, perhaps his only dinner table dissertation. He didn't allow for questions, remarks, or other interruptions from his table partner. Perhaps he is really deaf and can only talk, not listen.

An enormous platter with lamb covered in a mint sauce, beef, and veal arrived. I took the thinnest piece I could find, along with the asparagus and peas, and waved the rest away.

"In the afternoon, Mrs. Madison received word to flee. And that she did, grabbing up silver, the red velvet curtains she and Benjamin Latrobe had just bought for the house, and Gilbert Stuart's portrait of George Washington."

I turned my attention back from the asparagus to question, Is it a Stuart? Henry said the painter later denied painting it, though some people think it is a later replica by Stuart of his famous work.

"When Generals Ross and Cockburn and their two hundred men reached the White House, they expressed themselves as grateful to their hostess. The officers dined at the table by candlelight in the dining room, drinking, singing, offering toasts and curses at the Americans they still counted as outlaw rebels. The men raided the kitchen and larders in the basement to provision a grand picnic on the south lawn. And then, having used up the White House's facilities, they piled up the furniture and set fire to the building."

"What a fiery feast!" I said, and hastily turned my attention to King, the terrapin, and the canvasback duck. He went on with his joust.

"Think how wonderful, to dance attendance on your love, to spread your cloak over the mudpuddles of her life, to always give and never take! Marvelous! Ennobling!"

"I think you and I could use a Court of Love to adjudicate

the question," I said to Mr. King, who had helped himself to an inordinate amount of duck.

"Tell me, Mr. King, what of the idol? How can she reconcile receiving such tributes, oblations without offering any return? Such a person would be ignoble to accept such lavish offerings."

"But think of the inexpressible sensations of being passionately desired in the abstract."

"You think about them, Mr. King, I find it too upsetting."

I gave up with that story, and finished my dinner in contemplation of the snowshoes under my ice cream, leaving Mr. King to the mercies of Miss Rebecca Rae on his other hand. I heard him continue with the trials of courtly love to the surprised Miss Rae.

Despite Miss Rose's temperance views, no one was shorted on alcohol tonight. Six glasses—for sauterne, sherry, Rhine wine, water, champagne, and burgundy—sat at every plate. When added to those the cut glass saltcellars with their vermeil spoons and the silver pepper shakers for each guest, I was amazed room was found for the souvenir place cards: red, white, and blue ribbons, three feet long, three inches wide, with a picture of the White House at its top. The guest's name and the date were hand lettered in gold. Below was the presidential seal. As if all that wasn't enough to choke a horse, on the right of each lady's place was a corsage of eight large roses with a gilt bullet-headed pin. For every gentleman, a boutonniere centered with a single *Bon Silene* rosebud rested on the napkin.

After dinner, we shook hands again with the President and Miss Rose. The President said to me, "Mrs. Adams, do take your guest through the rose house my predecessor Hayes built—if you're not too tired, go the whole hundred feet. I walk there often."

"I hope Congress is going to let us have more money for the conservatory," piped in Miss Rose.

Mr. James and I did walk through the West Stair Hall down the steps to the Palm House, admiring the camellia, fern, and primrose clusters, and thence into the rose house, the grapery, and the orchid house.

Though I had dismissed King's espousal of courtly love, I found myself obscurely troubled when I stopped to think about it. I had an uncomfortable feeling that Henry's attentions to Lizzie Cameron had something of that quality. Was it love for love's sake? A travesty? An affair of the imagination? That would make sense.

"Mr. James," I said, "I have been listening at great length to Mr. King on the subject of courtly love."

"Ah, the *Roman de la rose*. You would make a splendid May Day queen with a choir of birds to sing songs in your honor."

"Now you sound like a knight of love yourself. You will quite turn my head."

"As long as it turns in my direction. There is of course an element of charm in the thought of unrequited love. Do you know the young critic George Bernard Shaw, like Oscar Wilde an Irishman come to London?"

"Yes, I have heard of him."

"Well, over a pint between acts at a play, he confessed a belief that the most satisfying love affairs were those conducted totally in the minds of the lovers."

I was saved from having to answer to this point by the Postmaster General who came up to speak at some length but rather well on the selection of designs for stamps. Henry, I had noticed, was talking animatedly to Mrs. Cameron's sister. Mr. James was completely engrossed in conversation with Miss Rose, I doubt not on her George Eliot book. Finally, in desperation to go, I asked the Postmaster to deliver me, as though I were an envelope—or perhaps a special delivery package would be a better simile—to Henry. Even then, I probably would not have been able to persuade Henry and Mr. James to say good night, but thank heaven, the Marshall came quietly through the crowd and urged us all to go home. I must give Miss Rose my fervent thanks for the dismissal.

November 25, 1885

CHAPTER 17

November 26, 1885

Thanksgiving for Henry James

∞

Dear Posterity,

I woke up at a respectably early hour this morning perhaps because I didn't drink King's Mexican hot chocolate last night. I was afraid if I did I would oversleep, especially after staying so late last night at the White House. I was particularly concerned to be up in time to have breakfast with Henry James—and to check on the Thanksgiving dinner. I wanted everything just right for our guest who dines (though obviously not at Thanksgiving dinner) with the aristocracy in those ancient country seats he's eternally writing about.

I needn't have worried. Cook came up this morning to bring me a cup of tea and report that Thanksgiving dinner is well underway, just as I'd planned it: turkey with truffle sauce, pork

loin, oyster dressing, corn pones, the vegetables she bought yesterday from her family's farm, pecan pie, angel food cake with a
cherry icing, mincemeat pie for the Northerners, with a healthy
swig of bourbon for the Southerners, and so on. Fortunately, we've
recently had delivery of a few cases of Madeira. I give thanks for
my talented and well-trained staff.

Novem-
ber 26,
1885

I've fished my journal out of its new hiding place, under my
summer hats, to record the events of this holiday.

What a treat to have Henry James come visit! He said last
night that he'd come all the way from England primarily to see
us. Wasn't that kind of him to say so, even though it's a gross
exaggeration. The White House dinner I am sure was an incentive.
I suspect he's thinking about it for another novel. And of course,
he's in this country to see his sister Alice and snub his brother
William. His visit gives some meaning for me to today's observance.
My sister and I have been fond of James since we met at Newport
when we were still young.

The last time he left for England, he wrote me a note saying
his last word to the United States was appropriately to me since
I was "the incarnation of his native land."

I took offense, since he was at that time leaving it because
he said he found the United States tasteless and boring. I forgave
him after I heard he called me a "perfect Voltaire in petticoats."
I would have forgiven him anyway after reading *The Portrait of a
Lady*, which he kindly sent me.

John and Clara Hay were to leave after the dinner last night
for home and a family Thanksgiving. I suppose they don't mind
traveling all night in their private railway car. We had a message
waiting for us after the dinner saying that La Farge had turned
up on our doorstep—as usual without his wife and umpteen
children. I don't really understand why he isn't celebrating Thanks-

giving with them or King likewise with his mother. Oh, well, perhaps King and La Farge are simply here because they know we observe what Henry thinks of as a quintessential Massachusetts holiday. As we have no children, I suppose I should be grateful that we are not faced with trying to be thankful for just the two of us—and of course the dogs. I am indeed very thankful for the dogs, who even as I write are chasing one another around the rooms and poking in my wastebasket this time, in the hopes of finding something edible. I know some people, especially those who have children, laugh at the affection I lavish on the Skyes. When I had vertigo recently, Boojum stayed right on the foot of my bed and wouldn't eat unless I fed him tidbits. Possum, now, is less sentimental. He would be delighted to eat me if mixed with potato. I have to love something that loves me back.

This morning, Henry and King planned to ride with La Farge. Good, now I'll have Mr. James all to myself at breakfast.

Is it possible that Mr. King's visit is in any way linked to the portion of Henry's letter Boojum brought me? Was it to King? Could they even now be engaged in some pursuit that—how did Henry put it in the letter: "I am not sure that what you ask could be accomplished without Marian's knowledge. And I'm certain it would not be possible with it . . ." What could he have meant? I have mulled it over and over again, without much success. Surely with such a salutation, the letter would have been to a woman, I think. If the letter was to Clara Hay, at least it wasn't about money. I wonder if Mr. King came to borrow money from Henry and John Hay? Most likely, as I concluded earlier.

I will be very glad to talk with my favorite novelist. Of all the people I know, I find it easiest to confide in Henry James. Every so often, when I'm writing in my journal, telling all to my imaginary descendant, Miss Posterity, I think perhaps I'm really writing to Mr. James and he's reading it and turning it all into novels.

I certainly felt this was true when I read both *Daisy Miller* and *The Portrait of a Lady*. The latter book was very hard for me to read because it was far too close to home. Yet I suspect this intimacy that James engenders is the secret of his vast popularity, surely among women like me. We yearn to understand ourselves: what is permitted to us, how far we can go without permission, what is expected of us, what is demanded. Women today are undergoing an evolution. If I had been born when Frances Benjamin Johnston was, I hope I would have been like her—brave, courageous, and most of all, confident of my right to live and work and succeed. Instead, I've found myself unable to go forward, backward, or even stay in one place. Perhaps James, out of his vast experience with turning real women into characters, will tell me how to turn myself, from a character in this book, this Life of Henry Adams, into a real woman. My husband is, I know, a good writer. But I strongly resent having my life plotted, my character described, my very conversation written by someone else. I believe I deserve to write The Life of Clover Adams.

Speaking of writing, I noted on the silver salver in the hall there were still no letters to be mailed. After capturing Boojum in flagrante delicto, with the second letter in his mouth, Henry may have deduced that his first draft of the letter was missing and has decided to conceal evidence of his current correspondents. Why should I care?

I took time this morning for a careful toilette. I have to make up in careful attention for my lack of beauty. As Henry once put it: women who read Greek have to pay more attention to their dress. I so want Mr. James, if not to admire my looks, at least not to be repelled by them.

How glad I am to see him! He is much the same as ever—a face like a well-read leather-bound book, soft to the hand, yet sturdy. He has just the right looks for a confidant.

"Mr. James," I said over late breakfast, rallying him in the manner of newspaper reporters on both sides of the Atlantic, who find him good copy, "is it true you came to the United States in November solely for the purpose of celebrating this peculiarly American feast?"

"Why not? I've crossed the Atlantic for less important reasons. I actually came over to study you a bit, Mrs. Adams, for my next book. I find you an ever present source of inspiration."

"A pretty speech indeed, Mr. James. One of my acquaintances—I won't say friends—asked if you were coming for more 'raw material' for your novels."

"I am serious, you know, my old friend."

"You and I are never serious. Would you like another cup of tea and our local newspaper?"

"If you are serious, I certainly will seriously accept. If we had been serious earlier our lives might have been vastly different, Mrs. Adams."

"Then I wish I had paid more attention to the practice of being serious, Mr. James."

"It would have been far better for both of us."

"I am not sure what you mean, but I think I am perhaps better off for not knowing."

"Knowledge can be a frightful handicap."

"If it is the wrong truth."

"Or the right information at the wrong time."

"Or the wrong information for the right people. Are there no characters, no plots in London or Paris these days?"

"None with your touch of genius."

"How kind you are. Though I'm not sure what you mean."

"You have intellectual grace. Ah, you ask, what is that? I suppose I mean that you look for meaning where no one else expects to find it. You never find it necessary to accept ideas handed down from other humans or other gods. You accept that you may have to make sense out of chaos. I suppose I am saying, in far too convoluted a way, that you have a creative spirit. You take everyday life and make a painting of it. Look at this table, the fruit chosen to go with the tablecloth, the Tiffany glass on the table set so the morning sun shines through it."

"How nice of you to notice. Few people do. And some who know that I arrange things just so find it arrogant, contrived."

"But how pleasant to know that you have made a secret that only the select will discover. Perhaps you and I are the only ones who will notice that at 12:05 on a November day, the sun and the glass will work together to make a painting of exquisite color on your table—ephemeral art."

"Actually, it comes by accident. I can't take the credit. Last year at this time, when I was looking for a place to put it, I just set it down. When I looked again, there was glory."

"Ah, that is what I mean. The ability to recognize grace when it comes. You use the same gift in capturing passing beauty in your photography. Your camera is like a net capturing a butterfly. What you are seizing upon is that moment when the subject's guard is dropped and his soul revealed."

"Yes, I do recognize grace—your grace in giving me such a fine gift, the greatest anyone can bestow: appreciation."

"That, Mrs. Adams, I have in abundance for you. You make of your tea parties high dramas. You choose your guests as I might make up characters for my novels. You plot your parties so that the participants can reveal their true nature."

November 26, 1885

"You know too much about me. I think we'd best talk about you. I find it amazing that you understand so much about the way women experience emotion."

"Are you one of those who think I was too unkind to Daisy Miller?"

"Well, it was a shame to kill her with Roman fever just because she wanted to see the Colosseum at midnight. But at least you let her innocence sleep forever in an angle of the wall of imperial Rome beneath the cypresses and the thick spring flowers. But I think your *The Portrait of a Lady* is far harder on Isabel Archer."

"Do you really? Well, I was only writing truth. I, of course, changed the circumstances somewhat with my novelist's warrant. But the characters were much the same as in life. And after all, I gave one aspect of the character a happy ending."

"You mean Henrietta and Isabel were suggested by the same person?"

"How perceptive of you to guess. Though it isn't surprising with your gift of understanding that you saw through my dividing the one person in two, to better illustrate the result of alternate choices and alternate universes."

"Isabel reminds me—a bit—of *Esther*, in that new novel of the same name. Naturally, your book is a thousand times better."

"I make no such claim. If I am not mistaken, the author has written an earlier 'mistresspiece,' set in Washington. Perhaps by the time the author of *Esther* has written as many books as I, she will be a far better writer than I."

"I know that is not possible."

"How can you know, Mrs. Adams? Do you know this author?"

"I think one can know a great deal about a writer from the work. Especially novels. They reveal as much about the author as her characters. I have the feeling that the author in question writes in stealth, wraps her manuscripts in bottles, and throws them in the sea for beachcombers to rescue and read. Perhaps she is incarcerated in some stern reformatory."

"Really? I would like to know more about this mysterious, imprisoned author. I am sure she warrants cultivation. So what do my novels say about me, kind lady?"

"That, kind sir, you are at pains not to give yourself away. That you look at emotion from all sides. That you never make a decision when you can avoid one. Yet that you feel very responsible for the people—real or imaginary—whose lives are entwined with yours. I think of you rather as the tree trunk on which the clematis grows. On the other hand, I believe your tree would never support an invasive growth such as moss, or worse, a woodpecker. You help people without allowing your own self to be injured. I wish I were the same. I understand Isabel marrying Osmond, it is a mistake I can imagine making, though good sense would mitigate against it."

"I know this about you—you are a very responsive and responsible person, even to your own detriment, dear Mrs. Adams."

"Do you now?"

"And I know Henry Adams. When you passed through on your way back from your honeymoon, I wrote to a friend—you'll forgive me—that your husband can never be a very spacious or sympathetic companion, though you had improved him. I added that you struck me as toned down and bedimmed from your ancient brilliancy."

"You described him very well. Not only then, but in *The Portrait of a Lady* as Osmond: 'The desire to succeed greatly—in something or other—had been the dream of his youth; but as the years went on, the conditions attached to success became so various and repulsive that the idea of making an effort gradually lost its charm. It was not dead, however; it only slept; it revived after he had made the acquaintance of Isabel Archer.' "

"If you're going to apply that paragraph to your husband, you should add the later bit: 'He always had an eye to effect; and his effects were elaborately studied. They were produced by no vulgar means, but the motive was as vulgar as the art was great. To surround his interior with a sort of invidious sanctity, to tantalize society with a sense of exclusion, to make people believe his house was different from every other, to impart to the fact that he presented to the world a cold originality—this was the effort of the personage . . .' And what about the description: 'a model of impertinence and mystification, his ambition was not to please the world, but to please himself by exciting the world's curiosity and then declining to satisfy it.' "

"Do you think of Henry—or do you mean me—as such a poseur?"

"I have never thought of you as one who pretends interests or friendships, my honest friend."

"Petty jealousy can be very annoying here. Clarence King, for instance, was denounced by Dawes in the Senate as 'an extravagant humbug' because he forgot to go to a reception to which he was invited. And then there are all the strangers who come to Washington without introductions, stand at the door presenting their cards, and expect me to put out another cup at our tea table. A man's house is not his castle in Washington but the public's beer garden."

"I grant you, Mrs. Adams, that such matters are delicate. But surely you have the right to choose who will drink your very good tea."

"To welcome people one does not like into one's own home, I say, is not only hypocritical but dangerous to one's morals. I am afraid that what I think of as intellectual honesty—other people may call bitterness. I am also possessed of a tongue sharp as a scalpel. It has made me disliked in some circles. My father-in-law has been quoted as saying that he pities rather than dislikes me. Still, he complains that I am a marplot—I suppose I have marred and sometimes ruined a plot or two in my day. I confide in you that I have found it more peaceful to leave to my husband the correspondence with his family. I learned on our honeymoon trip that my mother-in-law did not share my humor."

November 26, 1885

"Not ever being supplied with such a relation, I would not know, but wit among relatives can be dangerous, as I have discovered."

"When my father was alive, I would write him with as much wit as I could muster, because he liked the pointed phrase and the dissection of people's actions. He liked it so much that he would often quote my better remarks—that Morton was a self-made man who would have been better to have hired himself done. And my answer to why Roscoe was on the Committee of Foreign Relations: because he's unfitted for the domestic.

"Washington is a whispering gallery. My in-laws wrote Henry to complain that the Boston *Herald* quoted what I had said, attributing it to 'a hostess of liberal proclivities.' Of course, anyone who would be annoyed knew the identity of the hostess. Such incidents make Henry furious. His mother told my husband to see that I desisted from making withering remarks that disturbed their friends. William Walter Phelps—he's a New Jersey Congressman—told Henry's older brother that I am bitter because I am not welcome in 'refined circles.' "

"You surely do not pay attention to such japery—I have said of you that I approve of the fact that your salon on the whole keeps out more than it lets in.

"I think perhaps that Henry Adams is like an abacus: for every move, he pushes a bead, and only when he calculates the result is he willing to act. I think you are not an accountant nor a clerk."

"If I have a criticism of both Henry and me, it is that, like Osmond, we dream of large ambitions and put forth small efforts."

"Are you accusing Mr. Adams of indolence?"

"Not really. He works very hard on his histories."

"Of indifference to you?"

"Do you find him indifferent to me?"

"A mutual friend once told me that your husband confessed that his heart could no more be moved than a boulder, and that marriage was only possible as a convenience."

"Ah yes, convenience, is that what he sees in me? A convenient woman. A researcher? A housekeeper? A hostess? An heiress?"

"Fortune hunting? Forgive me again. I shouldn't say such things in his house."

"Our house, please. Hardly fortune hunting. Unlike your Isabel, I hardly have enough to make it worth his while. My dowry only makes it possible for him to devote himself to his histories."

"That for a historian, or a writer, is no small thing."

"Even at the expense of what he once called the 'brutalities' of marriage?"

"Does he practice such?"

"Only mental ones."

"Those are the worst kind. If he beat you, you could implore your brother to call him out. But mental assaults are harder to explain. I have known you a long time. I have always basked in your brilliance, your unwillingness to accept easy opinions, the trodden ways. But now you have the look of a sun in eclipse, not total, but annular."

"What is an annular eclipse?"

"One where, when the moon moves over the sun, a thin ring of the solar circle is left, like an illuminated frame. The effect is quite spectacular. Still, I miss the full force of your light. I comfort myself that an eclipse is a brief phenomenon."

I handed him the newspaper and put up a sheet in front of my face to keep him from seeing my embarrassment turning my face into a tomato. That was not what I longed to do. I wanted him to explain my life to me. To tell me that I was not asking too much. If I had the courage, or the wit, or been born in a different time, our conversation would have been far different.

Later:

After Thanksgiving dinner, the men lit their cigars and I retreated to my boudoir and the riotous affections of Boojum, Possum, and Marquis. As soon as they heard me in the hall, they raced to greet me—I suspect from the kitchen and the guilty delights of the garbage pail. They had a rather decadent air to them. They followed me upstairs looking like balls of tumbleweeds. I had to shut them in the bedroom until I changed to my robe to keep my dress from being pulled into threads by the violence of their passion.

As delighted as I was with their romp—it's so wonderful to be loved with such enthusiasm—I am very tired. I seem to have less and less energy. I believe my lassitude comes from sleeping so poorly. I have strange dreams and they sometimes scare me into hours of worry and wakefulness. King claimed the cocoa from his travels in Mexico is the very potion I needed. But indeed, I did sleep rather well last night.

Making notes on my conversation at breakfast with Henry James, I am struck by something he said. At the time, I tossed it off in my mind as a pleasant light flirtation. But did I make a mistake, long ago, in not considering that Mr. James might have held me in serious regard. Could that be? Is it possible that he really was interested in me romantically? Perhaps wished to marry me? All these years. I never really thought he had any interest in me other than friendship.

We were born in the same year and saw each other often in our early adult years. I was always enormously impressed by him—admired his writing and his deep sense of what was behind people's actions. I recall a long conversation we had once. He said that Dickens's books have clever, fascinating plots, memorable characters, but he thought the writer wasted good material. "He only eats the icing on the cake, leaving the cake itself to be thrown to the dog."

And perhaps that was my problem. I was so awed by Henry James's brilliance and erudition and deep philosophical insights that I thought he existed only in his books. I saw him as a self-sufficient creature who really needed only pencil and paper and his own amazing imagination to be content. I never thought before that he might be as alone as I. Or that together we might never have been lonely.

I wonder why James has never married. I am sure that many women would have been delighted to share their lives with the literary lion with the charming roar and sharp bite. How wonderful it would be to live with Henry James! To listen to him try out plots and motives of characters. To look up facts for him. And even—oh! how wonderful the thought!—to have him help me learn to be a better novelist. Certainly not in his class, but something better than I am. I wished I had told him I wrote my books.

Perhaps I will reveal all in a letter and ask his advice. That's one communiqué I would mail myself—Boojum would have no chance to deliver it into Henry's hands.

Bosh! He would never think such a thing. He doubtless finds me a bore—what did he mean by my "ancient brilliancy bedimmed?" If he means that Henry keeps my light under a bushel he is of course correct. But such a small, faint light is easy to obliterate with a puff—you don't even need a huff.

CHAPTER 18

December 2, 1885

Wrong Steps at the Decatur House Ball

∞

Dear Posterity,

"Isn't this the night you're going to Mrs. Beale's party?" I asked Henry at breakfast after Henry James departed for Massachusetts. I consoled myself by feeding Marquis bits of bacon with one hand and toast to Boojum with the other, to the music of delighted little yelps. Feeding my breakfast to the dogs is the best way to stay thin, I've found.

"Yes, what are you wearing?" he inquired with the tone of one who expects an answer he will not accept. Henry, even at such a late breakfast, is always grumpy. He doesn't really come awake till the sun goes down—when I begin to fade.

"My nightgown and robe, suitable for turning in early."

"You mean you're not going? To the Beales? Marian, this is really just too much! What will Mrs. Beale say?"

"She's said. She wrote me a note back at my regrets and said she was very sorry I had caught cold going to the White House. I should take good care of my health and not go out late till I'm better. And she'll expect me to come to the next ball they give. And she looks forward to seeing you tonight."

"How terrible of you, Marian. What won't you do next?"

"Oh, Henry," I said with as light a tone as I could manage, "you know me, I don't always feel like company. These dark, humid fall days make me sleepy and tired and my nose run. I'm sure you'll have lots of company, you are never lonely." I piled up my sentences, one atop another like pillows in a Turkish corner. Henry would have had to use a knife to pry a space for a comment. But he seemed to have little desire to divide my monologue into a dialogue.

"They'll waltz and you'll have a grand time. I well remember people said you were one of the three best dancers in Washington back when your father was in Congress. You know I don't enjoy that sort of large gathering, but you do, so there's no reason I should keep you from it. Don't trouble yourself, go off to your party. And tomorrow you can tell me all about it."

Possum growled at Marquis, who took the bacon away from him.

I expected to hear a similar growl from Henry. He looked at me sternly, as if by force of his will he could make me tell him what I was keeping from him. Henry was not fond of scenes, or indeed any sort of emotional struggle. Still, I believe he was writing a speech in his head—to say something, offer some reason, since I would provide none, and give an opinion, as befitted his position as the head of the house.

Finally, he delivered his dissertation, as long as mine and equally couched not as conversation, but as a speech, expecting no answer. It was as if the two of us were music hall comedians or monologuists playing the same bill, but in completely separate acts.

"Well, I had planned to go. Emily McLean has been by every day to remind me. She says she counts a great deal on my presence. Her mother is very anxious that I come—oh, and you too, certainly.

"Emily's so beautiful, you know, so fresh and lovely, that men of her age make bothers of themselves. They crowd around her and try to touch her, even now she's married. Just think, their wedding was a year ago in October! She can hardly breathe, she says, because of the pressure of their presence. When they dance with her, they hold her so close, she feels as though she's suffocating. Her husband doesn't take care of her properly. She really pleaded with me to come tonight. I told her I wasn't sure you would feel up to it since you haven't been well. But she said, of course, I must come by myself if you didn't want to. She promised to have supper with me—her husband will be deep in his business dealings, as usual.

"It's going to be quite a nice affair. Not too large—not really a ball, but a pleasant gathering for this time of year. Now that the McLeans have their very outrageous house, Mrs. Beale leaves huge balls to them."

I watched as Henry subsided. He sat a few minutes quietly. Had he already gone to the party in his mind? Or was he being still to let me know that he hadn't accepted my explanation, if that is what it was? I adopted a noncommittal face, with, I hope, no suggestion of desire to continue the conversation.

For the moment, Henry seemed as if he'd gone away, leaving

only his skin, like an apple peeling in the chair. I kept silent and watched as his foot began to tap in time to some unheard music—the evening's waltz orchestra apparently had already struck up in his mind and changed the rhythms from day to night.

Eventually, in his mind, the dance with the beautiful Emily must've been over. Henry gave up on his unheard melodies and my unspoken conversation. He stood up as if to leave. "If that's the way you want it," he said, and shrugged, a man who considered he'd done his duty and nothing more was expected of him.

At the door, he turned and said, with an air of confidentiality: "The party won't be half as much fun without La Dona. She was very disappointed at not being well enough to go. I must say her delicate condition certainly does become her. I've never seen any woman as beautiful as she is now. There's a radiance about her that's spectacular. It's as though she had a sun inside, glowing. Don't you think she looks wonderful? I always thought Emily was a close rival to La Dona in looks, but she certainly can't compete with her now. Yesterday afternoon I took over a bouquet of roses from the garden, just about the last, I expect, for this year. I told La Dona that she put them to shame, they should hang their blossoms in her presence."

I tried to decide if Henry intended to be so cruel. But his lips bore no mark of his taunt. His eyes stared directly at me, as if he had no idea of the offense he had given. Surely, though, not even Henry could be so dense. I dug my nails into my palms, trying to make the pain keep me from either dissolving like a sugar cube in a cup of hot tea or else throwing the Ming vase at Henry. The indecision about which to do fortunately kept me from doing either. I held my breath, counted to ten, stood up, and said very quietly to Henry, "How nice for you that she gives you pleasure. Good morning."

With that, I walked up the stairs, went in my boudoir, and without another glance, closed the door, resisting the impulse to turn the key. From somewhere, since I believe neither in hell nor heaven, I couldn't say where, I found the strength to stifle my cries of rage and hurt.

I heard his steps across the floor of the other room and the slam of the door as he walked out. He was well down the hall and into his study before I permitted myself a few long-denied and well-deserved tears. The drops were warm and moist on my cheek and salty when they hit my lips.

I hoped that the belles would step on his shiny dancing pumps and borrow his handkerchief to dry their tears shed for their unfeeling gentlemen friends. I disliked Emily Beale McLean as all other right thinking wives did. The only use I had ever found for Emily was as the role of Victoria Dare in *Democracy*, a woman who wanted men only for their names on her dance cards, the gifts they would bestow on her, and most of all, the envy her suitors would arouse in the hearts of her women friends. Emily enjoyed taunting men with her beauty and then making fun of them with her wicked, though not terribly clever, remarks. Clarence King was the only one who ever resisted her flirtation—and on her side a good bit more, I suspect. He gave her no reason to think he admired her, and when she declared her strong affections to him, he never again set foot in the Beale House.

When I saw Sarah Bernhardt's recent performance on a Washington stage, she reminded me of Emily. But then, I didn't care for the Divine Sarah either. Both look like fancy Parisian dolls, all eyelashes, curly hair, and bundles of clothes, owing their form to the Follies. Both are cunning in their own eccentric ways. Emily Beale McLean shares with Sarah Bernhardt a reputation as a beauty and as a woman who knows who and what she wants.

After a brilliant season, in which all the eligible men in town, and December 2, 1885 a remarkable number of ineligible men, hungered for Miss Emily's cotton candy seductiveness—all fluff and no substance—she topped her dance card with John R. McLean.

McLean bought the *Cincinnati Enquirer* in 1873 from his father before he came to Washington and attracted the wandering eye of the willful Miss Beale. McLean owns real estate, streetcars, gaslight companies, cemeteries, banks, newspapers, as well as Emily Beale. He paid a good price for her, but he could afford it.

He has everything she wants: money and the desire to spend it in the embellishment of his possessions, including his wife. As an enticement to marriage, he bought the mansion at 1500 I Street not far from her family's house on La Fayette Square, and set about to gild the interior as though it had been an Italian cherub. The house was elaborate enough for its previous residents: Senator Edward Morgan of New York; Senator Simon Cameron, La Dona's father-in-law, that horribly corrupt man whose son is in his father's image; and Grant's Secretary of State, the very pleasant Hamilton Fish, who lived there from 1869 to 1884.

I knew and liked Julia Fish well. How she managed eight children I will never know. Unlike a great many wives, she never neglected her social responsibilities. Every week of the season, they gave two formal, seated dinner parties and receptions by carload. She told me that they actually counted 1500 at one reception. As I once said to Henry, Mrs. Fish was hooked on being in the swim.

∞

In the evening, the maid came with my supper, but I sent it back, with word to the cook that the food appeared to be delicious but my appetite had failed. About 10:00 P.M., I heard Henry slam the front door. A quick trip to the window enabled

me to see him in the yellow gaslight across the Square and over
to General Beale's house. I could even see the unmistakable Emily
meet him at the door, as though she knew the minute he would
arrive. She grabbed his hand and they whirled on the doorstep in
a dance for all of La Fayette Square to see their joy in Clover
being left behind. Could she be Henry's "Dearest Love" of the
cryptic letter? I could well believe it. She's been after him for
years, ever since they met. She loses no minute to tilt her head
at him, stroke his hand, and ask his learned opinion while gazing
in his eyes.

All of a sudden, I couldn't bear solitary thoughts a bit longer.
With a burst of determination I didn't know was left, I pulled the
bell for the maid, pulled out my blue-green French faille dress
embroidered with gold thread in designs of Persian flowers. It's
rather bare—the French must have better heating than we do—
but I determined to wear it with a fichu. I had ordered it from
Worth on the basis of a fabric sample and a photograph just before
my father fell ill. I have never worn it. Wouldn't they be surprised
when I swept up the Beale staircase! I frantically began dressing,
not waiting for the maid. But I was all thumbs, trying to put on
this hated bustle. I almost ripped a flounce in my haste, fighting
my way through the folds, until the maid came to my rescue and
sorted it all out straight. Jane did my hair quickly, while I kept
saying, "Hurry, hurry, I must go in time for the supper."

Jane called the coachman and I rode the half block or so. I
wouldn't chance my gold shoes in the rough street. At the Beales'
door, the butler admitted me with some surprise. He knew me,
as did everyone on the Square, but I seldom crossed the Beale
threshold at this time of night.

As always, I admired the vestibule, the most beautiful in

Washington, as I handed my cloak to the maid. The house's December 2, 1885 designer, Benjamin Latrobe, was the capital's first professional architect, as distinct from gifted amateurs. He must have been very proud of the long segmental arch, going from the entrance to where the tunnel form meets a segmental dome. Rectangle, circle, and semicircle all project and recede in the moldings of the wood-framed and plastered ceiling, as if stepping forward and back in an elaborate dance. The decorations on the ceiling, a Beale addition, are frivolous cosmetics.

As stately as possible for one five feet, two inches, I went up the great stair to the ballroom, entering that grand salon, just in time to see Henry waltz by with Mrs. McLean, far too wrapped up in his dance to notice his wife.

I felt even more forlorn and lonely than at home. Why hadn't I remembered that it was easier to feel lonesome in a crowd than by yourself? No one saw me. I suddenly realized what it was like to be a ghost. A ghost at the feast. Transparent. They looked right through me. They forgot they knew me. All eyes were on Henry dancing with Emily.

I settled on a gilded bentwood ballroom chair, determined to study the painted ceiling, another Beale frippery, and decide once and for all if it were a fatal desecration on the Latrobe work of art.

After five seconds, I rendered the criticism: fatal. I could look no more. I stood up and went into the north drawing room, found another chair, and, again, for the lack of conversation, and to still the muttering in my mind, concentrated on another Beale embellishment, this time the parquetry floor decorated with a medallion cut of twenty-two different kinds of rare California woods, inlaid to make the California state seal, an inglorious female holding the state shield, a miner, a bear, mountains, and the Golden Gate. Encircling the picture was the word "Eureka!" in tribute to the discovery of gold.

Just when I had worn out all the possibilities of the pre- posterous parquet, the fulsome voice of Mrs. Beale bubbled over like a chunky stew behind me. "Why, Mrs. Adams, what a pleasure! I'm so glad you got over that bad headache of yours. Your husband told us it was very severe. Do you think it could be the mold? It blows in, you know, from the Potomac and hangs in the fog." Mrs. Beale rattled on. Still, I was grateful for the notice.

"Mrs. Adams, let me make you acquainted with Miss Simpson from Baltimore. I was just showing her my wedding ring. I know that you know all about it, but she doesn't. It's still a remarkable story to me after more than thirty-five years." Mrs. Beale held out her left hand and said, "How beautiful it is! The ring was made of the gold my husband discovered in California! Wasn't he won- derful to find gold?"

General Beale came up. He'd seen his wife hold out her hand from across the room, but it was also possible that he had a sixth sense that told him when there was an opening, if only a crack, to tell his favorite story. Everyone on the Square had heard it so often, they could repeat it by heart—and sometimes did. Henry was particularly adept at mimicking Beale. But there was no help for it, Miss Simpson from Baltimore was fresh game, she'd hear it unless she was brave enough to stop up her ears. I, for once, didn't begrudge old man Beale my attention—better than watching Henry dance with Emily. I sank back into the chair and prepared to see if just this one time, the General might not reach Washington on his race across the continent.

"I'll give you the abbreviated version of my landmark journey. It's really a book," said the General, taking a good-sized swallow of the bourbon from his glass and settling himself down on a chair as though it were a saddle. Neither the chair nor the bourbon, however, slowed down his story. "Henry Adams should write it all down sometime. It's history! December 2, 1885

"My story is adventure! Gold! Discovery! Danger! How the West was won! How California came to the Union! People love to hear about it. When new people come to town, sometimes I have to tell it a dozen times at one party! Waiter, get me another glass of bourbon. Mrs. Adams, Miss Simpson, pardon me, I was so busy storytelling I didn't notice neither one of you have anything to drink. Why, you'll be as dry as that desert I had to cross on my way across the continent. What'll you have? Waiter, you get the ladies some of that delicious rum punch my wife made, yes, and some of those sandwiches. We'll have oysters later, and terrapin, lots of shrimp and ducks. I shot the ducks myself, right over there on the Potomac, behind the White House. It's been a good duck-hunting place since I was a boy. But to get back to my story. You don't have all night, I know that, you want to dance.

"Well, it all began a-way back in July 1848 when I was assigned to the Navy's Pacific Squadron. We went out to California to find out if there really was gold out on the west coast or just glittering rocks, fool's gold they called it. Now I was just a lowly acting lieutenant then, a young man. Though I'd already been to California and back, through Indian territory—Indians who had no great love for the pale faces on account of how bad they'd been treated. My commodore got this idea to pull off a switch. You see, the army courier had been sent by ship to take the official news about the gold to Congress. But though the commodore was a sailing man, he thought that a brave and determined rider might make better time on the dangerous land route, and maybe just beat the army officer's time and save the glory for the commodore's command. I also suspect he had in mind to get rid of me. I wasn't such a bad caricaturist back then, and the commodore heard tell of me doing one of him with the legend BLOW THE MAN DOWN.

"Anyways, I was game—as well as young and foolish and hungry for fame. So I borrowed a deer fringe jacket from one of the Mexicans we had in the camp. I squeezed me some berries and wiped the juice on my face and hands. You couldn't have told me from a Mexican, not a bit of it. My own men didn't recognize me. So I rode hell-bent—excuse me, ladies—through the most arduous trails, up mountains and through jungles you never would believe, clear across Mexico. I could have kissed the dock at Vera Cruz, I was so glad to get there and get out of the saddle to rest my ass—excuse me, ladies.

"Once I hit Mobile, I had to commence running again. You'd never believe, with the whole authority of the United States of America's government behind me, what a time I had finding a stagecoach. I have often said, it was easier to find the gold than that stagecoach. But I finally did, though the amount of money it cost me was amazing. Amazing! You wouldn't believe it if I told you. So there I was, racing in a stagecoach to Washington, not sure I'd ever make it.

"And what do you know? I broke all the records from there to here. I made it from California to Washington in forty-seven days! Why, did I tell you that P. T. Barnum was so excited about my trip and the discovery of gold and the rush to California that he offered me a powerful lot of money for my bag of dust and nuggets? I didn't give them to him, though; I donated most of it to the Patent Office. I saved out just a little bit to make Mary a wedding ring. The senators told me that was quite all right—especially since the gold was all mine personally. Excuse me, ladies, I see Don Cameron over there and I have a message for him from

Mrs. Grant. You know the General's memoirs are selling like hotcakes. But if you have a minute or two later in the evening, I'd be glad to tell you how I brought camels to the American desert."

In spite of myself, I hadn't wasted my time—his story would work very well into my *Letters to Posterity from La Fayette Square*. Henry, even if he often makes fun of the General, secretly admires him and envies him his adventures. Henry would like to be an adventurer. That's one reason he esteems King, so much—the geologist who wanders around the world, one jump ahead of the panther, his creditors, and, I suspect, his cast-off women. Henry's adventures are all in his head.

The aforementioned bald head shone on the dance floor and turned in my direction. Henry looked directly at me and then looked again. He stopped cold, so suddenly that Mrs. McLean bumped into him—or was that deliberate? I wasn't sure. But I was certain that Henry was surprised, or perhaps appalled was the better word, to see me. The band stopped playing, Henry spoke quickly to Emily, and they both came over.

"For heaven sakes, Clover, what are you doing here? You said you didn't feel up to coming. I told Emily and everybody else that you were feeling poorly and yet here you are. Are you trying to make a liar out of me? What on earth did you have in mind?" Henry hissed, his neck twisting as he spoke. I kept a calm manner, as befitted a lady under an unreasonable attack from her husband.

Emily looked enormously pleased as she stood holding onto Henry's hand as if it had become glued to hers during the dance. When he had exhausted himself, she took over. "Well, now, Mrs. Adams, I gather you didn't feel as bad as you let on to Henry that you did. I told him I hoped you'd come."

Emily smiled sweetly at my husband, dropped his hand reluctantly, looked at her dance book, and turned to her next partner, who'd arrived to claim his prize.

Suddenly Henry looked very alone. And very small. I was almost sorry for him.

"Don't let me keep you from your next partner. I'm sure your card is full, you're always very popular with the ladies. I don't care to dance myself, as you know. Please go ahead."

"I shouldn't leave you here standing by yourself. I do have to present my apologies to my next partner. Oh dear, Clover, see what trouble you've caused."

"Greeting Mrs. Adams, Mr. Adams," Truxtun Beale, the son of the house, came over. He has been kind enough on occasion to take me to see his stables. Though he was thirteen years younger than I, we had a mutual regard, based in part on our mutual distaste for Emily. We both preferred Mary, his other sister.

We exchanged a few pleasantries about his mission to Persia. Truxtun Beale had already had an impressive career. His first step into the elaborate minuets of diplomacy came in 1876. President Grant, an old friend of his father, appointed that Western hero to be Envoy Extraordinary and Minister Plenipotentiary to the Austro-Hungarian Court in Vienna. Beale, despite his youth, served as his father's secretary, a service Henry had performed for his own father at the Court of St. James in London.

I decided to continue to make use of the evening to research La Fayette Square history. Besides, when—or if—Henry looked my way, I wanted both Truxtun Beale and myself to look animated. Mr. Beale was quite happy to spend his time with me—at least I required no map when he spoke of his travels. Tonight, I surprised him by asking for tales closer to home. And proud heir presumptive to the grand house that he is, young Beale was happy to accommodate me in a walk around the ballroom.

"I know, of course, that Stephen Decatur built your house —I think with the prize money he won fighting the Barbary pirates?"

December 2, 1885

"That's right," said the young diplomat. "He'd won lots of money, though he died before he got his prize for his most famous exploit—setting fire to the USS *Philadelphia* to keep it out of the hands of the Tripolian pirates."

"He died in a duel, wasn't it, at the Bladensburg dueling ground? What was the fight about?"

"He'd sat on the court martial board that had suspended James Barron from the Navy. Barron held it strongly against him at the time. Several years later, Barron challenged and killed him. Decatur was brought home to die in the front room."

"And a subsequent owner had to brick up the northeast window because his ghost kept peering out."

"Oh, so you've heard that story, too, have you?"

"Is it true?"

"Oh, I think not. I've never seen Benjamin Latrobe's drawings for the house, but I understand it's always been a blank window, indented only for symmetry. As you can see over there, on the inside, there's no evidence of a window."

"What a shame, it's such a good story."

"The house is full of good stories. His widow, Susan, by all reports was quite a girl. She lobbied well on her own behalf. But though she finally was able to get Congress to give her a pension, she never received his Philadelphia prize money. That's why, she said, she had to rent this house to Baron Hyde de Neuville, the French minister, and then to the Russian minister, Baron de Tuyll."

"I've heard it said that she once told Henry Clay that if the Russian's servants didn't stop digging up her shrubbery and flowering bushes and charging furnishings to her, she was going to cause an international incident that could lead to war."

"I suspect she did tell Clay something to that effect, maybe that's why he rented it from her himself. Later, Martin van Buren and the British Minister Sir Charles Vaughan lived here successively. This is surely the only house in town to be the ministry of Great Britain, France, and Russia. Just before my father bought it, from the Gadsby estate, Judah P. Benjamin, the Confederacy's Secretary of State, even lived here. Enough of history. Will you dance?"

These days, I never dance, having given it up some years before. But suddenly my arms went up to meet his as if I had no control over them. It had been a long time since I had been held close against a man's chest and felt the warmth of a man's body.

"How kind of you to ask me. I would be delighted."

We whirled around the dance floor. Beale must have brought back a magic carpet from his world tour, for my feet didn't touch ground, they were heel deep in fluffy clouds. And young Truxtun Beale was smiling at my pleasure, holding me a bit closer than the fashion. I wished the dance would go on and on and I could float in the clouds forever.

The music, like all incantations, did come to an end, breaking the spell and depositing me with almost a thump back on earth. I smiled up at my partner, who squeezed my hand. He leaned down and asked softly, "Shall we dance the next one, and the next and the next?"

"No," said Henry, who'd come up behind us and overheard the question. "My wife is going home. It's far too late for her. Her health is not up to these hours of dissipation. Come along Clover. I'll escort you home."

"I'm not ready to go home," I said firmly. "Mr. Beale dances so beautifully, I'm having a delightful time. Amuse yourself with the beautiful Mrs. McLean."

At that, Henry put his hand on my shoulder and squeezed it as he pulled me toward him, away from Truxtun Beale, saying between his teeth, "I said, it's time for you to go home."

As the pain sliced into my arm, the room whirled around me in some mad dervish dance with a mad throbbing beat echoing in my ears. I saw Henry standing there, holding a disembodied arm and smiling. And then, I knew nothing.

When I opened my eyes, Emily leaned over and whispered in my ear, "Feint or faint?"

Mr. Beale gave me his full but gentle support, holding on firmly despite Henry. I was relieved to see that despite my impression when I blacked out, my arm seemed to be attached firmly, though rather uncomfortably. Henry had yanked hard.

"My dear," said Mrs. Beale who'd come up to join in the excitement. "It's too hot in here. All these people dancing, why, we could have done without the fires. Truxtun, you just bring her this way to the little guest bedroom off the library."

"I think she'd be better off at home," said Adams, asserting his right to even a very limp wife.

"Please, Henry," I protested. "Not, not right now. Later."

Willy-nilly, I was half carried by, half walked with my dance partner, who refused to relinquish his catch. In the small bedroom, I was plied with smelling salts of a particularly virulent scent and enough pillows for a harem. Fortunately for me, Mrs. Beale had assumed command. Her son insisted on sitting beside me and rubbing my hand. Henry, with a deceptively bereft look as though some bigger dog had stolen his bone, stood at the end of the daybed.

"Thank you, Mrs. Beale, thank you, Mr. Beale, I'm sorry to make such a scene. Forgive me. Now everyone should go back to the dance, beginning with you, Henry, and Mrs. McLean."

When they all were safely out of the room, Truxtun Beale's attentions were renewed. He reluctantly released my hand, placing it gently on my chest. He fluffed up my pillow. Then he poured me a glass of brandy from the cut glass decanter on the table. He put his arm around my shoulder—with no protest from me—and held me while I drank the peach-flavored liquid. "Feel better?" he asked, as I felt a pink flush spread up my face.

"Much better. What a fool I am for making such a display!"

"Adams scared you. He had no right to come up behind you and pull on your shoulder that way. Anyone would've felt assaulted. Besides, you are a fragile lady."

He took my hand again, raised it, and brought it not the proper two inches below his lips but to them. He kissed the back of my hand firmly. Before I could demur, if that was what I intended to do, he had turned my hand over and kissed my palm.

I knew I should be indignant. Nothing else was proper. But the warmth of his lips against my cool hand was not a gift I could spurn. I had far too great a need.

I wonder from time to time what I would have done if the door had not opened then, just as his arm pulled me closer.

"Well, laddy dah, you two. You're having just too big a time in here," Emily teased.

Henry stood, looking rather abashed, still holding Emily's hand. Emily held the hand high, like a trophy, and whirled around him, her skirts whooshing as they went. "They don't need us here, Henry, let's go back to the ball."

No one urged them to stay, though some polite murmur should have been called for from me.

The spell that enmeshed my companion and myself, however, December 2, 1885 was broken, and I hadn't the courage to try to cast it again.

Mr. Beale obviously felt his chance was lost. He let my hand escape, went over and filled two plates, and brought them back.

"Some fool will soon come to interrupt us again," said my dinner partner. "Quickly, when can I see you again? I'd like to talk. I never have the opportunity to see you without masses of people, though you seem to understand me so quickly."

"I'll walk in La Fayette Park day after tomorrow, if I'm able," I said with as casual yet warm a response as I could manage. "I often do. I'll see you at Jackson's statue, about 11:00 A.M. Henry will be at the State Department then. How pleasant it will be to see you. You must come with more stories of the Square."

At that, the door opened and Mrs. Beale said to her son, "Come, Truxtun, let Mrs. Adams rest and you go dance with Miss Cleveland." Seeing it was all out of my hands, I relaxed against the cushions and thought I might indeed enjoy a pleasant evening of pampering.

With all of them out of the room, myself neatly tucked in, the gaslight dimmed, I listened to the music and felt the bed move like a bark, slipping into the stream and carrying me along with it, where I was not sure, but if there were a waterfall, well, it would all be very quick. I won't worry, I thought, as I was wafted into sleep.

❧

CHAPTER 19

December 2 or 3, 1885

I didn't know whether it was past midnight or not
The Moonlight Lover

∞

Dear Posterity,

I woke up, I supposed in the early morning, though there was no clock in the room. The curtains were pulled only loosely across the windows. Moonlight splashed across the room in a sparkle of light, as if someone had grabbed a handful of the Milky Way and thrown it across the room.

I sat up in bed, pushing the pillows behind me, and admired the moonlight. I slept so soon and well, I thought I must have drunk more of the peach brandy than I realized. Now I was quite awake, very sober somehow, though expectant, of what I was not sure.

As I watched, the moonlight waxed and waned as clouds

222

drifted across the moon. And then, it seemed as though the moonlight was suddenly possessed of an extra dimension. The golden
rays began to round themselves, like a small whirlwind sometimes
seen on a dusty road. How enchanting! And then I realized the
shape the flecks were taking.

They were twisting into the shape of a man, a man of tassels,
bars, and medals, with a silvery sword hung at his side. Had my
evening's cavalier changed into fancy dress and somehow slipped
into the room at a blink of my eyes, intent on I knew not what?
Then I realized that though the specks of moonlight were whirling
industriously, the figure they illuminated was insubstantial.

I saw quite plainly through the man's body to the curtains
where through a slit the moonlight sprinkled itself into the room.
I realized, as icicles danced along the ribs of my spine, that the
being was not of my night nor my time. Later, I couldn't remember
whether I was more afraid than curious. As I watched, he, if that
is the right pronoun, seemed to realize where he was. He looked
around with great familiarity and pleasure, as a man might look
when coming home from a long way off. Slowly his face changed
into a moody longing, an expression of someone who had wanted
something or someone very much for a long time but could not
find her.

As his eyes swept around the room, he caught sight of me.
He immediately moved toward me as I pulled the bedcovers up
to my neck. He came closer and closer until he touched my cheek,
crooning, "Darling Sue, darling Sue, how I love you, how I love
you. I'll never leave you again. Come with me. I am so cold and
you are so warm. Come with me and we'll be together for always,
always."

Not flesh against my cheek, but a cool breeze. I held my

breath, too afraid to cry out. I was paralyzed, stupefied, a sculpture dipped in bronze and mounted in place. I could not have moved if the room had been in flame.

The bedcovers slipped from my grasp. The chill moved over me like a physical force caressing every mountain and valley of my body. The pleasure flowed between us, to him, to me, from me to him, until our passion joined together into a force of such velocity, I, too, like my phantom, dispersed into a thousand flecks of moonlight. The moon moved through a cloud, the light was almost gone, only lingering to show me the sad expression passing over his face, a disappointment too deep to allay, the look of a child who had no presents on Christmas morn, of a lover whose emotion is not requited, a longing so deep and wide that it could never be filled.

The apparition withdrew from my bed even though I tried to hold him, but flesh is a poor restrainer of moonlight. He looked ashamed, humbled, embarrassed, no longer brave lover, intrepid spirit, wish fulfiller. He bowed and said, "Faith, I must plead for your forgiveness, you are not Susan, and I have taken a liberty to which I am not entitled. I came from a long way away, through rivers and oceans and rivulets of time. I thought, I hoped, I wanted my wife, but you are not she. Though I tell you, if our times had come properly together, instead of this strange meeting out of sequence, we would have joined in joy. I bid you good night.

"Oh, yes, fair lady, I owe you one word, I bring this message to you from a far place. I warn you, life is short and the end comes before one is ready."

The whirlwind circled again, rising, skittering, and finally turning into a tunnel spilling out the window.

And all things were as before, with me alone, the only creature in the room. I sat for a long time looking at the moonlight, flat now and empty. Slowly, I began to shake and warm tears squeezed from my eyes. I cried, but softly, for the man of the moonlight, for myself, the briefness of life, the ephemerality of love.

December 2 or 3, 1885

CHAPTER 20

December 3, 1885

Tryst with Truxtun Beale

∞

Dear Posterity,

Like the Queen in *Through the Looking Glass*, . . . sometimes I've believed as many as six impossible things before breakfast. This was not one of those times. Along with breakfast in bed, I regretfully put down the masculine attentions and visitations— both real and spectral—to Mrs. Beale's overgenerous dosing with brandy. Considering the brandy and the other spirits of the night, I felt well, better than I had for the past few mornings.

Jane brought over fresh clothes and a note from Henry. John Hay and Clarence King were expected. Henry had gone to the station to fetch and go with them to a luncheon at State. If I didn't want to order a hack, he would return for me at teatime. I made a rather hasty toilette. As I emerged into the drawing

room, a delegation of Beales awaited me—a pleasant display of
Southern manners. I was grateful that Emily McLean was not part
of the party. I suppose she'd gone to her own house and husband.

I almost collided with Truxtun Beale, who came in about
the same time. "I've come to pay my party call," I said as a joke
to Mrs. Beale, who had the air of one who had buttoned up in a
hurry and still wasn't altogether sure she was decently done up.

"Delighted, I'm sure, dear Mrs. Adams. You're just in time
for lunch. I had the cook make those croissants that you like in
the hopes that you would stay."

"Gracious, I couldn't eat a bite. Never in my life have I been
served so lavish a breakfast. Delicious! I won't be hungry in a
month of meals. I also have a house full of company—did I tell
you? I have to talk with my cook about dinner for our guests.
What I'd really like to do is to walk across the park—I certainly
need the exercise after all I've eaten in this house—and be at
home in time to receive our guests. Clarence King and John Hay
have come to stay with us a few days."

"Clarence King!" exclaimed Truxtun Beale. "Well, old Fortieth Parallel himself. May I please call? I would like very much
to discuss the future of the West with the three of them."

In the face of such enthusiasm, I, of course, invited him to
accompany me home to meet the famous Westerners.

"We'll send you in our carriage."

"No, thank you, Mrs. Beale, I'll walk."

"I'll guard you from aggressive squirrels, voracious pigeons,
and marauding monuments," said Truxtun.

"Anyone who can turn such a neat phrase on the spot is
welcome to walk with me any day," I said, and sent Jane back to
our house on the run to help Cook.

"I'm pleased to see you so pert. Have you recovered from

the ball?" Truxtun asked. His tone was rather strained but not unfriendly. Actually, he looked as if he were concerned that I was all in one piece. I'm not sure he didn't count eyes, arms, legs, and add them up in a total.

"I'm fine this morning," I said. "Off and on since Thanksgiving, I've had a strange sleeping sickness—oh, I shouldn't bore you with my ailments. But I woke up this morning feeling much better."

"Well, Mrs. Adams, you know by now that Southerners, even as far Nawth as we are here in Washington, love to hear about other people's illnesses, we all live in a perpetual malaise, and you do know misery loves company. Do tell us all your symptoms."

"Do, Mrs. Adams, unless my presence impedes you. Should I leave? Is this conversation limited to ladies?"

"No, thank you, Mr. Beale. It's simply that I have spent my nights in strange dreams—not nightmares, you understand—just odd fantasies. I now sleep very late, contrary to the habits of a lifetime. I can't imagine why. I've never needed such sleep before."

"That's the reason," said dear, kind Mrs. Beale. "I wondered. I look forward to seeing you in the park with those darling dogs. And indeed, I have missed seeing you in the mornings."

Mrs. Beale bustled me out to the top of the stairs. Truxtun Beale and I walked across to the Park. I wondered what Henry would say if he saw me. Walking in Lafayette Park is hardly secluded enough to be scandalous, roughly tantamount to appearing on the stage at the National Theater, or the East Room of the White House.

Even so, inexplicably I found myself trembling at the unaccustomed sensation of walking with Truxtun Beale. I began to chatter, covering up my emotions with inanities.

"Tell me, Mr. Beale, do you, as I, think of Washington as

an adolescent still with questions about what it's going to be when it grows up? I wonder if George Washington, when he commissioned Pierre L'Enfant's plan foresaw that now, ninety-four years later, it would be still much admired—but fiercely debated and often ignored by today's more politically adept planners."

December 3, 1885

He looked at me rather surprised, as if he had expected a different remark. But Beale is nothing if not polite, and he followed my lead in the conversation, but with no more of a to-do, took my hand in his. I did not protest. His hand is so much larger that his wraps mine completely.

"You know of course, Mrs. Adams, of Boss Shepherd, the most recent of these plantation overseers to have his way with us? He saddled us with a debt of $22,000,000, double the legal debt limit."

"Well, he's a bit before my time. We moved here after his spending spree." I said, moving my hand slightly in his, not as if I were trying to free it, but a slight acknowledgment that my hand knew where it was.

"That's right, during the panic of 1873, Congress removed Shepherd as governor and Congress instituted the commission form of government," said Truxtun—for so I called him in my shameless mind.

He squeezed my hand rather hard. I would have squeezed back, but caught as my hand was, I could only keep it still and enjoy the intense feeling he provoked.

"But I realize the debt is still with us," I rattled on. "I comfort myself that not only will I not live to help pay it off, but we have no children to be burdened with it into the next century.

"However, during Shepherd's pocketbook-emptying— reminding me in its remorseless extravagance of Clarence King's efforts on a national scale to set up the Geographic Survey—it seems to me Washington has acquired most of the accoutrements of civilization."

He relaxed the pressure on my hand and beginning with my wrists, his fingers moved on to the back of my hand, and then to my fingers, twisted my wedding ring, and he rubbed the tips of his fingers over my knuckles. When the tips of his fingers reached my nails, he turned my hand over and stroked each tip slowly, seductively. Gradually his hand worked its way to the palm of my hand, stroking it gently but firmly. I felt as though my hand was a generator sending hot electric shocks into my body. I could hardly stand the excitement.

"At least the Corps of Engineers has made some effort to drain La Fayette Park and pave Pennsylvania Avenue with wooden blocks. These are accomplishments, don't you think so, Mrs. Adams?"

The effort of following his words instead of his hand was almost more than I could manage. But I tried.

"I am right, am I not, that unlike some areas of the country, Washington doesn't suffer from a shortage of water. But the quality does not equal the quantity. The new reservoir at Smith Spring, east of Howard, began two years ago, I believe?"

I curled my fingers about as much of his hand as I could, lightly tapping them.

"Yes. The engineers are tunneling under Rock Creek to serve the dry eastern section of town. A friend of mine, Thomas W. Symons, is engaged in a study of the Washington water supply. The 550 miles of the Potomac collect foul matter from the farms along its route. Since the land is cultivated and the trees chopped down, all the dirt and fertilizer wash into the river."

The tips of his fingers made circles in my palms, massaging

the mounds, tracing the lines, gently compressing the fleshy parts, until I could hardly walk.

December 3, 1885

"Oh, I know that. In the winter, after storms and snowmelts, the water is so muddy and, I'm sure, contaminated, we have to both sieve it and boil it. It's clear in the summer, but both Congress and anyone else who has the price of a ticket out of town leave at Lent." I stopped in my tracks and looked up at him with, I'm afraid, a look of pleading.

"I believe you go to Beverly Farms? It must be lovely there, Mrs. Adams."

Suddenly, with a fierce motion, he shoved his fingers between mine, pulling them in and out, in and out, rubbing finger against finger, palm against palm, in the most intense sexual experience I had ever had. A hot wave washed over my whole body, pushing the nipples of my breasts into hard protrusions, reaching out to touch him. In my imagination, I could feel him bending over me, taking a nipple between his lips, rolling it between that soft tissue, and then, with his teeth, biting it. I was overcome. I fainted.

I must have been unconscious long enough for Truxtun to move me to the big tree. When I awoke, I was sitting on the bench with his arm around me, still holding hard to my hand.

"Are you all right?" he asked.

I smiled weakly. What could I say?

We sat there for a time—so short, so long. My excitement began to wane, but it left such a sunny glow. For the first time in years, I felt that another body wanted mine. And the feeling was delicious beyond all. I leaned as close as I could to his shoulder and began to relax in his warmth. Finally, after we had been quiet for perhaps fifteen minutes, I said: "The pinch pennies lambasted Shepherd . . ."

But before I could say anything more, he moved until his
face, his lips were almost touching mine. And he said, "shhhhhhh."

That was all, though now both hands encased mine. I began
to wonder, nervously, if he would never speak to me again. Had
I talked too much? Had I bored him? Offended him? When I was
about to apologize, or say something, anything to break the silence,
he said: "Did you ever hear the story of Congressman Sickels? Or
perhaps it is too violent and unsavory for so high-flown a lady as
your own self."

"Heavens no, Mr. Beale. You know I have a reputation for
an insatiable curiosity." I said with relief.

"I know the story only from my mother, who had it from
Benjamin Ogle Tayloe. It all happened in 1859, before my family
moved into our house. At the time, Judah Benjamin lived here.
Though he furnished the house grandly, Mrs. Benjamin preferred
Paris. She made but a brief sojourn here, before she left for Europe,
forever.

"Anyway, Tayloe, who lived on Madison Place, across the
Square, kept a close watch on every blade of grass in the Park. I
am very grateful he is no longer the watcher. One night, he noticed,
as he had often before, a moving light in the upper windows of
the house in the middle of our block. This was not the first time
Mr. Tayloe had noticed what must have been an oft used signal
of love. Down in the Park stood a shadowy form. From it flamed
a brief flash from a match. Tayloe had just spotted the man moving
toward the door of the Sickels house when from an unseen assailant
'Bang!' a rifle shot rang out in the early morning air, and a second
and a third. Before you could say 'Philip Barton Key,' the surreptitious visitor crumbled. Tayloe went down the steps, clothed in
not much more than fear and trembling, to see if he could help.

"Alas, Philip Barton Key, for that was indeed he, was dead

by the time Tayloe and his household moved the body into a sort of clubhouse nearby on Madison Place. Dr. Hagner, when he arrived, could do no more than declare what everyone knew, that Key was dead of a gunshot wound. No mystery clouded the case. Just as well, since the victim was the U.S. District Attorney as well as the son of Francis Scott Key, the lyricist of the *Star-Spangled Banner*. The murderer was General Daniel E. Sickels, then a member of Congress from the city of New York. Since everyone else knew of the affair between Mrs. Sickels, a hot-blooded Spanish woman, and Key, a dashing Don Juan, no one was surprised that General Sickels knew too. He had told his wife he was going out for the evening. Instead, he waited in the trees of the Park, lurking, until Key appeared and gave his signal. Of course, Sickels was acquitted 'for temporary aberration of mind' provoked by the waywardness of his wife and the ungentlemanly behavior of Key."

By the time the story ended, I was quite in control of myself, though still not completely of my hand. So I looked up at the darling face, smiled, squeezed his hand and extracted mine with some difficulty, and said, "Henry's rifle is at Beverly."

Truxtun pulled me up with both hands, laughing. We looked at each other and laughed again.

"I had better see you home," he said. "Before your husband decides to come after me with his bare hands."

"He couldn't reach your neck," I replied and was almost convulsed with wild laughter again.

"Just what is so funny that you are making a public exhibition of yourself?" the voice came from behind the La Fayette statue.

Henry came around it, his face red.

"Hello, Mr. Adams," said Truxtun. "Mrs. Adams charmingly permitted me to escort her across the park. I'm afraid the antics of that squirrel over there sent us both into spasms of excessive merriment. I understand, by the way, from Mrs. Adams, that Clarence King and John Hay are visiting you. I am a great admirer of both men. We Beales like to think we belong on both the Pacific and the Atlantic coasts. Mrs. Adams was kind enough to say that I would be welcome at tea this afternoon with your visitors."

Henry looked at me. I had regained control of myself and now presented a reasonably dispassionate attitude.

"My wife is not strong. I think she has been rather overdoing it recently. She's actually not fit to go to balls, dinners, and teas quite yet. As you know, it has not been long since her father died. And that has been quite hard on her."

"Henry!"

"Mr. Beale, I'm sorry to tell you all this in Mrs. Adams's presence. But I'm sure you understand why I cannot invite you to join us for tea. Two visitors are really far too many for Mrs. Adams. But as they came quite a distance and are our oldest friends, we are accommodating them. But Mrs. Adams is excused from constant attendance. I am sure that now she needs to go take a rest in her rooms with her shades down. We will bid you adieu. Oh, yes, if you truly wish to speak with King and Hay, I think you will find them at the Cosmos Club, where I believe you are a member. I understood they planned to stay there until four-forty-five. By my watch the time is now four o'clock. Good day, Mr. Beale."

Truxtun endured this soliloquy with dignity—and the blankest of faces. I felt as though I had been suddenly dropped into a cold spring and quickly encased in ice. I couldn't break though this ice cage to say anything. Henry took me by the shoulder, spun me around toward the house, with a hand at the base of my spine. I felt like a large hunk of crystallized, brittle, frozen water being pushed off the iceman's wagon. Henry's hands were the rough metal ice tongs. When would the ice pick pierce me?

December 3, 1885

Inside the door, Henry said to Jane, "Tell Cook Mrs. Adams will have her supper in her room."

She did a quick almost curtsy. Henry went into the drawing room. I took my time about taking off my hat and cloak and handing them to Jane. I fluffed my hair in the hall mirror, straightened my collar, gravely shook hands with Boojum to make up for not taking him to walk in the park. And then, my mind firm, ignoring Henry's injunctions, I went to the door of the drawing room.

Henry had already joined King and Hay, who, despite what Henry had told Truxtun, were in our house, not the Cosmos Club. They sat together, laughing over a book richly bound in ornate silk. They closed the volume as soon as I came into the room and welcomed them. I thought it expeditious to ignore their occupation. I suspected the volume was one of King's collection of Japanese pillow books, so called because they are intended to be left on the bride's pillow to instruct her in her duties. I should have bought one for Henry.

"I think you all have met Truxtun Beale. I went to a ball at his parents' house yesterday, became indisposed, and stayed the night. Mr. Beale kindly saw me home. Upon hearing of our distinguished company, he begged to come and make Hay while the King shines."

The two men groaned in unison. Henry seemed flabbergasted at the effrontery of my pun. He got himself together quickly and smiling at the other men, said, "I believe he did not put it quite so eloquently."

"Not eloquently enough for Henry," I said. "Who forbade him to come to tea, though I had invited him and wished to have him here with you. Henry went against my express wishes. I leave you to choose his punishment. If you'll excuse me, I have been

told to have supper in my room. Like Truxtun Beale, I'm not
invited to join the company."

As their laughter subsided into a stunned silence at my words,
I left the room.

On my way upstairs, I suddenly felt I looked the way King
described Emily Beale walking across a room—as though someone
had "tilted a coffin on end and propelled the corpse spasmodically
forward."

At that time before her marriage, when she thought she was
madly in love with King, Miss Beale affected a rather white powder
on her face and no rouge, and her voluminous skirts made her
gait a bit erratic. I, having no love for the then Miss B., found his
remarks hilarious, if not apropos.

I dismissed King and his attitudes, Hay and Henry from my
mind. My fury at Henry's rudeness to both myself and Truxtun
was overshadowed by the warmth of my flirtatious afternoon. I
danced around my room, a ridiculous performance for an aging
dowager of forty-two. I felt overwhelmed by the generosity of
young Mr. Beale's attentions to me. Apparently the fact that I am
his senior by a decade or so doesn't bother him.

I realize that Truxtun is only amusing himself, and, of course,
me. His attentions—whether they included my remarkable experience in the depth of the night in his house or not—are not
serious, nor does he expect me to take them so.

Still, a liaison with Truxtun, for however short a time it
might last, could certainly move my life from the tundra of Henry's
coldness to the tropics of Truxtun's sensuality—my, I am far gone
in an excess of sentimentality, but such is the extravagantly ornamental feeling of a woman aroused.

♣

CHAPTER 21

December 4, 1885

Séance

∞

Jane brought me tea at 2:00 P.M. and said she had peeked in at me several times but hesitated to wake me.

"I thinks, ma'am, you's plain tuckered out. All that writing, partying, and thinking you do. No wonder you need lots of sleep. Don't you stir yourself, it be good for you."

I really didn't think so, because once again, I felt heavy when I awoke, as though my head were a clay model dipped in molten bronze and then quickly cooled in ice water.

I remembered suddenly that at the dance I had arranged to meet Truxtun Beale in the park again this morning. I had missed the rendezvous. Then I thought of the scene in the park yesterday, the insult to Truxton, the assault on my dignity, and the affront to our guests. Obviously, after that humiliation Truxton wouldn't have expected me—perhaps Henry with a pair of dueling pistols.

Without thought of shocking Jane, I kicked my wastebasket, destroying my toe as a consequence. I collapsed on my bed and wept into my pillow, pummeling it with my fists.

"Ma'am? Can a fetch a doctor? Are you hurt? What can I get you?"

I tried hard to still my shakes, but it was still a time before I could reassure the maid—who didn't deserve to have such a scene spread before her. She, after all, had not been denied a longed-for meeting—nor hurt her toe.

I waved her away, out of the room. And in a bit I knitted my nerves together.

In the downstairs hall, Henry looked at me, and without changing the dour, noncommittal look on his face, went into his study and closed the door with a militant snap.

The Skyes are the limit. They came dashing at me from the top of the stairs. Jane who followed them down said, "Good morning, ma'am. The dogs have been waiting for you. They were powerful lonely yesterday without you. They barked all the night before."

They did look happy, doing their tumbleweed imitation all over themselves and me so I could hardly take a step. Their delighted little yips were music to me, far nicer than Mrs. Beale's band. While we were having our love feast in the hall, the door of Henry's study opened. He came out and said, "Marian, can't you control those dogs? How am I expected to get any work done with all that carrying on?"

I apologized, and, as best I could, led them up the steps and out of his jurisdiction. I slipped into my warmest robe and we all piled onto the chaise together and snuggled. Possum, perhaps in search of some misplaced crumb of croissant, gave my face a thorough wash, while Marquis and Boojum attended my hands. By that time, the rest of me was thoroughly covered with Skye hairs, turning my robe into something like an Indian feathered cape. Finally, the dogs were thoroughly worn out, and I was able to write these words.

December 4, 1885

In the early evening, Jane knocked on the door to say that Mr. Adams had said he was going over to the State Department to walk back with Mr. King and Mr. Hay. Cook wanted to know what we were giving them for dinner.

I hastily extracted myself from my doggy blanket, washed, put on a respectable outfit, and sent for Cook. She'd already gone through the larder, and we worked out a menu, good enough for people arriving without notice: oysters, fried chicken, cold sliced beef, Parker House rolls, preserved okra and tomatoes, squash, strawberry and rhubarb pie, apple pie, and chocolate cake. Fortunately, there's Madeira left over from Thanksgiving. I went downstairs to check flowers, etc., accompanied by my troop.

The dogs pushed the door of Henry's study open and I hurried to extract them before they got themselves and me in even more trouble. I would catch one, but he would wiggle away while I was trying to grab a second. Anyone who has three dogs needs six hands—at least. I had to stop to laugh because Boojum hopped into Henry's desk chair and took the earpiece of his eyeglasses in his mouth. Looking for all the world like a hirsute scholar, he turned to me for applause. When I could finally control my laughter, I removed the glasses, wiped off the stem, and being unable to resist, looked at the large desk blotter. I was saved from sin. The blotter was clean. Over in the fireplace I could see the charred remains of the previous one. But from the edge of the new blotter protruded a white bond paper corner. I pulled it out and read it:

"My Dearest Lover,

"The rusty iron minutes drip from the clock in a slow, measured flow as I sit pleading with them to plummet, to get on with it. As heavy and solid as the time, you'd think they'd cascade down my days. Alas, even the seconds are measured out parsimoniously as if they were grains of cocaine. How long can I endure the seconds, the minutes, the hours, the days, the months, the years, the life without you? My brain, my flesh stay in a constant agony of arousal without orgasm, threatening a holocaust of my hopes, leaving me but a few powdery ashes. Come, my adored one, come, let us cherish each other before life and love are dust, blown to oblivion by the tornado of the gods."

The letter stopped abruptly. I held on tightly to the desk to keep myself from shaking into cells of brain and blood, particles of flesh, a whirlwind of disintegrated parts. Lizzie? Emily? Clara? Someone I never knew, never saw, never heard? Who? Whoooooooooooooo? The word screamed in my mind. Who had called forth this anguished passion from the self-contained, self-important Henry? What unfulfilled passion kept him from loving me? Why? Why? Why?

Calling up a starch I did not know I possessed, I stiffened, put the sheet back where I found it, grabbed Marquis and Possum by the nape of their necks, called to Boojum to follow, and removed us all from Henry's sanctum.

Fortunately, we all were in the hall to greet our guests formally. My hasty greeting yesterday, before being sent to Coventry, hardly counted. "How good to see you," I said, grateful that I didn't belong to a religious sect who believed the Lord would strike you dead if you lied.

"How nice of you to have us," said Hay, ever the gentleman.

"I had more unexpected consultations with Secretary Manning. King was staying with us so I brought him along for the ride." King just grinned. I have to say Henry looked about as happy as I have ever seen him. He was beaming as if someone had just installed electricity in his head.

"Of course, we should've stayed at Wormley's. We were very rude to impose on you on such short notice."

Before I could say a word, Henry hastily said, "I told you yesterday, I keep rooms made up for you two. You're always welcome here. Marian, have you done anything about dinner or should I take them out?"

"We have plenty."

Henry sent meat skewers of sharp looks at me.

Dinner was hasty. Cook was evidently none too pleased to have constant houseguests. And the men had the air of wanting to get on with it.

As I was leaving the room to have my coffee in the drawing room away from the cigars, Henry stopped me. "Marian, I should tell you, I have asked Madame Zornsky to come over tonight and conduct a séance."

"What?" I said. "A séance, here?"

"Well, actually, we thought we might do it next door— quieter, no servants, dogs, and so on."

"Do come with us," said King politely.

"Heavens—I guess that's the proper word—no. If I don't believe in every word of the teachings of the clergy, I believe even less in those of the unordained. Besides, if there really is a choice between God and the Devil, I know which side I'm on."

"Oh, do come, Clover, it's bound to be fun. Madame Zornsky is supposed to be the real thing," said King. I wondered where his scientific attitude had strayed. As though he heard my thoughts,

Mr. King said, "It's an adventure. A scientific experiment. We want to see if she can produce anything that we can't explain. As you well know, when the three of us put our heads together, we can make a plausible answer to almost any phenomenon. And if you were along, we'd be bound to show her up."

I have no idea, even hours later, why I went along, except for the perverse feeling that Henry didn't want me to come. I must have taken leave of my wits, stunned by the shards of Henry's love letter bomb. As crazy as it was, at least it wouldn't be another night upstairs by myself, seeking answers to the conundrum of Henry, trying to fit my jigsaw pieces. I would not say to myself that I was hoping for another encounter with the man of moonlight from Decatur House, for he was not mine. I wished him in some Elysian fields with his Susan. I long to summon Mr. Beale.

I went upstairs and piled on as many warm clothes as I could, giving myself the look of a rummage sale counter. We walked next door, the men holding boxes of candles.

Madame Zornsky was already waiting at the door of our new house when we arrived. I started at the sight of her. I'd heard of the medium, as had everyone in Washington society. All sorts of high officials, members of Congress, lobbyists, and, it was rumored, even presidents, had reached with her across the chasm between now and then.

She was wrapped in a cape, rather say a huge blanket, with only a small amount of face showing—impressive, eerie, as though her reality was not ours. Her black form standing there so still in the aura of the yellow gaslight of the street could have been an unnaturally tall fire hydrant or some other object rooted to the street. When she finally moved she didn't shake hands but gave a quick nod to each, as though reserving her courtesies for her true friends, the expected spirits.

December 4, 1885

We gathered in what is intended to be the library, the floor complaining as we walked across it, straining unsunken nails and boards out of shim. The room was far from ready for entertaining. Stacks of paneling leaned against the walls, breathing out sawdust. Sanding the plaster had left a narrow beach around the wall. As is Richardson's design, few walls are flat. Bays, arches, alcoves, protrusions, and recessess add to the feeling that no surface is certain. A smashed windowpane sprinkled sharp points, reflecting the fire going behind the green marble mantelpiece. The gaslight has not yet been turned on in the house, so the fire was the only illumination.

"We brought candles," said Henry to Madame Zornsky. She turned her head away from Henry and looked a long time into the fire.

"I think not. The fire is light enough. I think we'd better go to the other end of the room, though it may be a bit cold for Madame Adams. Fire can upset the emanations. It's an element. Air, earth, fire, water. You have to be careful. It might call up an elemental, the salamander of fire, the sylph of air, the undine of water, or the gnome of earth. It is necessary to know what you're doing in these cases. Séances are not for those who are unable to control what they summon. Spirits unleashed can be dangerous."

Suddenly drafty currents seemed to gyrate around me.

"You look a bit pale, Madame Adams," said the medium. "Are you sure it isn't too cold in here for you? Perhaps you'd like to go back to more comfortable quarters? I wouldn't like you to catch the grippe."

Why did I say, "I'll stay?"

I didn't recognize the round table in the center of the room, nor the chairs. It seemed no time to ask. The table was not large, but curiously carved, with strange beastly heads in a circle around the edge of the top. I wasn't too sure I wanted my wrist within the reach of their bite.

At the instruction we sat in the circle, holding hands as one is expected to do.

"Unbelievers think we hold hands to prevent me from using mine to make fraudulent effects," the medium said. "For me the reason is the power thus created by the circle of people." She paused, closed her eyes, leaned her head against the high back chair. Such was the potency of her presence, no one moved, spoke, coughed. When the silence solidified, she said, with an almost cheery voice, "Mr. Adams, did you know you are a natural clairvoyant?"

He grinned. "Not actually."

"Well, you are. I'm never wrong. You may find it a bit upsetting when I go into a trance. You may come with me, whether you will it or not."

Henry looked apprehensive.

We sat for what seemed an eternity as the fire died down. But though the wait was long and tedious, it was not boring. Shadows of ourselves, chairs, tables, and some objects hard to identify danced on the walls in steps set to the crackle of the flickering flames. Madame Zornsky, as best I could tell, hummed to herself or perhaps recited a mantra. Her singsong became louder, and the sound echoed, magnified, bounced like projectiles from the hard surfaces of the chamber. I wasn't sure whether the words, in a tongue unknown to me, were a prayer or a curse. I would not write them down if I could spell them because I fear their energy. It is not necessary to be a believer to be a fearer.

All of a sudden the medium broke off her words as though something was choking her throat, bottling the words up on the inside. The words must be filling up her breathing space because December 4, 1885 she turned as blue as the sky reflected in the Tidal Basin.

As I watched, she began to writhe this way and that, as if to escape the domination of some spectral energy. I dragged my eyes away from her to look at Henry. He too looked as though he were in thrall to some phantom power. The other men looked perplexed but not seriously affected.

A whooshing sound began in the darkest corner of the room—framed by an arch, intended someday to hold Henry's choicest leather-bound tomes. Something, I knew not what, was gathering strength. It was not a shadow, nor was it substance, but a something in between.

The figure seemed to be a vacuum, drawing to it all the specks of the room, the plaster powder, the sawdust from the woodwork, even the crystals of the shattered glass. It was hard to make out exactly what its form signified. An entity, I supposed, though whether man, woman, or beast, I could not tell, but then the light was fast fading, and soon the dark would blind us. For the nonce, I could not take my eyes away. I had no curiosity for its effect on others. I knew with a strong certainty that it formed itself for me, none else.

The wraith was now in its final form. A sail? A swaddling cloth? No, of course—a shroud. Two white cloth folds reached out and said, "Clover."

I am not sure what happened next.

CHAPTER 22

December 5, 1885

The Locked Door

∞

Dear Posterity,

This is not exactly the sort of epistolary work I had in mind.
I don't understand what is happening. I am not sure how long my
faint lasted. When I woke up this morning—or is it afternoon?
—I wasn't sure how I came here.

Last night's events were too bizarre to be believed. I am very
sure that was not the ghost of my father. True, I fainted when
my name was called. But I suspect I might have anyway, what
with the cold, the unpleasant surroundings, and, let me face it,
the tension. I now have to wonder if the ghostly presence was
achieved by some sort of artificial alchemy I don't understand. I
have read of such frauds by nefarious mediums bent upon producing effects to persuade their clients. Surely it was not a per-

formance put on just for me? That would mean a conspiracy against my sanity. I cannot believe such a terrible accusation against Henry—or Clarence King and John Hay.

Henry woke me with a knock on the door. He came in, bringing a cup of chocolate with one of Mrs. Beale's marzipan croissants, and made his view clear, in the kindest, most pleasant of voices.

"Clover, I've been terribly worried about you ever since your father died. I know you're not your usual self. I see you sitting in company, rubbing your hand across your forehead. Are you having memory lapses? I suspect so. And this erratic behavior of yours. The way you treated Mrs. Cameron and Richardson. That wild last-minute dash to the Beale ball. Making a spectacle of yourself in La Fayette Park. And your faint, coma, or whatever it was last night. Are you having headaches? Delusions?"

Speaking in as measured and controlled voice as I could, I said, "Henry, I am perfectly well. My health, except for the ailments caused by this swamp we live in, is fine. I should never have put myself in the position to be so frightened as I was last night."

"Clover, this is ridiculous. Why were you frightened? Nothing happened last night to frighten you."

"What do you mean, nothing happened? The séance, Madame Zornsky, the creature calling my name?"

"I have no idea what you're talking about. We had supper last night with John and King. You left us when we lit our cigars. And then, when we came out of the dining room, we found you in a swoon on the steps. We had no reason to suspect anything or anyone scared you."

"Are you saying that I made it all up? Dreamed it? The séance in our new house? The medium? The cry from hell? It was not a nightmare, it happened! And now I am beginning to believe you made it happen. You, John Hay, and King." I shook with the intensity of my defense.

"Clover, what is the matter? We've always been fond of each other. At least I thought you were of me. The years since our marriage, with the exception of this one, have been the happiest in my life. We are part of a famous family, we're received everywhere. We have good friends and amusing acquaintances. I dance attendance on you perpetually. I laugh at your puns, I carry your camera."

"Have you forgotten already, Henry? I have no camera, it was stolen. I have no darkroom, it was destroyed."

"Poor Clover, you're imagining things again. It's all right there where it's always been, your camera, your darkroom. What do you want me to do? Just tell me, and anything that is within my power, I will do."

"Henry, I have tried to tell you for thirteen years. I have given up."

"Dear Clover, you must be ill. I have been very concerned about you. So I have asked Dr. Mitchell to join us. He has been of such help to John Hay. Hysteria, as you know, is a specialty with him."

Before I could protest—for all the good it would do me—Dr. S. Weir (what an appropriate name) Mitchell knocked, and without waiting for an answer, came in. He obviously had been waiting outside for his cue. He had all the charm of a medical tome, a thick, black look about him, his tie like the ribbon page marker. Indeed I did remember his previous appearances at our tea table, and his antifeminist arguments, presented as efforts to protect the "weaker" sex.

"How are you, my dear Mrs. Adams?"

"I am flourishing. If I were withering I would not think it

safe to tell you," I said with as cool a manner as I could manage.
A cool, crisp, controlled manner is best, I have found, in dealing
with his sort.

"Now, now, Mrs. Adams, you know I am your friend. We
have drunk tea together in your charming drawing room."

"I find our encounter this afternoon somewhat different. I
am not accustomed to meeting my tea guests in my boudoir."

"Oh, I grant that. Still, my visit here today is, shall we say,
a bit different." He spoke as though his words were coated in
sweet, slimy cough medicine. "Instead of drinking your tea, I have
come to invite you to partake from my font of knowledge about
conditions such as yours."

"What conditions are you talking about? You will excuse me,
but I am not aware of any of my conditions that need watering
with your knowledge." I kept my tone as even and low as I could,
knowing he presumed any high note in a woman's voice a sure
sign of hysteria.

"I think you do. Your husband and I have discussed your
case at great length. I have heard from your friends Clarence King
and John Hay who have long and intimate knowledge of your
episodes of depression and its converse, that manic hilarity, un-
becoming to a settled lady such as yourself. Perhaps the chief
symptom that betrays the extent of your illness is your diary. I
have not read it all myself, only some passages copied from it to
illustrate your problem. These reveal a deep-seated confusion.
However, I believe it is possible to effect a cure, provided you
come under my care immediately."

"How dare you, sir, read my private papers? Who gave you
leave?"

"Why, your husband, dear lady."

"He did not have my permission to read it himself, much

less show it to you. I now know who stole the gold key that unlocks my diary."

"Here, here, Marian. Steal? I am after all your husband, and what is yours is mine."

"Not my thoughts, Henry Adams." In spite of my efforts, I couldn't help shaking. I reached for the nearby table and held on for dear life, steadying myself to say: "Dr. Mitchell, I do not need your assistance. I am quite capable of managing my own affairs if I am left to do it. I see no need in our prolonging this conversation. I am sure you have patients who need you elsewhere. I would not keep you from them."

"I would not be doing my duty to my Hippocratic oath if I abandoned you now to your illness. I believe in the first place that you must give up this constant writing. Even the strongest feminine brain can be overtaxed by the exertions necessary to produce factual reports, much less fiction. The strain is particularly unhealthful for women of your age. Once a woman has passed beyond childbearing, then perhaps she might take up writing rhymes for her grandchildren, or songs for rocking babies. But trying to write an elaborate work leads to mental confusion, anxiety, and distasteful bodily changes for ladies of your years and attainments. Novels are not healthful for women to read, much less write. The confusion between fantasy and reality is too much for the soft, fragile feminine brain. Better for you to tend your roses, be charming for your husband, entertain your friends."

"So you think writing makes one unfit for life? Then pray tell me, my good doctor, what of your own book of poetry? Was it necessary for you to give up your practice because of rhymes chasing each other around in your brain?"

"Marian, enough. You must not speak to Dr. Mitchell so. He's only here to help you."

"Help me into a straitjacket, you mean."

"Oh dear, Mr. Adams, I am afraid that Mrs. Adams must have my rest cure. I personally think it would be best to take her to Philadelphia where I could most easily supervise her treatment in a proper nursing home."

December 5, 1885

"I will not go. You couldn't force me. I have no need of your ministrations. I am best served by your absence."

"If Mrs. Adams is going to resist going to a proper facility, then I cannot be responsible for her recovering completely from her aberrations. Such problems are deep-seated and take intensive control of the depression."

"I will not go!"

"Well, until Mrs. Adams can be brought to a more healthful and agreeable view, I will give you a prescription for the minimum course of treatment that perhaps could bring her around. Six weeks at least in bed. No visitors save for myself. No writing materials in her rooms. She should be kept out of the sun, and the moon, too, if possible. The curtains must be kept closed at all times. Since your house faces south, I believe the back of the house would be best, if you are going to insist on leaving her here. In any case, no reading matter that would upset her. I include in this, the Bible, a great source of agitation for females, especially those, as I remember Mrs. Adams among their number, who are so deranged as to dispute its messages. Your reading should be limited to the moral meditations I have prepared for you, Mrs. Adams, to ponder and memorize. One a day. I think you will find them charming and uplifting. No supper until you've recited your day's dose. At the end of this time, I am sure, Mr. Adams, if all my prescription has been rigidly followed, that the regime will make Mrs. Adams willing to undertake a more prolonged treatment directed to make her content with her lot, accepting of her place in the world, and no longer impelled to befuddle her brain with all this scribbling."

By the most extraordinary efforts, I managed to retain my composure, not screaming, howling, or even interrupting his extraordinary speech, a funeral oration to my sanity. I amazed even myself with my forbearance. I stood up, walked over to the door, opened it wide, and said to Dr. Mitchell, "I cannot think of any treatment guaranteed to kill me quicker. If you have any humanity, any human feeling, not to say perception as a physician and a philosopher, you will leave my presence this minute and take my husband with you. I have nothing further to say to either of you."

"Now, now, Mrs. Adams."

"It will take more than the two of you to incarcerate me."

Henry, his face turning as red as a bloody face from the waxworks, stood up and said quietly to me, "We will leave now, Marian. But we will be back."

"I will not be here when you come. I plan to leave this house as quickly as I can and never pass through any door that would lead me to your presence again."

"Don't be ridiculous. You can't go like this. Where would you go? With no warning to your family, hasty packing, and worst of all, without an escort."

"I am a grown woman. I need no escort. When I reach the train station I'll wire Nella."

"As ill as you've been? What would your family think of me if I let you go alone, unprotected, ill, on a night train?"

He took me by the arm and propelled me to my chaise. Dr. Mitchell nodded his agreement. Henry was, by the law of the land, the master of his house. No matter my income paid for it. At last, as I reached for a lamp to throw at them, they left.

For a time, I was so furious, I could hardly contain myself. I knew then that Henry planned to get rid of me. He would lock me up and throw away the key. Why? Why? What had I done to him?

I worked hard to regain my lucidity. I would not waste my efforts in further weeping or wailing. Henry had determined to put me away, gain control of my money, remove me from his life. That was clear. I would think calmly and collectedly about what had happened and what I must do.

I knew then I had to escape as quickly as possible. I should do as my grandmother did. Take myself and my small fortune off, live, as certainly I could, on my own means. And look for such pleasures as would come to an independent woman. Why not? I would not make the mistake Henry James's Isabel made. Once away, I would never never come back.

Praise heaven that my money was left by my father specifically to me, in trust. That would not be easy for Henry. He would have to live without my money. Could he afford the Richardson monstrosity? I am not so sure.

Money. That's a thought.

I looked in my reticule and found I had a surprising amount of money, far more than I usually had on hand. This was because I had taken a fair amount of cash to Massachusetts when I went to nurse my father in his final illness. Well, the money would be a help.

I could go live in my father's house in Boston, or in Beverly Farms, or even set myself up in a salon in Paris. I'm barely forty-two. My father lived to a great age. Except for this eternal catarrh—caused I'm sure by the dreadful climate of Washington—I'm healthy enough. Henry is the disease I must cure.

I began to pack. I called Jane, who has always been a staunch supporter. I thought best not to tell her too much, because I didn't want Henry to blame her.

"Jane, I must go to Massachusetts. A problem to do with the disposition of my father's paintings. I don't want to tell Mr. Adams right now, he would insist on going with me. I'd rather he not, he's enjoying his friends. I'll write him a note and you can give it to him later, after I've left."

"Ma'am, you want to catch the nine-o'clock train tonight?"

"That's right. Do you think I can make it?"

"Yes, ma'am. I'll have Brent harness the horses to the carriage, then I'll come back and pack for you. He will take everything down the back stairs."

"I would be very grateful."

"Shall I come with you to Massachusetts, ma'am? I don't rightly think you should go by yourself."

"I'll have a train full of company—and I should be able to get a compartment. Oh, yes, please ask Cook to pack me a supper. I won't be at dinner, I'm sure Mr. Adams told you."

"Yes, ma'am." And she hurried off.

First I put my journal and the original handwritten manuscripts of my books in my silk underwear case, in the valise. Then I added my shoes, pocketbooks, etc. Jane came back and undertook the serious packing of my Worth clothes in my steamer trunk. "I'll leave my summer things here," I said. "But I may need most of my winter clothes. You know what Boston is like."

By 7:00 p.m. I was thoroughly packed, even throwing in a print or two from my boudoir. I regretted I couldn't take more. But perhaps Henry would not be churlish and let me have them later.

I sat on my chaise, I hoped for the last time in this house, writing these notes in a small book I keep in my purse. Jane said the carriage would pull up at the kitchen door. She went downstairs to reconnoiter and came back with the report that the men were on their way to the Cosmos Club! I've never been so grateful to Henry, Clarence King, and the other founders of that male haven as I was then.

Here's Jane.

∞

Later.

I take up my pen again to write how my foray for freedom was foiled.

As I came down the steps, my bags and trunk in front of me, Henry stood at the base of the stair by himself.

"Good evening, Henry," I said, with as much aplomb as I could scoop up out of my disordered brain on an instant's notice. "Did you enjoy your stag dinner? Did Dr. Mitchell join you? I am sure it was more agreeable for my absence."

He smiled. "To judge by your luggage, you must be planning to give me your absence permanently. Have you then decided to go to Dr. Mitchell's rest home in Philadelphia?"

I thought distractedly that I had best not admit to the truth. He would think of a hundred reasons to prevent me. I would lie.

"Henry, you know of my moods and flurries. I have taken a passion to go to Boston and stay with my family for a bit. I think I will be much more settled in my mind after a time there. You won't be lonesome. Mr. Hay and Mr. King will keep you company for as long as you like. And then when they leave, you can come up to Boston and see how well I've grown. And we can talk about Dr. Mitchell's treatment then. Excuse me now, but I must hurry to catch the train. Good evening."

Henry waved to the servants to put my luggage down. He stood at the bottom of the stair, directly in my path. He advanced, his nostrils flaring. I had no choice but to go back to my room.

Henry has turned the key in the door to the hall from that side. I suppose I could tie the sheets together and go out the window. Or drop notes, "Help, I'm being held prisoner!" Jane is no use, I know now.

So here I sit, wide awake in my room. Wondering who would come to free me? Truxtun? Mr. Corcoran? the Bancrofts? I rang the bell. No one answered. I realized I am famished—no breakfast, lunch, or supper. I looked around the room. Have I no fruit? There is the hot chocolate Henry brought me earlier. Cold, I'm sure, but I have to have something. Oh, yes, and a croissant. Well, it'll have to do. There's no hope of escape until sunrise.

I didn't make it to bed before I fell asleep in my traveling costume, complete with hat, on my chaise. I wonder now if Henry put a draught in the chocolate to quieten my nerves and make me more tractable. I now think it likely my two or three previous infusions of chocolate milk were also doped, I'm not sure with what. King sometimes brings Henry cocaine, I know that. Would an infusion of coca leaves make a cocaine solution? Or could it be opium? I don't know that. Perhaps it's just that I'm worn out, and the cocoa makes me as limp and lifeless as a wet petticoat pinned on a line.

Before I worked out the thought, my mind became a jumble of confused images. Before I could sort them all out, I felt myself beginning to sink into a deep hole of darkness, going down, down, down in a spiral without end. I was blown and buffeted by dire forebodings, earthquakes, hurricanes, tornadoes, a dark well of noise and jolts.

Before I reached the bottom, if indeed there was one, I found myself climbing back, hand over hand, toward consciousness. By the time I reached the top, dawn had not sent even a sliver of pink to the top of my curtains. I woke up with a feeling of seasickness, no, airsickness, as though I were Icarus, flying, not with wax-attached wings, but a pair of disembodied wax-filled ears, ringing with a disordered cacophony. As I came awake, the dream seemed to be continuing. I heard strange knocks and small shrill cries and whimpering. December 5, 1885

At first I thought it must be the dogs, but I hadn't seen them last night. I hadn't dared to ask Henry where they were, well aware that in his present mood, if he knew I wanted them, he would keep them from me. I was sorry, because my bed was cold and lonely without a dog or two asleep on my feet, keeping them warm. I wished fervently they were with me now—they would fearlessly investigate the strange noises, as they did the annihilation of my darkroom. I pushed myself out of bed, threw my negligee around me, and headed in the direction of the noises. As I walked toward the door to his bedroom, the noises increased in intensity. Now I could hear moans, squeaks, and scuffling. When I reached the door, I heard unmistakably Henry's voice saying over and over, "Again, again, again."

I put my hand on the knob, even though I presumed Henry had locked this one, as he did the hall door. To my surprise, it turned. I opened the door. The three—Clarence King, Henry, and John Hay—were together in Henry's large bed, so intent on taking their mutual pleasures they paid no attention to me, the interloper. I stood for a long moment until, even with my inexperience, I was sure of what I had seen and what I must do. Finally, in an act culminating thirteen years of hesitancy, I turned and went out, closing the door. As I did, I heard Henry's anguished cry, "Clover." I replied softly, "Excuse me for intruding."

Back in my own boudoir, I held onto the comforter and shook. I felt as though I were back in that black hole of dreams, only now it seemed to be sucking me down into its pit. The waking vertigo is far worse than the dream. Only now I know that the threat is genuine, he has a real reason for getting rid of me. Sodomy is, after all, a crime. What would his family think if he were accused of being a sodomite?

I tried the hall door again. Locked. I went to the window, pulled back the curtains, and could see only blackness, except for the wan efforts of the sickly gaslights. I must get away. I must.

In an effort to think this through, I went to my suitcase and took out my journal—Henry has returned it. I took my pen from my purse, stretched out on the chaise, covered myself with my heavy burgundy comforter, and tried to make sense of what I'd seen and what it means to my life. My pen and my journal are my life raft and oar. I must use them to go in the right direction.

When did it begin, the long nights when he stays up till dawn when King or Hay visit? He says he talks with King or goes to the Hays' house. Or they stay late, they say, at the club. Tonight explains Henry's penchant for late parties and male company.

And the letters. "My Dearest Love" indeed. The only thing I'm not sure about, was he writing to King or Hay? What was the plan? That they all go away together? I wonder why they decided to take their chances now and have their orgy here, in this house, with *me* in the next room? Perhaps the danger gave zest. Now I understood the sleeping draught and why they thought themselves so safe to disport themselves as they would. How many other times have they drugged me? No wonder I fell asleep in my chair, and had such strange dreams and an aching head. With the drugs to prepare me for the séance, they would be sure I would be so devastated that my word would not be accepted—I could be easily sent off to Dr. Mitchell's madhouse. But my hold on reality is stronger than they thought. And their passion for each other was certainly beyond my knowledge.

So little is understood of why people love, much less who they desire, I do not blame Henry for his choice. I do blame Henry for the years he deceived me into thinking that his lack of interest in my body was all my fault—he would love me as I wanted him to had I only been beautiful—as beautiful as Mrs. Cameron, or as seductive as Mrs. McLean, or as exotic as the Egyptian belly dancers King talks about—anyone but my poor drab self. Henry made me blame myself for the fact that I never stirred his desire—that at my touch, my pleading touch for warmth, for love, he pulls away, almost shivering.

December 5, 1885

Henry married me, promising a love he had no intention of giving. I could have accepted a companionable marriage, though I would've yearned for children always. If he had only said, "I am sorry, I have misled you as to my attentions, you are free to stay with me and live as friends, or you may go and seek someone else who can give you the love and children, which I cannot."

It is not only his lack of desire for me but his hatred for me that has plunged me into the seventh circle of Hell. He is a child who doesn't want to play with a toy but doesn't want to allow anyone else to enjoy it either. He derives his satisfactions by torturing me with my supposed inadequacies and chaining me, a prisoner, to him.

I am sure that somewhere deep inside he turned against me, began to hate me, because he at last understands I am not to blame for the deficiencies of his life, the terrible lack of love—and I suspect most of all—fame. He hates me because he can not bear to hate himself. Were he able to throw off the demands of his family dynasty, he might be able to accept the sadness of being childless. Were he willing to be discreet and choose as partners those who have no obligations to others, he could certainly live a sexual life satisfactory to himself. Most of all, he could have been

content, were he to learn to accept his achievements as a writer
and historian and not suffer this raging hunger gnawing in his
heart because he was not a president, nor minister, nor secretary
of state. Poor Henry, he so craves glory.

The knowledge that you have harmed someone, that you are
responsible for doing them serious injury, is the most harmful and
long enduring cause of hatred. It is easier to forgive someone who
has wronged you. Today, I no longer hate Henry—certainly there
were times when I did, when I accepted his accusation that I was
responsible for the inadequacies of his life.

Now I understand everything and forgive everything. And I
feel liberated. I know at last I am not to blame. He has no use
for my body, or any other woman's, no matter how beautiful or
yielding. I can go on with my own life, and I no longer need to
worry about his.

I heard the key turn in the hall door. And without a knock
Henry, impeccably dressed in smoking jacket and velvet trousers,
walked through my door as if it were any night and he were any
husband, a habitué of his wife's boudoir.

"What do you want, Marian? I asked you that once before
and you wouldn't say. We must bargain now. There is no other
way. I'll begin. You will agree to say nothing about what you think
you have seen tonight. I don't know what wild story you have in
mind to tell. Of course, no one would believe you anyway. But
even lies have a way of disrupting lives, and I don't intend that
you harm mine with your mad fantasies. But if you are wise and
don't talk about our affairs, keep your calm and behave reasonably,
I will tell Dr. Mitchell you are better and we have decided to do
without his services."

"How dare you say I lie? I can no longer endure such treatment."

"What do you want?"

My list of necessities was immediately in my mind, as if I had flipped through the book of my heart and found the right page at once.

"I intend to make a new life for myself. I hope to divorce you and remarry. I don't have anyone in mind, nor have I ever been unfaithful to you. But I want a child badly. And I don't have much time to conceive and give birth, so time is crucial.

"And I intend to have, as well as a baby, another book, at least one more. I plan to have *Democracy* and *Esther* republished under Marian Hooper. My lawyer can deal with you on separating our finances.

"And that's it. Say whatever you intend to say. But I will not stay here. Certainly not since you have taken to jailing me, trying to scare me into madness, threatening me with an insane asylum.

"When daybreak comes, no matter what it takes—bribery, shouting out the window, climbing out the balcony, I will leave you. You and King and Hay can end your pretense and live happily ever after, without me to interfere."

Henry looked at me and said, "You are completely unreasonable as usual. Well, be it on your head. You've made your decision. And thus mine. I will facilitate your journey to your karma. You will leave at dawn. I will be glad to see you go." He left the room.

I have shoved a chest in front of the connecting door. I'm going to bed and console myself.

Dawn. Dawn. I can hardly wait to escape. I'll take the train to my sister. I am free, free forever.

At last, exhausted, I slept.

❧

CHAPTER 23

December 6, 1885

I'll See You Again

∞

Dear Posterity,

My nose woke me up. I could not breathe through it. My whole upper respiratory system felt full of plaster, now turned to stone cornices over my eyes, fallen iambic columns where my ear channels had been. My mouth was dry, cracked and stiff. I stood up, sometimes that helps.

From my window, I couldn't actually see the sun rise. Though I looked, hoping for a few pink rays to spread a soft throw of light to cover the dirty sheet of winter decay now laid upon La Fayette Park. I watched for a few minutes, but all I could see was a pink finger here and there, the morning laying its hands gently on the night, softly, easily, not snatching at the darkness, but carefully picking it up a little bit at a time lest it be frightened by the glory of the light. I am such a sun lover that not until that December 6, 1885 minute had I ever thought that the night, which seems threatening and terrifying to me, could itself be afraid of the sun. The secrets of the night are revealed by the sun. Little can be hid from its light. One must live so as to never fear the light on your deeds.

No reason to hurry now. Surely he will send a servant to help me with my baggage. After last night, he will be more than glad to let me go, to get rid of me, to assent to a life apart. For if he tries to stop me, I will be the sun to Henry's night.

I am about to leave this room, this house, this street, this capital forever. I am glad, very glad indeed to leave. So why do I not get on my way? No protracted good-bye is indicated. Still, I find myself looking out the window to La Fayette Park. I can see very little. Just the small blaze of the gas lamps guarding the White House.

The day must not yet be here. In the laundry house in the rear, the maids are asleep on their virgin pallets. They need their rest before their hard day, up and down the steps, fetching and carrying the detritus of our lives. I fear I have not been an easy mistress. In the carriage house, the coachman and his wife will likely be enjoying their domestic bliss. I envy their warm love under the quilts. In the alley behind us, the milkman with his horse and cart will soon come clumping through the mud and the odoriferous evidence of the previous horse's passage. The gaslights on the street send forth their yellow glow, turning the rare passerby into a jaundice victim. The sounds, the smells, the sights of the sun are beginning.

I shook myself, trying to throw off my shell of lethargy. Before the day actually comes, I had better get myself up and prepared for the final encounter. I lit the gas sconce. I dressed quickly.

I tried the door, still locked. I went to the door, crouched down beside it, and put my eye to the keyhole. I saw no light through it. Henry must have left the key in it. I wonder what excuse he gave the servants for locking me in.

I remembered, even in my distress, something I once read. I found a stiff piece of paper that I had intended to use for sketching. I slid it under and beyond the door. Then I took my buttonhook and poked it through the lock. I heard a gratifying thunk! The key was now on the paper. I pulled it very gently through—fortunately there was enough of a gap to allow it to slip through. I stopped when I heard noises. Then I realized it was only the milkman leaving the milk at the back door. No servant would be up yet—I hoped. One more tug brought paper and key through. I was free!

I turned my attention to a review of my last night's packing. Jewelry, money, best clothes, a book of eighteenth-century sketches, my journal, my letters from Henry James, my family, and a friend or two. What am I missing? What big, important, essential jewel of my life am I missing? I walked through the house in my mind, in imagination, picking up and laying down objects. Even in my mind, I didn't violate the holy of holies, Henry's study, where he worships his own intellect. I wonder if he knows he's lost his last worshipper. Indeed I have tried to be that.

And then I realized I hadn't taken my nose drops. No wonder my nose had turned into a death mask. I found the leather case. Took out the nose drops, leaned back, and hastily put a dropper full in each nostril.

First came the odor of bitter almond, then the unbearable pain. And now I know what has been saved from the destruction of my darkroom—the bottle of potassium cyanide. I can feel it burning through my head, my brain. Soon it will reach my heart.

I have very little time left to write, though I doubt posterity will have these pages. Perhaps—I will quickly put them in my secret drawer.

But Henry has won. Now he will have it all forever—he will claim my books, burn my journal, tear up my letters, sell my pictures, spend my money—and obliterate my memory.

But I will have my revenge. I will haunt him every day of his life.

Author's Afterword
Is Fiction Truer Than Fact?

"Was It a Case of Suicide?"

The thought that the respectable man of letters Henry Adams may have murdered his wife came to me in a sudden shudder akin to the experience called "someone walking over your grave." That feeling down my spine may be the best confirmation I can produce. Even so, the hearsay evidence, the only testimony at the time, available in 1885 newspapers in fuzzy microfiche records, suggests that indeed the historical record of Clover's death and what led up to it, as Henry James said of Clover's salon: "on the whole left out more than it took in."

The published record of events of that tragic Sunday morning, December 6, 1885, goes like this:

Washington in 1885 was a Southern, churchgoing town.

Clover and Henry Adams, however, never went to a house of worship, not even to Benjamin Latrobe's handsome St. John's, called the Church of the Presidents, across Sixteenth Street. Still, they most assuredly would have given their six-member household staff the morning off to go to their own. So when Henry took his toothache to his dentist that morning, Clover would have been alone.

Where she was, what she was doing, whether she was alive or dead when he left can never be known.

When Henry came back to the house (as *The Washington Post* reported on December 7, 1885), there on his doorstoop was a friend (probably Rebecca Dodge) come to see if Clover, in the polite phrase of the time, was "receiving" visitors. Henry went up the stairs to his wife's boudoir. She was lying on the floor, on a rug near the fire, still warm, but without response. Whether she was still alive at that moment is not certain. Adams picked her up and put her on the sofa, left her, and went two blocks away to fetch Dr. C. E. Hagner. Dr. Hagner could not resuscitate Clover. The next day *The Washington Post* reported, gently, that she died from "paralysis of the heart."

Two days later, the enterprising correspondent of *The New York Sun* added: "Although she was still warm, they could not revive her. The fumes of the poison and the empty phial that contained it told plainly enough the cause of her death."

"Was It A Case of Suicide?" demanded the headline in *The Washington Critic*. The sensational story reported: "The certificate of Coroner Patterson and Dr. Hagner in the case of Mrs. Henry Adams, who died suddenly in this city on Sunday last, is to the effect that she came to her death through an overdose of potassium [cyanide] administered by herself. A *New York Sun* correspondent states further that there is no doubt Mrs. Adams intended to take her own life. She was just recovering from a long illness, and had been suffering from mental depression."

Certainly that is what Henry led everyone to think. But the evidence for suicide "while of unsound mind" is not convincing to me. Because of the Adams prominence as the grandson and great-grandson of presidents and the friend of the mighty, no questions seem to have been raised at the time.

My view of the stability of Clover's spirit comes from the few letters that survived her, despite a massive burning by Henry Adams.

In the spring of 1885, as readers of this novel know, Clover and her sister Ellen, called Nella, had spent a month comforting their dying father, Robert William Hooper. Though the sisters had nursed their father round the clock, Clover felt up to calling on an Adams nephew to partner her Hooper nieces in dancing classes. So she *was* able to turn her attention from his sickbed for a short time. On the evidence of her letters, Clover was as reconciled as she could be expected to be to her father's death on April 13. Clover wrote to Clara Hay in May of the "gaiety with which my father walked to his grave. His humour and courage lasted till unconsciousness came on the 9th and on the 13th he went to sleep like a tired traveller." (As cited in *Henry Adams: The Middle Years* by Ernest Samuels.)

Much has been made of Clover's closeness to her father. And the usual evidence offered is her Sunday custom of writing him. Those who think that strange, too dependent, overzealous, must belong to a less dutiful generation than I. Anyway, the letters certainly read as though she enjoyed writing to a knowledgeable and appreciative reader, flexing her splendid gifts as a political pundit, a gossip writer, a party reporter, and the chronicler of a salon (with recipes). The letters are an invaluable account of the society and culture of La Fayette Square, the center of the capital in the 1880s.

During the summer following her father's death, Henry wrote friends inelegantly that she was "off her feed." Back in Washington in October, he added, "My wife goes nowhere," though Liz Cameron wrote of Clover bringing her roses. After Clover's death, melancholia was the generally ascribed cause of her summer indisposition. Evidence suggests she may have had a different medical problem.

All through *The Letters of Mrs. Henry Adams* (edited by Ward Thoron) she writes about her upper respiratory problems, especially her difficulties with her Eustachian tubes, a cause of vertigo, a disagreeable condition.

Washington stands on the line where both Northern and Southern trees and flowers grow. Pollen, heavy doses of river and swamp mold, and high humidity make the capital unhealthy for sufferers from ear infections, sinus, and asthma, as I well know.

Usually, Clover and Henry spent their summers in Beverly Farms, Massachusetts, away from the allergens of Washington. But their summer house, Henry said, held too many associations with her late father. So Henry hid Clover away, isolated from relatives and friends in the spring spas of the Allegheny Mountains in West Virginia. To his confidants, Henry Adams wrote about the glories of the oak trees, especially one just outside their door, in Sweet Springs, Monroe County. Did Henry realize the effect of oak pollen on allergy problems?

After Clover's death, attention shifts to Henry's own actions, reactions, and mental stability. Adams "behaved as if tormented by some obscure sense of guilt," wrote Samuels (in the third volume of his authoritative biography). "What followed in the wake of that calamitous Sunday suggests an overmastering impulse toward expiation and self-mortification."

Adams had introduced his wife to photography, which in that day necessitated the use of potassium cyanide to develop the glass negatives. So obviously he knew her darkroom contained deadly potions. If Henry honestly thought his wife was suicidally depressed, why did he take no measures to lock away the poison? Samuels, the scholar, unlike myself, the novelist, makes no suggestion that Henry was seriously at fault. But the biographer does write, "How painful also to realize that it was her act that made him a marked man, obscurely suspect."

After Clover's sad body was found, Adams sent a note to a neighbor asking her to keep all callers away. He sent no word to his best friends, John Hay and Clarence King, choosing instead to endure the night alone. A neighbor, Nicholas Anderson, wrote to his son, Larz, December 9, 1885, "I can imagine nothing more ghastly than that lonely vigil in the house with his dead wife." Why did Adams choose to reject all company on such a night? What was he hiding? Was he composing a pseudo-suicide note? Clover's loose, free-form handwriting would be no trick to imitate.

Henry did telegraph his brother Charles, Clover's brother Edward Hooper, sister Ellen (Nella) Gurney, and brother-in-law Ephraim Whitman Gurney. They arrived the next afternoon, Monday, December 8.

The letter, unfinished, unsigned, unposted, said to be found open on Clover's desk, was given to Nella. It concluded (according to her), "If I had one single point of character or goodness I would stand on that and grow back to life. Henry is more patient & loving than words can express—God might envy him—he bears & hopes & despairs hour after hour—Henry is beyond all words

tenderer and better than all of you even . . ." (As quoted in a
letter by Nella Gurney in *The Education of Mrs. Henry Adams* by
Eugenia Kaledin and others.)

When Henry came downstairs to dinner the evening the
relatives arrived, he wore a brilliant red tie. Dramatically, he tore
the mourning band off his left arm and cast it under the table,
rejecting visible signs of sorrow. (From an interview with Mrs.
Robert Homans, an Adams niece, as Samuels recounts in *Henry
Adams: The Middle Years*.)

In the following days, Henry replied to Hay's telegraphed
condolences: "Never fear for me."

On New Year's Eve 1886, Henry determinedly moved into
his part of the joined-at-the-corner new Hay-Adams mansion on
La Fayette Square and Sixteenth Street. The Hay family followed.

Adams inherited the Beverly Farms cottage, which Clover
had paid for, some $40,000, and Clover's one-third share of her
father's fortune of half a million dollars (worth more then than
now). He had been named by Robert William Hooper as one of
three trustees of his estate. Clover's will made a complete and
unlimited bequest of her estate to Henry. Henry "followed the
Brahmin custom of putting the entire estate in trust, naming himself
as beneficiary, but he treated the income and, at his death, the
principal as belonging to his wife's five nieces." (As Samuels explains
in the middle volume of the Adams biography.)

That Christmas he gave Lizzie Cameron a piece of his dead
wife's jewelry.

In June 1886, Henry went to Japan, staying until October.
John La Farge, the artist, went along, traveling at Henry's expense.
The trip was the first of many escapes he made with La Farge, Clar-
ence King, and John Hay in search of the islands of forgetfulness.

In the thirty-three years following Clover's death, Henry

wrote no novels. He did write (among others) *Mont-Saint-Michel and Chartres* with a large contribution of research by Ward Thoron (privately published first in 1904, trade edition 1913); and *The Education of Henry Adams* (privately published in 1907, trade publication in 1918). The autobiography posthumously won a Pulitzer Prize, as later did the Henry Adams biography by Samuels.

In his last years, the sage of Lafayette Square enjoyed life in his Washington house with John Hay and family, his nieces, "nieces in wish," and peripatetic politicians and pundits.

Henry often sat on the granite bench in Rock Creek Cemetery to contemplate the Saint-Gaudens statue. On March 6, 1910, he wrote Elizabeth Cameron:

"Yesterday I went out to Rock Creek hoping for a minute's content and repose, but the ocean of sordidness and restless suburbanity has risen over the very steps of the grave, and for the first time, I suddenly asked myself whether I could endure lying there listening to that dreary vulgarity forever, and whether I could forgive myself for condemning my poor wife to it. The grave itself has become a terror." (From *Henry Adams: Selected Letters*, edited by Samuels.)

Patricia O'Toole, in her wonderfully researched book *The Five of Hearts*, relates a tremendously important fact she found in the Henry Adams papers in the Massachusetts Historical Society. In the H. D. Cater collection of the papers was a long overlooked (suppressed?) interview with Henry's secretary Aileen Tone and his niece Elizabeth Ogden Adams.

On March 27, 1918, a little more than a month after his eightieth birthday, the women found Henry Adams dead in his bed. The two went through his desk, looking for funeral instructions. Instead, they found a "partially filled bottle of potassium cyanide, the instrument of Clover's suicide."

What Was the Sexual Preference of Henry Adams?

My novel about Henry and Clover Adams may be the first
to spell out the possibility of sexual relations between Adams and
his closest male friends. The truth, if that was ever ascertainable,
about his preferred pleasures, their nature and nurture, has been
buried for almost three-quarters of a century. However, his letters
and his life, and most of all, the despair and the death of Clover,
have led scholars to much speculation over the years.

Henry's actions and writings may be interpreted in many and
varied ways to suggest: homosexuality, bisexuality, asexuality, or
impotence. And even—dare I say—necrophilia, as suggested by
the following letter, unclassifiable as to satirical or serious. Adams,
at the time a Washington journalist and lobbyist, wrote his longtime

274

friend, the English nobleman Charles Milnes Gaskell on January 13, 1870:

> Your humble servant is supposed to be attentive to one of these young women, just on the threshold of twenty and in fact not without fine eyes and no figure. Perhaps in your vulgar mercenary eyes her chief attraction would be £200,000. In mine her only attraction is that I can flirt with the poor girl in safety, as I firmly believe she is in a deep consumption and will die of it. I like peculiar amusements of all sorts, and there is certainly a delicious thrill of horror, much in the manner of Alfred de Musset, in thus pushing one's amusements into the future world. Shudder! oh, my friend, why not! You may disbelieve it if you like, but I assure you it is true that every sentimental speech or touching quotation I make to her, derives its amusement from the belief that her eyes and ears will soon be inappreciative. Is not this delightfully morbid? I have marked it for a point in my novel, which is to appear in 1880. Meanwhile my attentions are not limited to this, or any other, individual. I sometimes wonder how I ever cared for anyone. My heart is now as immoveable as a stone, and I sometimes doubt whether marriage is possible except as a matter of convenience.

(From *Letters of Henry Adams, 1858–1891*, edited by Worthington Ford.)

∞

Other letters, all in the collection of the Massachusetts Historical Society, bear on the subject. A letter, many years later in 1890, to Elizabeth Cameron again speaks offensively of marriage:

"How I pity at times that imaginary lady, my possible wife.

How quickly and comfortably I would suck the blood out of her . . . an innocent victim to my ennui."

In Cambridge, on February 8, 1872, two weeks before becoming engaged to Clover Hooper, Adams, thirty-four, wrote Gaskell a certainly serious and revealing paragraph:

"In this Arcadian society sexual passions seem to be abolished . . . I suspect both men and women are cold, and love only with great refinement. How they ever reconcile themselves to the brutalities of marriage, I don't know."

∞

When he does write Gaskell on March 26, 1872, about his engagement, the description sounds certainly less ecstatic than economic:

"She is very open to instruction. *We* shall improve her. She dresses badly. She decidedly has humor and will appreciate *our* wit. She has enough money to be quite independent . . . I don't want you to marry, though. One of us surely should remain single for the good of all."

Henry seemed anxious to reassure Gaskell that his marriage would make no difference to their relations. He wrote on May 30, 1872, about Clover:

"I think you will like her, not for beauty, for she is certainly not beautiful, and her features are much too prominent; but for intelligence and sympathy, which are what hold me. She is quite ready to like you indefinitely, and as she is fond of society and amusement, I do not fear her separating me from my friends."

Again, four days before their wedding, on June 23, he reassured Gaskell:

"You need not be afraid of her coming between me and my friends, for I believe she likes agreeable men as much as I do."

∞

Henry was certainly in no hurry to marry. Early on, when he was a student in Thun, Germany, on August 6, 1859, from Thun, Adams wrote to his brother Charles, "The women are all ugly here and I'm not vulnerable that way. Besides I've made an oath that if I can help it I'll not fall in love until it's certain I can't get along any other way. I've come to the conclusion that that's a double edged sort of amusement that cuts a little deep occasionally." (From *Henry Adams: Selected Letters*, edited by Ernest Samuels.)

∞

Adams's closest friend was John Hay, Lincoln biographer, balladeer, New York newspaper editor, McKinley's minister to England, and secretary of state. Their mansion joined at the corner of Sixteenth and H Streets was a public announcement of their enduring link, though, it is said, the rumor of an interior door between was not true.

"Adams clung to Hay as one more contact with the world of large affairs," writes Samuels in his biography of Adams. "The salutations of their letters tell the story of deepening dependence as each tried to outdo the other in affectionately facetious epithets. Adams would play variations like the following: 'My Son John,' 'Sweetheart,' 'Dear Heart,' 'Dear Oasis,' or 'Dearly Beloved.' Hay would riposte with 'My Own and Ownliest,' 'My Beloved Mentor,' 'My Cherished Livy,' and the improvisations flew back and forth with an almost feminine verve."

Henry Adams, Selected Letters, edited by Samuels, produces more such appellations: "Mon Cher," "Dear and Envied Mortal," "Querido" (beloved), "Dear Infant."

And on October 8, 1882, "My Dear Hay-oh, Your name naturally prolongs itself into a sigh as I think what fun I should have had if I had been with you in England. . . . Then we would have scaled Heaven and gone down into Hell . . .

"Robert Cunliffe is one of my few swans; I am very fond of him, and have always found him a gentleman to the core, which is muchissimo dear. The universe hitherto has existed in order to produce a dozen people to amuse the five of hearts."

Hay's biographer, Tyler Dennett, makes an almost identical point: "One cannot fail to detect in the growing volume of letters from Hay to Adams, with their salutations, 'Dearly Beloved,' 'Apple of Mine Eye,' 'Light of Mine Optics,' 'Guide and Philosopher,' 'My Own and Only One,' 'Tres Cher,' and again, 'My Beloved,' a note of almost effeminate dependence strangely in contrast with both their radically differing views and Hay's poise and habits of decision so soon to be disclosed in his official career. The entire relationship with Henry Adams presents one of the most striking contradictions in Hay's complex life.

"Perhaps the most important service which Adams did for Hay was to pass him on to his English friends."

At the time when Adams was in English society, during his father's ministry (1861–1868), "English society tolerated homosexuality only so long as one was not caught at it," Richard Ellmann wrote in his biography of *Oscar Wilde*. In April 1895 began the notorious trial of writer and aesthete Oscar Wilde. The result was his imprisonment for "homosexual offenses."

Yet at the time, homosexuality was not always considered an exclusive choice for life. Wilde himself married and fathered two children. Earlier, at Trinity College in Dublin, Wilde acquired a knowledge and a preference for classical Greece's acceptance of a dual sexual nature. His tutor, J. P. Mahaffy, characterized homosexuality as an "ideal attachment between a man and a handsome youth, and acknowledged that the Greeks regarded it as superior to the love of man and woman," according to Ellmann. This view would seem to reflect a view of woman as inferior even as a sex object. Mahaffy acknowledges Wilde's help in "improvements and corrections" in the preface of *Social Life in Greece from Homer to Menander*. Ellmann writes of the attempt in the 1890s of Lord Alfred Douglas as editor of *Spirit Lamp*, the Oxford literary magazine, to remake it with the "covert purpose of winning acceptance for homosexuality."

In *The Education of Henry Adams* certainly there are passages that seem to indicate such tastes. His most vivid description comes in his account of meeting Clarence King during a Western trip in the year 1871.

Adams, riding a mule in Estes Park, lost his way when "Darkness caught him before he could catch his trail." His mule, "cleverer than himself," found his way to the only cabin in the park. As the mule stepped up to the cabin door, two or three men came out to see the stranger. Adams writes (always in the third person):

> One of these men was Clarence King on his way up to the camp. Adams fell into his arms. As with most friendships, it was never a matter of growth or doubt. Friends are born in archaic horizons; they are shaped with the Pteraspis in Siluria; they have nothing to do with the accident of space . . . In the cabin, luxury provided a room and one bed for guests. They shared the room and the bed, and talked till far towards dawn.

King had everything to interest and delight Adams. He knew more than Adams did of art and poetry; . . . His wit and humor; his bubbling energy which swept everyone into the current of his interest; his personal charm of youth and manners; his faculty of giving and taking, profusely, lavishly, whether in thought or in money as though he were nature herself, marked him almost alone among Americans. He had in him something of the Greek—a touch of Alcibiades or Alexander. One Clarence King only existed in the world.

A new friend is always a miracle, but at thirty-three years old, such a bird of paradise rising in the sage-brush was an avatar. One friend in a life-time is much; two are many; three are hardly possible . . .

So little egoistic he [King] was that none of his friends felt envy of his extraordinary superiority, but rather grovelled before it, so that women were jealous of the power he had over men; but women were many and Kings were one . . . The women were jealous because, at heart, King had no faith in the American woman; he loved types more robust.

If King was homosexual, and the evidence points that way, he certainly was not exclusively so. His secret common-law marriage under an assumed name with a robust black woman produced six children.

∞

At another place Adams notes: "Since 1879, King, Hay and Adams had been inseparable. Step by step, they had gone on in the closest sympathy . . ."

Adams actually met Hay in February 1861 in Washington, "recognizing him as a friend." But it remained until the season of 1880–1881 that the three became close, and with Clover Adams and Clara Hay formed their mock secret society called "The Five of Hearts." However, as Dennett notes, Hay was closer to Adams than to King (though Hay lent the latter an enormous sum of money over the years).

Immediately after Clover's death, Hay wrote Adams a moving tribute to Clover and added, "I can neither talk to you nor remain silent. The darkness in which you walk has its shadow for me also. You and your wife were more to me than any other two. I came to Washington because you were there . . ."

Dennett says, "One of the great disappointments of his [Hay's] life had been when Henry Adams and John La Farge went off 'like schoolboys on a lark' " to the South Pacific, August 1890 to September 1891. Hay sounds very forlorn, even jealous, in a July 20, 1890, letter quoted by Dennett: ". . . That pleasant gang which made all the joy of life in easy, irresponsible Washington will fall to pieces in your absence. You were the only principle of cohesion in it. All the elements will seek other combinations, except me, and I will be left at the ghost-haunted corner of 16th and H."

In December 1891, Hay wrote to Henry in England to tell him to come home and he added, "But what can I do? I can say I hunger and thirst for the sight of you but that is all."

∞

Adams in *The Education* . . . pays tributes to his friends. Of his years at Harvard where he met H. H. Richardson, he writes:

"Life is a narrow valley, and the roads run close together. Adams would have attached himself to Richardson in any case, as he attached himself to John La Farge or Augustus St. Gaudens or Clarence King or John Hay. . . . certain men with common tastes were bound to come together. Adams knew only that he would have felt himself on a more equal footing with them had he been less ignorant, and had he not thrown away ten years of early life in acquiring what he might have acquired in one."

And later he writes that Clarence King said that nature would have attained perfection except for "the inclination of the ecliptic; the other was the differentiation of the sexes, and the saddest thought about that last was that it should have been so modern. Adams, in his splenetic temper, held that both these unnecessary evils had wreaked their worst on Boston. The climate made eternal war on society, and sex was a species of crime."

". . . in his own reticent New England manner," writes Eugenia Kaledin (in *The Education of Mrs. Henry Adams*), "Adams eventually managed to imitate Walt Whitman's bisexuality by using his own self to express the doubts and disillusionment of every man and woman in society, just as Whitman had expressed their hopes."

∞

Many allusions have been made to the mutual devotion of Adams and Elizabeth Sherman Cameron. When I began my novel, I certainly considered the possibility that Henry was the father of her only child, Martha. But the more I thought about it, and the more times I read Samuels's essay, "Henry Adams and the Gossip Mills," the more I agreed with him.

Samuels points out that Martha would have had to be conceived by October 21, 1885, at the latest, whereas the Camerons did not open their Washington house until November. Cameron had six children by his first wife. Clover and Henry had none. Samuels goes on to say, "It was highly unlikely that they were lovers in the technical sense after 1900. Conceivably at some earlier period in their long intimacy, possibly after his return from England in 1892 and Mrs. Cameron's nervous breakdown in 1897, the inhibited courtier played the role of Lancelot. In that rather unlikely event the episode must have been a fleeting interlude in their enduring attachment . . ."

Samuels does contrast the "prosaic domestic details of his letters to his wife" and the "wide-ranging literary imaginativeness of those to his romantic idol. The contrast suggests the potent alchemy of unfulfilled love."

No doubt that Adams enjoyed the company of women—but he preferred women who had no sexual interest in him, as he had none in them. His pose as Lizzie's "tame cat" made him less vulnerable to those who would marry him off. The pose as one who practiced "courtly love"—a pure, spiritual adoration, untainted by the demands of the body—doubtless appealed to Adams—and likely to Cameron.

Adams served as escort for Mrs. Cameron and her unaccompanied women friends in Paris. Then as now, "walkers," as they are called, men with no sexual designs on nonnubile women, are often welcome escorts for those possessed of limousines and tickets to charity events. And, of course, there are many people who are simply friends, lovers in mind and spirit instead of body. Samuels remarks, "The varieties, vagaries, and the graduations of the relations that subsist between men and women passeth both numbering and understanding."

Arline Boucher Tehan who has studied the question at length in *Henry Adams in Love* suggests that Cameron preferred foreplay to consummation, certainly flirtation to commitment. Lizzie, at twenty, was enticed into her marriage to the boorish Senator Donald Cameron, forty-five, by a prenuptial agreement. Her consolation prize was the income from a then generous $160,000 in securities. The marriage, Cameron's second, was generally acknowledged as a business deal between her uncle John (brother of General William Tecumseh Sherman) and Pennsylvania Senator Cameron to rescue Lizzie's father Judge Charles Sherman from "certain difficulties he had gotten into." As the novel suggests, Lizzie managed much of the time to keep her husband at a distance. Eventually in 1814 Cameron agreed that his wife could live permanently in Europe, a safe distance from his first wife's children, who hated and despised her. He settled a "sizable sum" for life on Lizzie, and made their daughter Martha a beneficiary in the Cameron Trust, sharing with her half-brother and sisters.

Mrs. Cameron, though having many admirers, preserved her Victorian reputation. Tehan writes of Mrs. Cameron's "French . . . handling of the role of femme-fatale" and quotes Elisina Tyler's observation, "Although she liked to flirt and tease, to kiss and cajole, she never went all the way."

Lizzie Cameron perceived that Adams had other loyalties. She wrote to him after Hay's death in 1905: "I cannot be what he was to you, but I can be less cranky than I am." In Tehan's judgment, "She cared enough for Henry Adams to spare him the devastation of a marriage that might have been even more tragic than his first."

In the years after Clover's death, Henry made many long trips, as much as five months to a year at a time with his male friends, John Hay, Clarence King, Sir Robert Cunliffe, and Chandler Hale. In 1886, he traveled with painter John La Farge to Japan and again in 1890–1891 to the Pacific coming back by way of France. These trips were a considerable influence on Adams, according to *The Mind of John La Farge* by Dr. Henry Adams, a relative, writing in the catalog of the 1987 exhibit at the Smithsonian's National Museum of American Art.

"Probably no other American painter played such a role in shaping the achievement of a major American author, let alone two . . . Both Henry James and Henry Adams were mannered and exasperating writers who have always been viewed with suspicion because of their aloofness, their compromised masculinity, and their distaste for the crudeness of American society. La Farge has similarly been attacked as snobbish, effeminate and un-American."

∞

Adams's taste for androgyny is expressed in the Adams Memorial in Rock Creek Cemetery, though he only paid for it, not created it. Burke Wilkinson in *Uncommon Clay, The Life and Works of Augustus-Saint Gaudens* (Harcourt Brace Jovanovich, 1965) has written that the sculptor used both men and women as models for the sculpture. He adds, "Not being exactly of the earth earthy, Adams decided for himself that Saint-Gaudens intended the statue to be neither man nor woman."

When in 1904, Theodore Roosevelt, at a White House dinner, referred to the monument over Clover's grave as a woman, Adams wrote him this no–thank you note:

> If you were talking last night as President, I have nothing to say. Whatever the President says, goes. But! After March 4 [inauguration date and the end of Roosevelt's term] should you allude to my bronze figure, will you try to do Saint-Gaudens the justice to remark that his expression was a little higher than sex can give. As he meant it, he wanted to exclude sex, and sink it in humanity. The figure is sexless.

Roosevelt explained that he asked because "there has been some question in the minds of people whether the figure was of a woman or was non-human." And he added, "I think that the acceptance of sex often obviates the danger of over-insistence of it."

Who Wrote the Novels?

Who wrote *Democracy* and *The Bread Winners?* was the most popular parlor guessing game of the first half of the 1880s, and a favorite item in gossip columns of the day. Both books were wildly successful for the times. *Democracy*, called the first Washington novel, was a best-seller at home and abroad because it was an insider's view, a drawing room snicker at the tarnish on America's Gilded Age as manifested in the Capital. Much of the talk concerned who was who—which characters in the book were patterned after important figures of the day. No one was surprised that the book was published anonymously, an often practiced device of the time, especially when putting the author's name to it could result in the social equivalent of being boiled in oil.

The Five of Hearts, the inner circle of Lafayette Square, had a wonderful time playing the game of whodunit. Clover did indeed photograph the major suspects—except perhaps herself—with the book held cherished in their arms. Adams wrote many letters denying his own and his wife's authorship and suggesting that multitudinous others were guilty.

When *The Bread Winners* came out, anonymously, several critics suggested it was written by the author of *Democracy*. It was criticized as being anti-unions and putting down those who aspired to a better life. In 1907, two years after John Hay's death, his wife credited her husband with the authorship of *The Breadwinners*.

Esther, because of Adams's insistence that as an "experiment" the book be published without fanfare and without link to *Democracy*, was less controversial. *Esther* is a much more personal, intimate book, about personal philosophy rather than politics. Yet here again, the knowledgeable could put real names to the characters: Clarence King, John La Farge, Lizzie Cameron, and most certainly Clover as Esther.

Henry Adams never publicly claimed authorship of *Democracy* and *Esther*. That was left for his publisher, Henry Holt, to do in his memoirs.

I began *Refinements of Love* in the firm belief of Clover's authorship of *Democracy* and *Esther*. No reading or writing that I have done along the way has dissuaded me from that belief. Indeed, I am convinced.

Democracy and *Esther* strongly present the dilemma of the well-educated woman kept from using her knowledge and talents by the restraints of the time. Adams was not sympathetic to such a view. Indeed, in his late works, he seems to say that women's worth is dependent on their role as mother.

The best evidence for Clover's authorship is provided by

reading the novels themselves, especially in conjunction with her letters to her father, unfortunately out of print. The writing style, is unmistakable. Otto Friedrich, in his biography *Clover*, does not go all the way as I have in claiming the books for Clover. Still, he mentions that some descriptions in the book, especially of nature and clothes, are very like her letters.

The world, which has been enriched, and sometimes appalled, by the masses of letters by Henry Adams, would be well served by an expanded edition of Clover's, restoring the expurgations of the earlier edition, and including letters which turned up after Thoron's edition.

∞

The letters of Clover mentioning *Democracy* to her father, Dr. Robert William Hooper, are classics of "methinks the lady doth protest too much." Here are a few:

DECEMBER 21, 1880:

"I am much amused but not surprised at your suspecting me of having written *Democracy* as I find myself on the 'black list' here with Miss Loring, Arthur Sedgwick, Manton Marble, Clarence King, and John Hay! We hear that King has been cut by Blaine and Gail Hamilton, for his supposed authorship. John Hay says he has 'given up denying it'; that 'it will be known after the 4th of March.' Miss Loring has still the inside track, but Arthur Sedgwick is running hard. All I *know* is that *I* did not write it. Deny it from me if anyone defames me absent, and say to them, as Pickering Dodge of his parrot: 'If she couldn't *write* better than that I'd cut her—head off.' "

December 4, 1881, a year later; she is still keeping the subject alive:

> "By the way, Mrs. Heard was much interested to see Miss Beale on Thanksgiving Day, having heard of her in Newport as the authoress of *Democracy* in collusion with Herbert Wadsworth, whom she accused of it after Miss Beale had gone. He looked very conscious and embarrassed and when we told Emily Beale she only gasped. So her fury of last year may have been a blind. . . ."

January 31, 1882, Clover admits to writing *Democracy*, though in a tongue-in-cheek tease:

> "Simple Mrs. Bigelow Lawrence. I'm curious to see her course as to Blaine; it was thought last spring here that if Blaine were a widower she would not long be a widow. Emily Beale declared at dinner Sunday that the novel called *Democracy* was a horrid, nasty, vulgar book, written by a newspaper man not in good society. . . . Harriet Loring says, 'Clover, your aunt Tappan says you wrote it and that Carrington is Henry Sayles.' I said, 'Yes, I did, and *you*, Harriet, are the Dare girl. I hope you don't mind.' Then she gasps, 'Why, no. It's Emily Beale.' 'No,' I answered, 'I meant her for you.' Then I went up the street quietly and she down it very softened in manner. Aunt Tappan is *Minerva* in the novel I am writing now—I shall call her Minny for short!"

Henry Adams wrote the most vitriolic letters denying the books. Here are a few, all from *Letters of Henry Adams*:

JUNE 8, 1882, to John Hay:

> ". . . I receive no end of messages and letters from there [England] asking whether my wife wrote this work of the

Devil. Hitherto I have replied with indignation that my wife never wrote for publication in her life and could not write if she tried . . ."

Henry Adams many times playfully accused John Hay of writing *Democracy*.

SEPTEMBER 3, 1882, Adams wrote:

". . . in any case I give you the fullest authority and a power of attorney on my behalf to repudiate for me and for my wife all share or parcel in the authorship of that work, which we regard with loathing, as must be the case with every truly honest citizen. Only yesterday my wife learned that even your good and pure Senator George H. Pendleton resented it. When things have got to this point, there is no longer room to hesitate. Every virtuous citizen must join me in trampling on these revolting libels. For your sake I regret, but you must confess that you and Miss Loring and Harriet have drawn it on your own heads . . ."

He seemed miffed by suggestion that his wife wrote the book.

JANUARY 7, 1883, to John Hay:

"I understand that there are some new novels, but I never read novels—nor write them. I understand from my sister-in-law, Ellen Gurney, that Hon. J. G. Blaine at a dinner party in New York said that Mrs. H.[enry] A.[dams] 'acknowledges' to have written *Democracy*. You know how I have always admired Mr. Blaine's powers of invention! *The Republican* in a list of reputed authors puts J. G. B.'s name first with Gail

as collaborateur. You of course figure in it, and 'Miss Hatty
Loring,' and 'Mrs. Adam' (of the British Legation)."

Henry Adams made many critical diatribes against the work,
as in this letter:

MARCH 4, 1883, to John Hay

"Now that Arthur Sedgwick, we are told, acknowledges the
book, I can say what I did not care to say to you so long
as you were the author, that the book is one of the least
sufficient for its subject, I ever read. Since it came out we
have had half a dozen dramas here that might reasonably
convulse the world . . . Therefore I repeat that your novel,
if it was yours, is a failure because it undertook to describe
the workings of power in this city, and spoiled a great tragic
subject such as Aeschylus might have made what it should
be, but what it never in our time will be."

The supposition that *Democracy* was a teatime project of the
Five of Hearts brought forth this letter.

APRIL 20, 1883, to John Hay:

"Several times within the last fortnight I have been told a
story that you and King (sometimes one, sometimes both)
had heard the manuscript of *Democracy* read in a house in
Washington, had been asked to write a chapter, and so on
with variations (such as that King had written the account
of Worth's clothes in that veracious work) and finally, what
was more important, that you both said the house in question
was mine. In each case this story seems to have come from
Tom Appleton. I have in all cases emphatically, and in your
names, denounced it as one of Tom Appleton's lies, and

offered to stake my existence on the fact that neither you nor King had ever said anything of the sort. I had no hesitation in doing so, because I knew that the part of the story which concerned me was untrue, and as that was the point of it, I was safe in denying for you the whole."

Henry Adams was particularly upset with reports reaching them that Edward Lawrence Godkin, associate editor of *The New York Evening Post*, had admitted to knowing the secret. Adams wrote several letters to Godkin, with notes added by Clover. Here's one, November 28, 1880, of the latest on the subject, introducing the possibility of a joint effort by the couple. Henry Adams wrote:

"You are not likely to hear it again discussed. Yet if it should come up, and you should be embarrassed by it, you are welcome to say that you have my denial of my wife's authorship. As yet no one has suggested to me the idea that we wrote it, and I do not intend to volunteer a lie about it; but should anyone do so, I shall unquestionably bluff him off, and you may take this too for granted. If asked, I shall deny until I am ready to avow . . ."

One of the funniest events came when Henry's brother, Brooks, decided he had a great scoop—that *The Bread Winners*, like *Democracy*, had a "coarse half educated touch," and resembled Thomas Nast's political cartoons. Thus, Brooks reasoned, it must have been written by the same anonymous author. H. A.'s response is amusing:

FEBRUARY 2, 1884, to John Hay:

"I want to roll on the floor; to howl, kick and sneeze, to weep silent tears of thankfulness to a beneficent providence which has permitted me to see this day; and finally, I want to drown my joy in oceans of Champagne and lemonade. Never, not even, since Cain wrote his last newspaper letter about Abel, was there anything so droll."

Ward Thoron, editor of Clover's letters, wrote in the 1930s: "Henry Adams's novel, *Democracy*, was turned over to the publisher in the spring of 1879, and published anonymously in 1880, when it ranked as the 'bestseller' of the year. The secret of its authorship was probably known only to his wife, Hay, and King, and was well kept. Very late in his lifetime he admitted his authorship to his nieces, Mrs. Thoron, and Mrs. E. O. Adams."

Well, maybe so. I am quite prepared to believe Henry Adams claimed it, in particular to admiring young women.

Indeed, there is no smoking gun or wet pen to provide a final answer. But I have my convictions, and I hope you may agree with me.

Thank You Notes

I think of a historical novel as an ornate gilded frame holding an old mirror. The reflection is wavery, crackled, with spots where the silvering has been lost, but here and there are glimpses of what may have been.

This novel is based on my intuitive response—a novelist's license—to the study of Clover and Henry Adams by brilliant and hardworking scholars over three-quarters of a century. For their scholarship, I am grateful. But the specters of long-dead characters and long-ago events I have seen in the mirror of my imagination are not to be blamed on anyone else. I summoned them up myself.

The best view of Clover Adams is given in the remarkable set of letters she wrote to her father over the years of her marriage.

They are witty, splendid examples of social and political reporting, and an important source for information about life in Washington in the 1880s. Someone should edit a new, more inclusive edition of them.

The Letters of Mrs. Henry Adams is only available in secondhand bookshops. Ward Thoron, who married a Clover niece and researched *Mont-Saint-Michel and Chartres* for Adams, edited the collection (Little, Brown and Company, 1936). A few more letters have turned up since and been used to good purpose in several books.

The Massachusetts Historical Society is, of course, the great guardian of the Adams family papers. I am grateful to Louis L. Tucker, director, who graciously granted what he called my "novel" request to use excerpts from the letters of Marian Hooper Adams and Henry Adams, and from *The Education of Henry Adams*. Clover's letters are mostly to her father, Dr. Robert William Hooper. The voluminous letters of Henry are to almost everybody else.

The love letters found by Boojum and Clover in Henry's study were written by me and have no basis in fact. The other letters by Henry (quoted in chapters One, Four, and Twelve— and indeed all the letters quoted in the Author's Note) are his own, from the Massachusetts Historical Society which so kindly gave permission.

The Five of Hearts: An Intimate Portrait of Henry Adams and His Friends, 1880–1918, by Patricia O'Toole (Clarkson Potter, 1990) is encyclopedic, invaluable, and fascinating. The 1990 exhibit at the Smithsonian's National Portrait Gallery, organized by O'Toole and encouraged by its director Alan Fern, gave Clover the long-awaited exhibit of her excellent photographs, along with other pictures and memorabilia of the players.

Henry Adams in Love: The Pursuit of Elizabeth Sherman Cameron, by Arline Boucher Tehan (Universe, 1983) not only is the definitive portrait of the beauty, but also gives important clues to understanding Clover and Henry Adams. *The Education of Mrs. Henry Adams* by Eugenia Kaledin (Temple University Press, 1981) sets Clover with other women of the late nineteenth century.

Ernest Samuels and his wife Jayne N. Samuels know more about Henry Adams than anybody. Samuels is the author of the definitive and delightful three-volume biography of Henry Adams—*The Young Henry Adams* (1948), *Henry Adams: The Middle Years* (1958), and *Henry Adams The Major Phase* (1964)—and of the one-volume edition, *Henry Adams* (1989), all published by Belknap Press of Harvard University Press. He served as an editor on the six volumes of three thousand Henry Adams letters published by Harvard University Press (1982–1988). Jayne Samuels was an assistant editor. They worked together on the Library of America's 1983 one-volume collection—which includes *Democracy* (originally published in 1880), *Esther* (1884), *Mont-Saint-Michel and Chartres* (1913), and *The Education of Henry Adams* (first trade edition in 1918)—producing a splendid chronology and notes. Samuels's newest book, *Henry Adams: Selected Letters* (also Belknap, 1992) is a wonderful volume of "greatest hits." Samuels also wrote "Henry Adams and the Gossip Mills," in *Essays Presented to Bruce McElderry*, edited by Max F. Schulz et al. (Ohio University Press, 1967). This substantial and witty work convinced me that Elizabeth Cameron's daughter was not Henry's, though early on I thought it possible.

Henry Adams and His Friends, A Collection of His Unpublished Letters, edited and with an introduction by Harold Dean Cater (Houghton Mifflin, 1947) is helpful, though it took O'Toole, going through the Cater Collection at the Massachusetts Historical Society, to come upon the story of the nieces finding the vial of poison. *The Letters of Henry Adams (1858–1891)*, edited by Worthington Chaun-

cey Ford (Houghton Mifflin, 1930) was another fortunate secondhand bookstore find for me.

*Clover: The Tragic Love Story of Clover and Henry Adams, and Their
Brilliant Life in America's Gilded Age*, by Otto Friedrich (Simon and
Schuster, 1979); and *Descent from Glory: Four Generations of the John
Adams Family* by Paul C. Nagle (Oxford University Press, 1983)
introduced Clover to me and made her unforgettable.

John Hay: From Poetry to Politics by Tyler Dennett (Dodd, Mead,
1933) draws an interesting picture of this important and versatile
gentleman. Hay's great-grandson, James Symington, the musician,
author, attorney, former protocol chief and congressman, and proc-
tor of the Alibi Club (a reclusive and exclusive men's establishment
in Washington), graciously allowed me to see a handwritten Hay
poem framed on its walls.

Most of what I know about Henry James comes from his
novels and Leon Edel, author of the five-volume James biography
(1953–1972) and the delightful 1985 one-volume *Henry James: A
Life* (Harper and Row). The writings of Henry James were illu-
minating, especially those said to have been inspired by Clover:
Daisy Miller, A Portrait of a Lady, and *Pandora*. The James novels are
available in paperback and in Library of America editions. Richard
Ellmann's biography, *Oscar Wilde* (Knopf, 1988) was a help, not
only in understanding Wilde but the aesthetic and sexual customs
of his time.

I have used several real stories that still linger about Lafayette
Square. Much information on the Adams collection, the W. W.
Corcoran houses, and the Hay-Adams house and others, their
architects and occupants, is brought together in the scholarly and
charming *Sixteenth Street Architecture, Volume I*, written and researched by Sue A. Kohler and Jeffrey R. Carson, and introduced
by Charles A. Atherton, executive secretary of the Commission of

Fine Arts, the publisher and the great shaper and protector of taste in the Capital. James Goode's high-interest *Capital Losses* (1979) *Best Addresses* (1988), and *Outdoor Sculpture of Washington, D.C.* (1974), all Smithsonian Press, are essential to anyone who wants to know the good stories about everything in town.

Andrew S. Keck's "Uncle Henry's Mind: Henry Adams and His 'Bronze Figure,' " from *Records of the Columbia Historical Society of Washington D.C., Volume 52* (1989) told me much about the Adams Memorial history.

Our Neighbors on La Fayette Square by Benjamin Ogle Tayloe (1872, from the library of the American Institute of Architects, in cooperation with Octagon) and *Early Recollections of Washington City* by Christian Hines (1866, from the collection of the Historical Society of Washington, D.C.) were both reprinted by the Junior League of Washington in 1981 and 1982, respectively. Another Junior League project, *The City of Washington*: *An Illustrated History,* by Douglas Woods Sprunt, Judith Waldrop Frank, Niente Ingersoll Smith, et al., edited by Thomas Froncek (1977, Knopf) has been reprinted (1992) by Wings Books.

Two publications of the National Trust for Historic Preservation contain delightful stories of Beale and back: *Decatur House* (1967) edited by Helen Duprey Bullock and Terry Morton, and *Decatur House and Its Inhabitants* (1954) by Marie Beale, Truxtun Beale's second wife. Mrs. Beale was famous as one of the three Mrs. B.'s who ran Washington society for many years. She was the last private resident of Lafayette Square.

Susan Mary Alsop's *Lady Sackville, A Biography* (Doubleday, 1978) gives a charming view of Washington and Victoria in the 1880's.

The history of Hiram Powers's *Greek Slave* comes from the Corcoran Gallery of Art records.

I read and was horrified by "The Yellow Wallpaper" by Charlotte Perkins Gilman (published in January 1892 in *New England Magazine*; and in 1980 by Pantheon in the *Charlotte Perkins Gilman Reader*, edited and introduced by Ann J. Lane) years and years before I discovered that Gilman had actually been a patient of S. Weir Mitchell, novelist, neurologist, and poet of Philadelphia and Baltimore. His diabolical and demeaning treatment for women and especially women writers is well described not only in the short story, but in Gilman's own biography, *The Living of Charlotte Perkins Gilman* (1935; reissued by University of Wisconsin Press, 1990, with an introduction by Lane). Mitchell's visits to the Adams house are mentioned in Clover's letters, though there is no explicit evidence that he treated her. I do have my suspicions.

Mary Lou White, researcher and mystery reader, found Clover and Henry Adams's, W. W. Corcoran's, and Emily Beale McLean's newspaper obituaries. Kim Klein helped me find many obscure books in the Library of Congress and the local libraries. Judith Martin and Virginia Devine read an earlier version of *Refinements* and encouraged me to go on.

My information on film developing comes from the Smithsonian's National Museum of American History's exhibit of a photographer's studio of the period, which I saw in the informative company of photo curator Eugene Ostroff and my husband.

The White House dinner—menu, decorations, etiquette, and so on—is the result of much research over more than quarter of a century's writing about entertaining at the White House, with much help from former White House curator Clement Conger and associate curator Bettye C. Monkman. *Entertaining in the White House* by former colleague Marie Smith (Acropolis, 1967) was wonderfully helpful. *The Original White House Cookbook, 1887 Facsimile Edition*, republished 1983 by Devin Adair, first published by Saalfield

Publishing Co., confirmed all the things you've heard about gargantuan meals. The magnificent two-volume *The President's House* by William Seale (The White House Historical Association, 1986) is a work of great scholarship and a pleasure to read.

I acknowledge with appreciation my agent, Carl Brandt, for his wise editorial advice, taste, patience, and understanding of Clover; my knowledgeable editors, Cornelia and Simon Michael Bessie, for their encouragement, belief in the book, and skillful editing; and our daughters, Camille Booth Conroy and S. Claire Conroy, who listened to many reruns of the story.

Most of all, I thank Richard Timothy Conroy. He interrupted the writing of his own hilarious Mysteries at the Smithsonian novels (about a very different Henry) to: read and edit every word of this novel many times, make inspired criticisms and corrections, listen to all my wild imaginings, cook dinner and play the piano while I wrote, drive me wherever I needed to go, and be, since 1949, the best husband, friend, and editor.

About the Author

Washington Post style section staff writer Sarah Booth Conroy has walked across Lafayette Square and around the other squares and circles of the nation's capital for more than a quarter of a century. The facts she has reported fill her Chronicles column on present and past people, parties, and places. The fiction she has imagined to explain, elaborate, and expand those facts fill this novel—and others, she hopes, to come.

The writer has received awards for her articles from the American Institute of Architects, the American Association of University Women, as well as the Reader of the Year Award (1990) from the Mystery Writers of America.

She lives in a large bookcase in Washington, D.C., with her husband, Richard Timothy Conroy, author of the series Mysteries at the Smithsonian. They have two daughters, S. Claire Conroy and Camille Booth Conroy.